SE JAKES

RUNNING WILD

HAVOC MOTORCYCLE CLUB

A HAVOC NOVEL

Riptide Publishing
PO Box 1537
Burnsville, NC 28714
www.riptidepublishing.com

Running Wild (Havoc, #1)

Cover art: L.C. Chase, lcchase.com/design.htm
Editor: Sarah Lyons
Layout: L.C. Chase, lcchase.com/design.htm

ISBN: 978-1-62649-154-0

First edition
June, 2014

Also available in ebook:
ISBN: 978-1-62649-153-3

SE JAKES

RUNNING WILD

HAVOC MOTORCYCLE CLUB

A HAVOC NOVEL

This one's for LS, because he fostered my love of music, especially the Grateful Dead, whose touch is all over this book.

Cry 'Havoc!' and let slip the dogs of war.
—Shakespeare, *Julius Caesar*

TABLE OF
CONTENTS

PROLOGUE

DON'T NEED LOVE

Every single time he broke into my house, I had to convince myself it wasn't a dream.

I never knew when he'd show, couldn't plan for the times he'd yank the sheet off me before the mattress shifted under his weight. His hands were big and rough on my bare back, and when he flipped me over and skimmed between my legs, that heated rough on my cock was heaven.

So was the big, hot body on mine.

I didn't know if I should be stopping it. But why would I? Hot sex, no commitment. Hell, no talking. Most of the time just a soundtrack of classic rock, punctuated mostly by the Grateful Dead, which made the whole thing so goddamned hot. It was the perfect nonrelationship for a guy like me, since my lifestyle was completely nonconducive to relationships.

But this guy wasn't just any guy. No one in my twenty-four years had ever had the balls to pull this kind of break-and-enter shit with me. I was impressed. Fascinated.

He was a shadow. I was used to moving through places unnoticed, but even though he had it down to an art form, he definitely wanted to be noticed when he came into my bed. And he was strong. Stronger than I was, which was no easy feat.

He was tattooed. Always bore a couple of bite marks after we finished. I couldn't help myself—I liked the idea of leaving my mark, but then, I was always hoarse the mornings after he visited, so I guess we were even.

He liked to study me in that brief space of time postsex before I crashed. I could see the appreciation in his dark eyes, and it made me squirm. He'd notice that I was somewhere between embarrassed and enjoyment, and he'd chuckle, low and husky, and that made my cock hard. Again.

I wanted to ask him why the hell he kept breaking in, but I didn't. It was obvious to me—he wanted to fuck. And I was acquiescing when I normally wouldn't have. I liked control, all types, all the time. But during these visits, it didn't matter.

He made me dizzy. Pliant. Incoherent.

I could tell he liked me that way. Expected it.

He'd take his sweet time—always did—but I always got what I needed when I needed it. He didn't hold anything back, would stop me from thinking, worrying. Took all the shit from my shoulders for those hours.

The whole thing was a free fall every single time. I pleaded for it, gave it up with no shame because sex shouldn't have shame. And I wasn't ashamed of this at all . . . but I didn't know if I was supposed to be his secret . . . or if he was mine.

Why the hell did I think about it this hard, this much?

I was getting seriously laid on a regular basis. More orgasms than anyone had a right to. Fucked blind and dumb.

Fucked to sleep.

And then he'd leave. I never knew how long he stayed, pretended I didn't give a shit. But I'd wake up in the morning and tell myself he'd stayed for a while after I went to sleep, even though I had no idea if he had or not. Because I pretty much passed out by the end of it, the good kind of exhausted where I was so comfortable I probably had a stupid smile on my face when I did so.

Did he tire me out purposely?

Furthermore, how did he get into my place? It was locked down tight. In my more lucid moments, I thought about adding another dead bolt, more locks and a different security system, all at once, just to see if he could still get through.

But what if he couldn't?

It was what stopped me every single time.

CHAPTER 1

YOU DON'T HAVE TO ASK

"Bertha's tonight!"

Noah's voice blasted through the house, and I stirred in bed, struggling to yank myself out of a dead sleep.

In the Army, I'd learned a lot from the Special Forces guys, including how to shove myself into REM sleep. They'd warned me I'd be giving up on sleeping normally again, and they'd been right. I'd been out for three months now and still slept lightly, usually waking in an instant and always alert.

Except this morning, like random others over the past eight months, my head ached and my body felt like lead. I untangled myself from the sheets and lay on my side, cheek pressed against the cool mattress, my naked body splayed across the messy bed.

The clothes I'd worn last night were scattered with the pillows on the floor, the shade opened just enough so I could see I'd slept through my entire day off.

And I was alone. Except for the rose, which was the only thing left on the night table. There were also more of them in the living room from last week, shoved into a glass since I didn't have any vases, and I couldn't just leave them without water.

Red roses. I fucking blushed every time I looked at them, and every time more were delivered. They never came with a card, but I knew who they were from.

I heard Noah fucking around in the kitchen, then he yelled again, "Rush, did you hear me? Berthas's tonight. Come on, it's late."

"Yeah, way too fucking late," I muttered, reached to the floor to grab a pair of sweats and yanked them on, simultaneously annoyed that I'd ever given him a key, and willing him to deliver me coffee by the sheer power of thought.

He walked into the bedroom without knocking. Noah was an inch shorter than my six-foot frame and broader too, his hair longer than it'd been in forever—mine wasn't buzz cut, but it was longer and messy, just the way I liked it, while his dark hair was tied at the nape of his neck. Mine went between dark and light brown, depending on the amount of sun I got, and my eyes were the color of good, strong whiskey. His were hazel and were now attempting to scrutinize me.

He'd been my best friend since juvie, but the only thing that kept me from kicking him out this morning was the coffee he handed me before turning to survey the room. "What the fuck, Rush?"

I could ask the same of him, had been planning on it for a while, and now it was going to be a matter of self-defense and deflection, two of my best skills.

But first, coffee. Because I already knew what Noah had been up to the past few months—and I suspected it'd been going on a hell of a lot longer. But when he'd started, I'd still been caught up in my own shit, wondering what the hell I'd do with my life once I got out of the Army. Plus there was all that sex keeping me pliant and distracted. "Fuck Bertha's. We can just go back to Cy's."

"Yeah, after that fight you started last night? I don't think so." Noah shook his head. "And you didn't even drink."

I hadn't, ever since I'd decided that the first late-night tryst was the byproduct of an overactive, alcohol-fueled imagination. Had to be.

Didn't explain the roses, but it'd made me feel a whole lot better. Actually, *better* wasn't the right word for it. *Disappointed* when he hadn't come back the next night, even though he'd left no indication that he'd ever come back. But he'd randomly snuck in a couple nights later.

And many nights after that.

If he was going to sneak in and fuck me, he could at least have the decency to be predictable.

I took several sips of coffee. "Yeah, you and Linc had no problem joining in." Linc'd been in Basic with all of us, assigned to the platoon Billy and I were in (Noah wasn't, but ended up in the Sandbox with us anyway), and he'd left the Army the same time as me and Noah.

Noah grabbed a chair, sat next to the bed, put his feet up, countering, "You threw the pool table into the front window."

Yeah, okay, there was that. "I told Cy I'd give him the money," I muttered, then took another giant gulp of coffee. I'd had to fight, because everything twisted up inside of me had no place else to go except barreling into someone's face.

With my hand still wrapped around the mug, I rubbed my bruised knuckles, the ones Ryker had kissed last night, while Noah continued to bitch. "And then you left me there with Linc—you're lucky *we* didn't have to call *you* to post bail. And now I find out you left so you could get laid. And you got her flowers? Nice touch."

Of course he'd naturally assume I'd gone home with one of the girls we'd been shamelessly flirting with last night. Noah was straight, but he'd known I was bi forever, and I'd never been so much partial to either sex as much as partial to sex in general. Lots of it, with lots of partners, and rarely the same one twice, because who the fuck needed that kind of complication?

I hadn't, until eight months ago, when I'd become satisfied enough. And obviously, it had become complicated, at least in my mind.

"Bertha's. Tonight. Eleven. The band's awesome—tribute to Guns N' Roses," Noah continued obliviously, like repeating it enough times would automatically make me say yes, which, although annoying as all fuck, was a good thing.

Because at least he'd veered off my sex life.

"Don't you think it's better we stay away from shit like that?"

Noah finished his coffee and rolled his eyes at me. "We're going to drink and dance. Besides, we don't have to answer to anyone."

Bertha's had been off-limits to us when we were in the military because of its rumored associations to Havoc, a motorcycle club with alleged criminal ties. We weren't so much not allowed in there as strongly advised by our CO to avoid it if we wanted to live. With our dicks intact.

Now that we were out, there were no restrictions, except for those we set for ourselves. Noah and I hadn't talked about it, but for me, those were few and far between—like the options I had to make a living that didn't include stealing. But I still avoided Havoc like the plague.

I'd lived in this area long enough to know that the rumors about Havoc being a one-percenter club were actual truths. But a new president had come in a while back and cleaned it up—they were supposedly legitimate now, although who the fuck knew what that exactly meant. Didn't mean they weren't dangerous as fuck. Which I was completely drawn to.

I was also smart enough to know when to court it and when to stay away.

Speaking of which, I got out of bed to get away from Noah for a few minutes, took a piss, washed up, and headed to the kitchen. Hopefully, I could talk Noah into cooking something to go along with the coffee.

Noah followed me, picking up our conversation right where we'd left off. "What's the problem with Bertha's? You had fun last time we were there."

Yeah, that was exactly the problem. We'd gone that one time when we were both still in the Army, the illegal nature of the visit making it way more fun than it'd normally be. And that's the exact night when those late-night visits and the goddamned roses started. "It's dangerous to hang around that place."

"Seriously? Dangerous? You're worried about danger now? After you picked a fight with three guys after *you* screwed *them* over at pool?" Noah shook his head, his brow furrowed, because danger was what always amped me up. Noah knew that, and was typically the one to help me feed the need for it while keeping me somewhat safe. We were a good team like that.

I took out bacon and eggs from the fridge—the only food in there—and put them in front of Noah, a not-so-subtle hint. "What are you implying?"

"Don't be dense."

But I would, because then I wouldn't have to admit what happened that very first night. And last night. And all the nights in between that.

"Rush?"

I looked up at Noah, who was staring at me funny. "What?"

He pointed to the delivery guy he'd let in—and I'd been so deep in my own thoughts I hadn't even noticed—and I froze. Not that I didn't expect it, but fuck, in front of Noah? Really?

And, like he knew, the delivery guy grinned when he said, "Flowers for Sean Rush," because obviously he thought it was great that I'd gotten them. *Again.*

Noah grabbed the big box—bigger than normal—and pushed me out of the way to put it on the table. I tipped the delivery guy by lifting Noah's wallet from his back pocket and taking a couple of bucks, then pointed him to the door. It was only fair since Noah was already opening the box, demanding, "Who the fuck's sending you long-stemmed roses? The chick from last night?"

Thankfully, there was still no card. Hell, I still didn't need one.

Ryker was sending them. They came every morning after he made me come. Anyone might think he was courting me, but I knew better. The fucker had to be making fun of me. Didn't stop me from letting him into my bed though. "Long story. And fine, Bertha's tonight."

"You're just saying that to get rid of me." Noah smirked as he turned one of the roses in his fingers—this time there were eight roses instead of the usual single one. He touched a thorn and hissed when it pricked him. "Someone's into you."

"Yeah, right," I muttered, walked to the counter, and started cracking the eggs, badly, because I knew he'd intervene.

He did, putting the rose down in the box with the others. "What do you mean, 'Yeah, right'? In the real world, red roses mean serious business."

I wasn't living in the real world. I was sucked into a dream world where a man too big to move as silently as he did broke into my house, and I did nothing to stop him. I was actively encouraging it with my silence.

I was doing the same thing with Noah now, because I knew the fucker was stealing cars. Again.

If I had to pinpoint it, I'd say it started right after Ryker fucked me for the fourth time, which meant about five months ago. Because that's how I measured things now—in Ryker time. As in, the time before Ryker fucked me, followed by the time Ryker fucked me for the first time, the second time, and so on. I also knew what was different about each time. Because for the most part, (except for the pieces that were missing from our first night pre-first-fucking), I was clearheaded about what happened and when—and they were all excellent fodder for those times when Ryker wasn't around, and I was forced to jerk off and pretend it was as good as Ryker doing it for me.

I shook my head, trying to get away from the all-Ryker-all-the-time show. "I know you're stealing again."

Noah didn't turn away from the stove, like scrambling the eggs was the most important thing in the world at the moment. And while I couldn't lie that I wasn't starving, the truth was, he didn't turn because he was guilty.

When we'd gotten arrested together at seventeen, the judge told all of us—me and Noah and Billy—to stay away from cars. But come the fuck on—how was that even possible? Fixing, racing, and stealing cars and bikes was what I was good at. My gift, so to speak. Noah and Billy had started because of me, so I didn't know if they really loved all of it, or just the stealing part of things.

So when I left the Army, I'd tried to find a way to do some of it. Legally. And when I'd told Noah what I wanted, he told me he'd heard about a new garage here—and he'd gone to meet the owner right before I'd met Ryker. I'd wanted to move to Florida for a fresh start, but Noah hated change. So we'd agreed to stay close to where we'd grown up for a while. Work at Edmund's on high-end cars. Keep our noses clean.

I knew we were both fucked up. I thought it was the PTSD. That we missed the Army, missed Billy. I was wrapped up in my own secret, and I made every excuse in the book as to why Noah was acting secretive, when in my gut, I knew what Noah was doing and what the problem was.

And now, I waited, because we'd spent a lot of nights huddled together—in juvie, in jail, in the Sandbox—at first pretending not to be scared, and then too tired to care about fear. That would normally be the time guys would confess their deep, dark shit, but hell, we already knew each other's deepest, darkest secrets.

Until now, when we're both actively keeping secrets from each other. The only one he didn't know about was Ryker, and I wasn't sure why I kept it to myself. There were times I really wanted to tell Noah, ask his advice . . . but maybe I knew he'd tell me to get the hell out of it. He'd force me to realize what I already knew—Ryker left every single time.

Noah finally turned around. "Are you pissed?"

"At myself, for not asking you about it sooner."

"I only kept it from you because *you've* been fucking white-knuckling it, Rush. I didn't want to be the one to throw you over that edge. Just because *I* couldn't stay away . . ."

"How long?"

"How long have you been getting fucked and getting roses?" Noah countered.

"Nice one." I stared up at him. "Since we went to Bertha's."

"Same."

"See?" I slammed my fists on the table, so fucking pissed at how off I'd been. That would never have happened pre-Ryker. "Fuck that place."

"We were both just getting what we needed." Noah slid a plate of eggs in front of me.

"So what happened to make it a problem?"

I started to eat while Noah attempted to deflect with a muttered, "Nothing, it's fine."

I pointed my fork at him and smirked. "Right. You can stop any time you want to."

Noah rolled his eyes. "Things got out of control really fast. I mean, for months now, it's been fine. Odd jobs—small ones," he added quickly. "But last week, there was a bigger call than I thought I could handle and . . ."

He paused, like he didn't want to say anything more, so I added, "Edmund told you that you were in too deep to back out now."

Noah's brows raised. "You know about Edmund?"

"I know he's got a rep from before he showed up here." Just because I hadn't stolen a car in this area in years didn't mean I didn't keep up with this shit. I'd been trained by the best, a guy named Al who'd become a legend because he'd killed himself in a stolen car during a police chase rather than being caught and going to jail. People knew my rep, and they told me shit, kept me up with the business, even when I pretended I was done with it. Because every car thief knew that there was no *done with it.* We were lifers. "You've got to get yourself out of this—he's going to get you in deeper every time."

Noah rubbed his eyes tiredly. "I know. I'll figure out a way to handle it, Rush."

"Right—with my help."

"I won't drag you into it."

"I'm offering."

Noah sighed. "I'm always getting you into trouble."

"And I always get you out of it." It was our familiar pattern, and even though I told myself I was offering to help Noah steal cars because I wanted to save his ass—which was true—I also needed to steal a motherfucking car. I couldn't deny it any more than I could stop breathing, and it felt good to admit it, even if it was only to myself. "When's the next one?"

"Tomorrow night. And I can't pull it off by myself," Noah admitted, and he looked as tired as I felt. "It's the Ferrari."

Every car thief has a car that nearly broke them, one they tried to steal over and over and it fucked with their heads. Every car thief except for me, because Al had trained that shit right out of me. "I'll do it."

"Thanks, Rush," Noah told me, and I wanted to wipe the guilt from his eyes. Until he said, "Now it's your turn—spill about the roses."

"My turn? I'm going to steal a car to help you and that's not enough?"

"No," Noah deadpanned.

I pushed my plate away. "I'm almost positive they're coming from the same person."

Noah looked at me like I was an idiot. Which I was. "We talking guy or girl here? And couldn't you just ask?"

"It's a he. And we don't do much talking, so fuck you and your logic."

Noah smirked. "Okay, how about afterwards, then? Or in the morning? You must have a few minutes where you actually speak."

My cheeks got hot, and Noah was staring. He knew I had very few inhibitions in bed, if I had any at all, which was questionable. I was loud and explicit with what I wanted, what I liked, with men and with women.

"Let me get this straight. He comes in here in the middle of the night, has sex with you, and then leaves."

And that pretty much summed it up, although it didn't sound that cheap when I thought about it. I groaned and buried my head in my arms, then heard Noah's quiet sigh.

When he spoke again, the sarcasm was gone. "It's going to be all right, Rush."

Was it? I honestly didn't know. But I was done keeping this secret. I lifted my head and looked at him. "After that night at Bertha's, I came home drunk. I got into bed, passed out, and thought I'd had the best dream ever. And then the first rose came. Actually, when the room was torn apart in the morning, I was kind of suspicious, but when the rose came, I knew." I got warm just thinking about it—the good kind of warm, like a safe memory wrapped around me, even though what was happening felt anything but safe. "Nothing happened the next night or the next, but then it happened again and again and again. I tried to tell myself that I was going to stop it the next time, but I couldn't. Didn't want to, actually."

"It's that guy from Havoc—the big biker you and Linc made the bet about."

"Fucking Linc," I muttered. "Why are we friends with him again?"

Noah snorted and shook his head like he didn't know either. "So what's the actual problem here? I mean, Havoc or no Havoc, you've got someone who's sneaking in here at night, giving you a great ride, and leaving before you wake up."

My face got hot hearing my thoughts echoed back to me. They sounded so stark. So exposed. "The problem is . . . fuck. Sometimes . . . most of the time, I want him to be here when I wake up in the morning." Noah whistled low under his breath and stared at me. "What? Say something. You're freaking me out."

"Sorry. It's just . . . you're *feeling* something, Rush. Fucking finally."

He was right. The asshole was right. It'd been a long time since I'd been anything but numb, starting from when Billy was killed in Iraq. Billy, Noah, and I'd been tight since we'd met in juvenile detention, and when he'd been killed in Iraq, it had ripped me and Noah up pretty badly. We'd both been making shitty decisions since. Shittier than when we were teenagers, so that was saying something.

I'd been trying to tell myself that I wanted Ryker there because I'd started to feel slightly used when I woke up alone, but that wasn't it at all. I didn't feel used. I was lonely. And I'd been coming home earlier, staying in more, hoping for him to sneak in. This past week, he'd visited twice, and that had solidified my feelings.

But it'd also proven that the guy on other end of the roses only wanted sex. Because eight months of nothing else? How could I justify it otherwise? "Maybe I do feel something." I picked up one of the roses out of the box, rolled the stem along the pads of my fingers, balancing the sharpness so it had just the right amount of sting. "But he doesn't."

Noah frowned, glanced at the roses and back at me. "I forgot that you never date—you just screw."

I nodded. Never had a commitment, never wanted one. Ever. Until now.

Maybe.

"Rush, this guy's sending you red roses. In the real world of love and dating, that means serious business. You don't just send them to someone you want to see on a casual basis."

"He's making fun of me."

"Seems like a lot of trouble to go through. I mean . . . would you let him fuck you if he wasn't sending the roses?"

I closed my eyes and sighed.

"I'll take that as a yes. To me, it looks like he's trying to seduce you, and maybe trying to tell you how he feels about you."

"Then why wouldn't he just come right out and say it? Why the sneaking around, the secrecy? It doesn't make sense."

Noah shrugged. "Guess maybe he knows you better than you know yourself. Although that's not hard to do, Rush."

"Fuck you, *Noah*." Because I did know something about myself—both Al and my father had drilled into me—and it was that a guy like me was better off alone.

In return, Noah placed the roses in the middle of the table, right in front of my face.

I groaned and buried my face in my arms. Again.

And then I got ready to steal a car.

CHAPTER 2

THE THINGS I USED TO DO

Just before two in the morning, Noah put the cameras on a six-minute loop and we entered the lower level of the luxury car dealership several towns over that housed some majorly expensive cars in need of regular maintenance and minor repairs. Including the '87 Testarossa that waited for me, her gleaming cherry red a siren's song.

"Better hope she runs," I murmured, more to myself than to Noah, as I ran my hand along the front bumper. Noah glanced over but didn't say anything. He had his superstitions. I had mine. It was our usual routine, honed over time, and it should've felt out of practice, rusty and odd.

It didn't, and that worried and comforted me all at once.

We weren't using keys, since they were locked up more tightly than the cars. Thankfully, predictably, she was already unlocked, so I didn't have to do anything but unscrew the panel below the steering column and twist the right wires together. Although alarms and locks were infinitely more complicated on today's models, there wasn't much I couldn't get into, given the time and tools.

The engine purred to life, the *vroom* going right to my cock. In the past, I might've said stealing was better than sex, but post-Ryker, no way.

Ryker.

I'd debated telling him about my propensity for car theft, and how the need had been getting stronger every damned day, but decided that he wasn't my keeper or my conscience. Hell, maybe he would've encouraged me. Or maybe he wouldn't answer if I told him anything real about me.

Although what was more real than sex?

I heard Al's voice inside my mind, clear as day, snapping me back into reality.

Mind on the game. Eyes on the prize.

"She's in for new brake pads," Noah informed me.

I pulled out of the space by the lift and went forward a few feet, then hit the brakes hard. They responded with a slight slip, but they'd be fine. One of the first things I'd learned was never to rely on the car, but rather what I could make the car do for me.

And I didn't need brakes to stop a car.

Granted, things turned out better when I did have them.

"Let's go." With fifty seconds to spare, I eased the car out into the darkness and the garage shut behind us automatically. We waited a beat, and when no obvious alarms rang, I started out along the back roads. The last thing we needed was a police chase—I would've aborted the job in a hot minute.

The rain had just started, a drizzle that left the roads slicker than normal, but I really wanted to open her up.

So I did. We fishtailed a few times, but hell, that was part of the rush. Noah laughed, probably the first real laugh I'd heard from him in a long while.

The engine was perfect—inaudible—and the ride was as it should be from a car of this magnitude, a smooth, supple dance on the road. It was almost too smooth, too slick for my tastes, something I didn't mind visiting but wouldn't want to drive on a daily basis. I needed rougher. Harder. I was American muscle cars, all the way.

We were twenty minutes out from the docks in Shades, where we'd deliver. And then the familiar dull ache would begin as soon as the adrenaline wore off.

I steered the car off the next exit instead of continuing along the highway.

Noah grumped, "You were worried and now you're pushing our luck. Just head for the docks." He always got this way with the Ferraris.

"We've got plenty of time."

"Rush, what the hell are you planning?"

I glanced at him. "We're racing her."

"Are you fucking kidding me?" Noah asked. "No, you're not—Christ, you're supposed to get me *out* of trouble, not in deeper."

"We'll be fine," I told him, and I was calmer than I'd been in a long while, like the weight was finally off my chest. "There's a race starting in twenty minutes."

"You planned this," Noah accused.

"I got us an invite. We can race and still make the drop-off with time to spare."

"Dammit Rush, we can't afford . . ."

"First prize is inching up to ten thousand. Serious cash. On top of what you'll make for the boost . . ."

"Fuck you, Rush," Noah muttered. But I noticed he'd stopped protesting, so I turned up the radio and found some eighties music. I liked to match the music to the car. I swear they performed better when they recognized their own decade.

I took the back roads that wove together the towns of my childhood. I'd lived in this general area my whole life, just outside of Shades Run until after the Army. I'd been worried that moving too close would bring me too much temptation. And here I was, ready to race where I'd first learned to.

Who said you couldn't go home again? Although I'd always thought the expression should be, *You can't ever really leave home. Ever.*

Granted, these days my home was more of one than I'd had growing up. I'd done that purposely. I wasn't going to live hand to mouth, scraping by, and I wasn't even attempting a relationship, never mind kids. All I'd ever wanted besides a clean place of my own was fun, minimal responsibility, and enough money to keep myself out of debt and trouble. And I'd succeeded, and enjoyed it, even after the arrest and the forced enlistment. I thought I was fine, that I'd left behind the stealing and the scars of childhood.

I got the first inkling that I wasn't fine when I left the Army. I thought maybe the military had disillusioned me, but turns out I'd been severely disillusioned all the fuck along.

I'd always had trust issues. Post-Army, they were a hell of a lot worse. But I'd settled into working at Edmund's with Noah, along with going out and pretending I had all I needed. Because hell, it was more than a lot of people had.

The nights Ryker came into my bed were the only times I didn't have to pretend—didn't need to pretend. Of course, *that* scared the fuck out of me, but not enough to stop it from happening.

Sex with Ryker was a lot like stealing cars. The first time, I was also scared as hell, but I still wanted it. Badly. And the fear was overridden by the pure fucking pleasure of it all, the rush, the fix, the pulse-pounding grind of all that power under me, vibrating through me like it needed to become a part of me. Which it did.

The second time? Fucking heaven. Because I knew what I was doing. Knew what I'd feel. And all the times after that? My body learned to recognize the signs of an impending boost. I craved it like a junkie . . . the same way I craved Ryker. Make no mistake, both were an addiction, and I honestly wasn't sure which was more dangerous. Or if it mattered.

"We're almost there," I said to Noah. I had to cross the main drag, keeping an eye out for any police presence. The guys who ran the illegal races would be monitoring the channels for any activity, so we were relatively safe, but I wasn't taking chances. Even Noah was back into the old rhythms, which included watching the side mirrors while checking for alerts from his phone. The players might change, but technology was always on our side.

I went down two quiet streets, and then it opened up into something that looked like a movie set with the requisite muscle cars, brooding guys, bad girls, and music. Set ups like this happened in a matter of minutes and they were broken down just as quickly, all parties knowing that scattering when the cops showed was the only way to freedom.

The lights—street, head, and some interiors—kept things feeling more intimate than they ever could be.

A quick glance was all I needed to see that the game had changed in the last six years, and I didn't recognize a lot of the faces here. Good. Before, I'd usually raced farther from home, but we couldn't have risked a longer trip tonight. This was a one-off. I just needed to bleed this shit from my system.

"Why are there MC guys here?" I asked.

"Looking for you?" Noah ducked when I went to slap the back of his head. "Okay, sorry. And I have no idea. Didn't think any of them were into cars."

Ordinarily, they weren't. For an MC member, a car was a cage. I gave another quick look and noted that the jackets bore the Hangmen's symbol. They were a relatively newer MC, located about an hour south of here. And I hadn't heard them butting up against Havoc much, but then again, I tried to keep my nose out of *that* shit. Because knowing too much about criminal shit for me, beyond the superficial amount necessary to keep me out of trouble, was just another enticement to commit it, like being near a lit cigarette was to a former smoker.

God, I fucking wanted a cigarette.

"Want me to register with BT?" Noah asked me when we'd parked.

The fact that he knew who BT was told me that I hadn't really had to twist his arm to come here. But he loved this part of it, the gambling, the socializing. The bullshitting. He could talk the devil into selling him souls when he was really in the mood to do it, mainly because of his exuberance. Shit like this excited him like a kid at Christmas.

It was twenty minutes before start time. A lot of guys came here early so they could hang out and party. Intimidate the competition. In my experience, those guys lost more often than they won. I kept my business and pleasure separate—because racing was a pleasure, but I was all business about it.

It was a risk, but a more calculated one than spending years in the Sandbox, where every day you were in danger just by walking off the FOB.

I spent ten minutes working under the hood. There wasn't much to do at all—couldn't fix the brake pads at this point, but I knew how to compensate for their failure. Why I hadn't gone into stunt driving was something my old CO asked me a couple of times. He knew people in California, he told me. "They're fuckin' nuts out there, but you'd fit right in."

And I'd thought about it. But hell, fast driving led to shit like this. A gateway drug.

"She's pretty." The guy who'd spoken leaned against the bumper, and I glanced up, took in the leather cut . . . and the patch above the left breast that said President and had the Hangmen's symbol of the skull and crossbones, with the knife sticking out of the skull's head.

Shit.

He was tall and lanky—I couldn't exactly call him handsome, but there was very much a stand-up-and-listen-to-him vibe happening. His hair flopped over his forehead, his green eyes drilled into mine and held my gaze for a second too long, and I knew what that second meant. "Just borrowing her."

Which technically wasn't a lie. But hell, mine wasn't the only borrowed car here tonight. Guaranteed, I'd see that pretty yellow Mustang on the docks later tonight too, along with that tricked-out Hummer with the dark windows and expensive rims. I didn't want him to spread the word that I was into the imports scene—I sure as shit didn't need that kind of trouble.

"Don't think she'll take mine, though," the Hangmen's president said.

"You're driving?" I asked.

"No. I leave that to Jethro." He pointed to a guy with a bandanna wrapped around his head who looked older than me, and not MC related. "We like to see how the other half lives."

I snorted. Finished up under the hood while he still hung around, no doubt checking to see if there were any aftermarket additions, and then he handed me a cloth to wipe my hands on. As I pushed the rough material between my fingers, he said, "I'm Casey, by the way. You need anything, you can give me a call."

"I don't have your number," I told him.

He grinned at that, said, "Yeah, you do," before walking away.

Because yeah, I did. All I'd need to do was drive over to the Hangmen's compound. Which I wasn't about to do.

"Am I wearing a sign that says, 'MC guys, come fuck with me'?" I asked Noah when he came back.

"You're serious?"

I threw my hands up in the air.

"Just drive, Rush. Figure out your love life on your own time."

"Fuck off," I told him, and got behind the wheel.

Noah came to the window. "Are you really ready?"

"I'm fine. Did you see who's racing me?"

He gave a wry grin. "Hangmen's got someone standing in for them in this one. It's not the first time, either, according to BT."

What was the MC's deal these days? But hey, all's fair. I glanced over to the Porsche Boxster, and the guy with the ratty AC/DC T-shirt, black bandanna wrapped around his hair, and ripped jeans eyeing me as much as the Testarossa. A lot of the MC guys—a lot of guys from this world in general—were on the DL. Way more than the average person would think. Since it was mostly guys with their women here, it was pretty damned easy to spot the gay or bi guys. And yeah, he'd pretty much been my type, until my type'd become tattooed motorcycle guys.

Well, a certain tattooed MC guy, because Casey didn't push any buttons either.

I shook my head at myself and got my goddamned head in the game.

The rules of street racing were pretty easy—rev and drive as fast as you could in the short distance allowed before any other civilian cars got involved. Sometimes there were as many as four cars racing, but this stretch was narrow. Here, cars went in heats of two, with the fastest two of the night racing one another. But tonight, it looked like it was just me and the Hangmen's car—the others were apparently just for show. Too pretty to possibly fuck up.

Tonight's dig was a half mile–long stretch of straight road ending just a quarter mile before it opened up into a major intersection. Which meant the lack of brakes could carry me into the danger zone if I didn't hold it together.

Jethro and I waited in our cars until most of the crowd dispersed to meet us at the finish, leaving me, Jethro, some of BT's guys and some of their women, including a pretty blonde who was the flagger. As soon as she threw the flag down, I took off like a rocket, the car responding to me the way I did to Ryker. I just tried to hold on as I let her do her thing. In my rearview, I saw smoke, watched the Boxster fishtail a little, then hit a pothole and shimmied. That was the problem with true racing cars—take them off the track and they didn't translate to street all that well. Still, he caught up admirably and it was a close one, but I crossed the imaginary line that occurred wherever BT stood with his white flag. I didn't notice much else—these races always happened too quickly, and when it was over, it was very similar to recovering from an orgasm.

I won. The brake pads were really damaged, but I spun out and stopped on a dime. Then I backed slowly into a space and got out. Noah gave me a hard slap on my shoulder, and I looked into the crowd to see Casey staring at me. Hard.

Then he nodded, a subtle *Nice work*, and I did the same nod back before something else—*someone* else—caught my eye.

My head jerked to the side, and for a second, I swore I saw him. The crowd was swarming, dancing and celebrating, and I looked for the tall man with the tattoo on the side of his neck . . .

Jesus. Now I was hallucinating him. And then I looked back at the car, and I imagined myself spread out naked on the hood, with Ryker on top of me, and Jesus Christ, I was losing my mind.

Had to be, because my adrenaline raced into overdrive. After BT gave me our cash, I split it with Noah and we said our good-byes. BT leaned in the open window before I drove away.

"Be good to see you back here," he said, looking at me meaningfully. "I can supply the cars. All you gotta do is race 'em."

Neither me or Noah committed with anything more than nods. Right now, I was too high from the win to care about anything but that feeling, and since I was too jazzed, I made Noah drive to the docks.

It started to rain again, harder than before, which was a pretty great cover for our bright-red stolen car. When we pulled up to the spot, we got out of the car for the handoff. One of the big men stepped out of the shadows to drive the car away and I waited, watched Noah talking to another guy animatedly for a few minutes.

Then he was striding over to me, a smile on his face. "Done."

"We're not done till we're paid," I reminded him.

He showed me the envelope and yeah, we were done. I stuck my hands in my pockets that were already stuffed with a roll of cash as we walked in the rain toward the parking lot, where Noah, thinking ahead, had dropped his car.

"Want to grab some drinks?" he asked once we were a safe distance from the docks. "Maybe Cy'll forgive us for the fight if we buy some rounds for the house."

Even though it'd been less than twenty-four hours since Ryker's last visit—or maybe because of that—I was feeling a little off. Antsy. Horny. I checked my watch and said, "I think I'll just head home."

"Okay," he said, like it wasn't a big deal. And then he asked, "Is this Ryker shit going to change things between us?"

"What do you mean?"

"You're already different."

"Like how?"

"Can't explain it. I guess it's the kind of shit being in love—"

"I'm not in love!"

Noah rolled his eyes. "Being in 'like' does to people."

"Did I not just complete that job in record time?"

"Yeah, even with your brief thoughts of Ryker."

"How do you know I was thinking of him?" I demanded.

"That shit's written all over your face."

I shrugged. Sighed.

Noah softened. "I get it. You want to spend time with him. But dude, he ever going to come see you in the day?"

"I thought you said that didn't matter."

Noah stared at me steadily. "You matter. So I want you to matter to *him*."

CHAPTER 3

DEAR MR. FANTASY

I was on edge, but a night at the bar like Noah suggested wasn't going to fix it. The stealing, the racing . . . instead of satisfying me, it made me want more. Like it always had.

Instead, after Noah dropped me home, I made the drive back around to the old neighborhood. It was just outside the site where we'd raced and near the Havoc compound, forty-five minutes from where I lived now, but Shades Run might as well be a world away.

My truck was a nondescript old Ford, but she was built like a goddamned tank. Speed wasn't always the answer. I drove through my old block slowly, my window down, no music on to distract me, to make me more revved up than I already was. This slowing down took conscious effort. Always had. Nothing had changed here either—the same apartments and old houses, the same small-community feel. And Havoc's presence still blanketed everything, at least to me.

I stopped in front of my old building, the place where I'd seen the Havoc guys for the first time. Even then, I'd known I was on the edge of something.

I was still on that edge, but I wasn't sure what it was, or if it even mattered. All I knew was that I was back in the game, and there was never going to be any getting out of it.

I'd been eight when I'd caught sight of three men riding Harleys and wearing leather jackets emblazoned with the Havoc logo, the snarling dog of war.

That was before Mom split and Dad went to jail. Now, I stopped in front of the stoop of the building where we'd lived, where I'd been when Dad had first pointed them out and said reverently, "They're the good guys and the bad guys."

"How can they be both?" I'd asked.

"Because they are. Best you stay away from them."

"Because of the good or the bad?"

"Hush, Sean. Just hush."

I drove away from that memory, still moving slowly through the potholes that would never be filled. As I grew older, and into more of a bit of a juvenile delinquent, I learned more about Havoc, or at least the rumors. Because they really did stay in the hills, to themselves. Unless there was trouble.

I saw them as a symbol, a beacon, which was stone-cold crazy, because who the hell saw a notorious, violent biker gang as a beacon for anything?

One summer's night, about two years after that first sighting, me and some of the guys from the building—and what seemed like the entire neighborhood—had been hanging out after dark. It was too hot to go inside, and no one could settle in. Least of all me. That's when the roar of motorcycles cut through the night. Most of the people hid, including my friends, but I sat there and watched.

A few of them turned, almost surveying me. I froze, but they drove by.

"Jesus, Rush—you're not supposed to look at them," one of the bigger kids—I think his name was Mike—told me.

"I'm gonna follow them. Cover for me," I'd called over my shoulder as I threaded my Schwinn through the neighborhood. The bikes were moving slowly through town. Roaring. Intimidating. Searching. I followed at a respectable distance, more balls than brains. It was like the town shut down because of them. I saw people hanging out their windows once the bikes passed their buildings, peeking past curtains, relieved and now curious.

Finally, the Havoc guys stopped their bikes in front of a building that was near my school. One of the bikers got off his Harley and stood facing the door, waiting.

Now, I got out of my truck and stood there, the way the biker had. He'd probably been my age then, biding his time for the fight he'd been about to have. I flexed my fists as I looked up the steps, like I was expecting the doors to open. I was practically bouncing on my toes, and I actively fought not to scan the parked cars to see if there was anything of interest. Because I would steal one of them, for the hell of it, desperate to re-create that perfect goddamned high.

Later, I found out what the guy who'd been targeted had done. He'd fucked with one of Havoc's old ladies. There was a brutal beauty to the beatdown. One on one, not excessive. A lesson. But still, the biker had plenty of backup. *Fuck with us, you get the brunt of our whole family.*

I'd heard through the neighborhood grapevine that the guy had gone to the police. He was found dead two days later. Suicide. Had they scared him enough—or had they come back to finish the job? I'd like to think the former.

I didn't always believe violence was the answer, but there were times when nothing else would suffice to save the people closest to you. And that night, seeing those Havoc guys—the leather jackets, leather pants, dark T-shirts . . . I wanted all of it. The way they moved like a team and watched out for one another. The way they didn't have to say a word and still their brothers-in-arms knew exactly what they were thinking.

Years later, I thought I'd had that with Noah and Billy. For a little while, anyway. The bond grew stronger in the Army, but it wasn't enough to make me re-up.

Finally, I got back in my truck and drove out of the neighborhood and up toward the hills where Havoc was rumored to rule. I used to do this with the cars I stole, and all these years later, here I was still searching for them.

Except when I had one of them in my bed.

The only thing that comforted me about not having moved forward was that I was a pacifist compared to my father, who'd taken people out of their cars at gunpoint. He was currently serving a life sentence for murdering several people in cold blood during a bank robbery gone wrong. And really, he hadn't needed to shoot anyone, his lawyer told me. He knew he wasn't getting away—he'd been surrounded.

The psychiatrist told me my father was a sociopath—no conscience at all. And no, he'd quickly added, that wasn't always genetic.

There was truth in his statement—I definitely felt guilt. Although not about stealing cars. When I stole them, they were always empty—none of that carjacking shit for me. I took high-end and classic cars—took them from men and women who could afford ridiculous luxury items. Sometimes I made money off it, but more often than not, it was about the pure fucking thrill of it all.

So that part was, most likely, genetic. And never going away.

It'd been so incredibly easy to slide back into the old ways. One job, one night doing two of my favorite things, and I was hooked.

I'd been hoping the magic would've faded, that post-Army—the job that was supposed to have made me into a responsible adult—none of it would be fun anymore. Then again, to me the only fun part of the Army had been the cars. And the explosions. Well, the ones we'd created.

Boosting's an addiction, one I swore I was born with, and both Billy and Noah helped foster it. I remember Noah calling me from the first car he and Billy'd taken, while being chased by the guys they'd boosted the car from, because they knew I couldn't say no to helping them at that point. I'd already been training with Al and trying not to rub my delinquency off on them.

After that, we tried to be smart, or at least I did. Only small jobs, just enough to bleed off the adrenaline-fueled need.

Drag racing was another one of those things the three of us dabbled in. We'd borrow the high-end cars, jack them up a bit, and then return them before anyone noticed. Unless we wrecked them (which happened), in which case, we just left the totaled wreck for the police to find.

And we'd gone merrily along that way. Until we'd gotten caught.

And then we'd gotten lucky, thanks to a sympathetic judge who'd let us funnel into the Army. The military appreciated my skills, and so I'd actually become a better thief. But I didn't want to stay in. I saw too much shit, too many friends go down. I even avoided the monthly calls to work black ops for a private contracting firm—Prince Industries wanted young guys, and I'd seriously considered it, but I hadn't wanted any more trouble. I should've known I'd get into trouble one way or the other, but I figured staying in the good old US of A, working on cars was the safer bet. I was so fucking wrong.

It was all about channeling it, Linc would tell me. Linc was like, part hippie, part metrosexual. He was my age. Taller, lankier. A smooth talker. And he definitely fucked anything that moved, except for me. Not for lack of trying at first. And he was a definite delinquent. Which, of course, made him more than okay in my book. I could see him now, with an M14 strapped around his neck—without the safety—a bone in his hand, telling me that I could become the best version of myself.

I wasn't sure why I was still friends with the asshole.

Finally, I went home to an empty house, still flying. I stripped and got into bed, still smelling like grease and car exhaust, and fuck it, I was fooling myself if I thought I could sleep. Especially when my sheets, my pillow, my blankets, they all smelled like Ryker. I turned on my side, buried my head into the pillow.

Last night with Ryker had been intense. The bleed off of adrenaline from the bar fight I'd started—started in the first place because I was so fucking jumpy and it was either fight or steal a car—hadn't calmed me like it normally did. Not the way it had before Ryker came into my life and my bed. So I'd still been clawing at the walls when he'd shown.

As if he'd known (and really, how the fuck could he?), he'd flipped me over onto my belly. Grabbed my hands behind my back. Slapped my ass hard enough for me to struggle . . . and hard enough to realize I really fucking liked it. Then he'd driven into me and there was nothing I could do but take it.

As usual, there'd barely been any talk, just a complete fuck-me-hard fantasy that'd left me wrung out and happy. I could still feel his hands where they'd smacked my ass, even though he hadn't left marks.

Well, he had, but they'd faded by the time I woke.

Another vision flashed in front of me—that cherry-red Ferrari, me helpless and spread across the hood, and Ryker fucking the hell out of me. Holding my hips as he filled me. Like he was claiming me, punishing me . . . for stealing, for racing, for talking to the other guys while he was there.

With the sheet pushed to the side, I grabbed the headboard with one hand, jerked my cock with the other, pretending it was Ryker's hand, Ryker's mouth. I imagined he was here, watching me. I wanted that, wanted him to know I was fucking myself thinking about him.

Would he care?

Jesus, way to ruin it, Sean. Whether he cared or not wasn't the point. Would he watch? Tell me what to do? Order me around? Or just put me into the positions he wanted?

Being tossed around like a rag doll wasn't something I'd been used to at all—and I'd be damned if I ever came out and admitted with words that I liked it with him. But I guess my acquiescing said it all. And more.

Still, tonight I'd reclaimed a part of my life I'd missed and mourned. My body still buzzed like a livewire of electricity ran through me. I couldn't stay still, couldn't be satisfied by my own hand, but I'd have to try.

"God, you're so fucked up," I muttered to myself, and then Ryker's big hands were pressing my shoulders to the mattress.

"So get yourself unfucked," Ryker told me, forcing my hand away from my cock as his body weight pinned me, his blue jean–clad cock rubbing mine, both of us hard.

I bucked up, determined to say no this time. Except I couldn't pinpoint exactly why I wanted to, or if that *no* was for something else. And suddenly, the fight wasn't about stopping him. Not at all. The fight was me stopping myself . . . me getting out of my own goddamned way.

Even though it was pitch-black, I could feel Ryker watching me. Reading my goddamned mind like he was so good at doing when we were fucking. He waited there calmly, and I could still feel his hands pinning me, but he wasn't attempting to do anything else. "Waiting for you to tell me to go."

But I hadn't. And I wouldn't. I just couldn't vocalize anything when he was here, like I was afraid talking would somehow break the spell, make him realize how fucked up I really was.

Ryker was silent for several more seconds, then asked, "Were you thinking about me tonight?"

Whether he meant just now or at the race, I could honestly murmur, "Yeah." Because it was dark. Because I could convince myself that this was still my dream, my fantasy, and nowhere near my reality. Maybe I had fallen asleep and this wasn't really happening. Either way, I kept my eyes closed to keep reality far, far away.

"Tell me," Ryker demanded.

I couldn't admit that I'd been out stealing and racing cars—although, hell, maybe he already knew. "I was thinking about last night. And I was thinking about you fucking me on the hood of a car."

"What kind of car?"

"Does that make a difference?"

"I don't know—does it?"

Hell yeah, it did. "A Ferrari. Bright red. I was on my back, and you were standing . . ."

I stopped because, fuck, I'd said enough.

"Keep going, Sean. Tell me everything."

Sean. He'd called me Sean from the very first night. He was the only one in forever who didn't call me Rush, and I wanted that to mean something. It spilled out in one long, breathless story. "You were at the race, keeping an eye on me, and afterwards, you came over, pushed me down on the hood, told me to strip. I didn't want to, because everyone's watching. But you don't care. And I'm naked and you're still dressed. You only pull down your zipper, and you fuck me on the car, holding me down."

"You were jerking off thinking about that," he said after a long beat, his eyes dark with arousal, and dammit, how long had he been here? I flushed thinking about that, and only his hand giving my balls a tight squeeze stopped me from coming immediately.

"Yes," I managed.

"You'd let me fuck you in front of all those guys?"

"Yeah. No. I mean . . . for this . . . yes." Christ, I couldn't make him understand, not when I was this full of pent-up need.

But Ryker's voice growled through the dark, "No more fantasies without me."

And I almost came right then. Because holy fuck.

He pushed off me then, and I was about to protest—and yeah, I got the irony in that—but he moved back so he was standing at the foot of the bed. And then he yanked me down toward him, my body sliding along the sheets.

He put my calves over his shoulders. Stuck a pillow under my ass to make it the right height, and I swallowed hard when he told me, "Taking you for a ride."

Jesus. My cock leaked, my breath hitched, my muscles flooded with adrenaline I thought long spent. I could let everything else fade away, until I was on the hood of the Ferrari, with Ryker between my legs and the throb of my heartbeat in my ears.

I swear I heard the men around us murmuring. I heard Ryker's zipper go down. I heard the snap of a condom, the click of the lube bottle's cap, and then he was sliding a finger inside of me, and then a second and third to open me.

I was still sore from last night—but the burn was that hissingly good kind of pain I craved. I was a goddamned ticking time bomb. Shaking. Sweating. In the dark, he reached out and tweaked my nipples hard, and I arched into the pinch, wanting more. He gave it, the slow burn on my nipples and my ass, firing me up.

He rubbed his cheek, rough with stubble, against my calf before biting my skin, then licking the tender spot as he held me tightly in place against him. He didn't move, his cock nestled and pulsing against my ass crack like a car revving at the starting line.

Impatiently, I thrust my hips, using my hands to leverage myself... and that's when Ryker grabbed my arms and said, "Leave them over your head. I'll chain you down if I have to."

And as much as that intrigued me, there was no way I could handle it. So the threat worked, in that I put my hands overhead, grasping the sheet while he impaled me on his cock, stretching me with a steady push that forced a moaned "Fuck," out of me as a shudder rippled through my body like an earthquake's aftershocks.

"Still so tight," Ryker murmured.

My hips surged up and pushed against him, as if I could force him any deeper. "Fuck, Ryker, I need this."

Ryker stared at me in the dark, and for the first time *since* the first time, I realized that he goddamned knew that. And what the hell did that mean?

What did I *want* it to mean?

Was he trying to break me? If that was the goal, well hell, he'd achieved it the first night when I'd begged him, over and over, to let me come. Even as he was letting me come. That's how crazily incoherently addicting he was for me.

"Keep fighting," he told me now. "See where that gets you," and I hadn't realized I'd been slowly writhing against him, too full with him, my heart and body racing, a fine sheen of sweat covering my entire body. All I needed to do was let go and let my body take it all in.

No reason to fight the ride of my life.

When I stopped moving, I was all too aware of the rise and fall of my chest. After a beat, Ryker pulled back so his cock was almost completely out of me. "And Sean?"

I managed a "yes," my voice strangled.

"Fuck the Ferrari. That's too tame a car for you. Too smooth. You need a rougher ride. Always have."

And then his strong arms wound around my thighs as he simultaneously yanked me to him and slammed against me with a swiftness that jolted me. And from there, he didn't let up. It was bone-grinding, nonstop, out-of-control, could-barely-keep-my-hands-on-the-wheel sex. I was fucking flying as he rode me, trapping me, my calves on his shoulders, my thighs flush with his chest, my heartbeat in my cock.

My whole body ached and hummed, and I was getting loud. I was never sure exactly what I yelled out during sex with Ryker, but it definitely spurred him on.

And I was helpless against him, impaled on him, my ass filled and my gland singing every time he hit it. He held my hips still so the only motion was his, the only friction, my ass on the blanket, and I groaned when he sped up.

The guy strummed every fucking nerve of mine without trying, like he was a goddamned to-be-feared '68 Dodge Charger R/T with its big engine rumbling through me, fucking me smoothly, the same way it would the streets. I was his gearshift, steering column, and he infused me with power I didn't think I had.

There were no brakes. I didn't fucking need them.

He was everything I could want. Hell, everything I didn't know I'd wanted. And when that threatened to spill from me, I wound my hands into my hair, tugged hard, slid my hand down and bit the edge of my palm because fuck . . . I wouldn't give him the satisfaction. Not tonight. Not when he fucking knew . . . and he knew too goddamned much. I might've just decided that, but I didn't care. I didn't need to be rational when a hot, tattooed biker was breaking in to my place and fucking me senseless.

Two nights in a row.

I was reduced to sensation, to the pounding of Ryker's cock against my gland. He was a massive shadow, his arms wrapped around my thighs, pulling me hard against him even as his hips pistoned. I was overheated—on complete, searing overload.

For a brief second, it was obvious that he almost lost control too. His hips stuttered, a groan escaped his throat, and it was more than I'd ever remembered pulling from him. So I clamped down harder on his cock, wanting to make him come first.

He retaliated by fucking me blind, deaf, and dumb, so much so that I became the poster child for the expression *rode hard and put away wet*, my orgasm ripping from me without anything touching my cock, the cum spurting in hard, hot jets along my stomach and chest. I swore I tumbled into a second one, that's how goddamned drawn out it was, and at some point, I reached over to grab his arms. They still held my thighs in a viselike grip, but the second I touched him, he went over the edge, pulsing inside of me. He closed his eyes and emptied with a series of short, hard thrusts, and by that time, my entire body was one big tremble of overworked muscles.

I'd always been able to keep my cool under pressure, never lost it, not when the cops were chasing me, or someone was trying to kill me in juvie. Nothing shook me, not until I got to Iraq—and even then, I could contain it to just the Army.

But Ryker completely knocked me down, scooped me up, and decided I was his. Of course, I'd always assumed that was only after I decided I wanted him. That first night, I wasn't going to stop until he was mine. He was my conquest, my Kryptonite, my power source, all rolled into one.

Tonight I finally realized that I might've been the one in *his* goddamned crosshairs the whole time.

CHAPTER 4

KEEP YOUR DAY JOB

Edmund was satisfied enough with the job to lay off Noah, but I didn't kid myself that it was the end of the story. For now, though, I'd keep working at the garage with Noah to keep an eye on both of them.

The rest of the week was a typical one—too much work to possibly fit in, and still, somehow I managed to get it done by Friday afternoon. Being a perfectionist worked in my favor sometimes, even though a big part of it was keeping myself too busy to notice the soreness of my body and Ryker's absence. The fact was, I hated falling behind, and some of Edmund's clients were bitchy enough to make my life hell. Never mind that most of them didn't drive their damned cars, but stuck them in their marble-floored garages, taking them out for a spin every once in a while and then bitching when they stalled out.

In order for anything that pretty to run right, you had to let her run, often and hard and well. I guess the same could be said of me too. I didn't like to be penned in, so I felt for the damned cars. When they were in my possession, I made sure to spend some quality time with them out on the road. Most of their owners wouldn't notice the odometer change, but I knew how to turn back time anyway.

Today's ride was a sweet '84 Camaro. Totally old school. It'd been custom-made for the lead singer of some LA hair band, and judging by the undercarriage, it had seen some major accidents. But that didn't affect her drive much, and I took her out on the highway, opened up and blasted eighties music to egg her on.

It was worth it. My body was still vibrating from the ride when I pulled into the nearly deserted garage to find Noah waiting for me. Smirking.

"I saved your ass from Edmund," he informed me when I turned the music down.

"Edmund knows what I do." I remained in the Camaro, the leather smell enveloping me. "She went a hundred and ten on the open road without losing any torque."

"I'll bet." Noah was as into cars as I was. It was one of the things that'd drawn us together from the start, even though he liked to steal more than vehicles, while I remained a purist.

Noah was also tense as hell.

"What's going on?"

"He's got another job for me."

"Did you try to get out of it?"

Noah hesitated, enough for me to know that he hadn't, not at all.

"Come on, man . . . what the hell's going on with you?"

"Same thing that's going on with you." His words were clipped. Tense. "You got right back into it. You're more like yourself this week than you've been in forever."

"Maybe that's true, but it's not juvenile shit anymore, and I'm not ending up like my dad."

"You seriously don't think we should spend the rest of our lives working on cars for rich people who never drive them, never mind appreciate them?"

"Who the hell said anything about the rest of our lives? We're twenty-four years old."

"And we're stuck."

"We just got out of the Army. It takes time to adjust."

"I don't want to readjust," he said firmly. "I want what we had before." I stared down the guy who'd been my friend since we'd been fourteen, and he gave as good as he got. "I'm sorry, Rush, but I'm not going to lie to you. I know you tried to help me get out—and you did. I just didn't realize I didn't want out."

"Fuck." I stared straight ahead out the windshield to the big *Edmund's* sign. "I was always a free agent. I'm not working for anyone."

Noah nodded. "I get that. But it's a different game today."

"And I'm not in it," I told him.

And I meant it.

Until Noah went missing, and I got a call that I needed to finish his job if I ever wanted to see my friend again.

CHAPTER 5

SING ME BACK HOME

The job was a 1970 Chevrolet Chevelle SS 454. 360 horsepower. 500 ft-lb of torque. Under normal circumstances, I'd be jerking off thinking about all that power and all that goddamned torque slamming my body into the seat.

Knowing that Noah's life was possibly in danger put a brutal stop to that.

Of course, Edmund merely insinuated the danger by telling me he'd been trying to reach Noah all day with no luck at all, that Noah was supposed to be doing a job for him tonight, and since he was now suddenly unavailable, someone needed to step in. It was all very friendly-like. If I was imagining Edmund's goons from the docks holding Noah until I got the job, Edmund would no doubt tell me I was overreacting.

"I figured you'd want to help your friend out of a jam, whatever that may be. I really hope nothing's happened to him—that would be truly terrible." Edmund managed to sound as slick on the phone as he did in person.

I closed my eyes as I listened to Edmund outline the whens and wheres of the job. Normally, it was parked in a six-car garage in a private house in a gated community. Tonight, the owner was taking her out, and I'd find her, valet-parked in a lot behind a wedding hall. I'd grab her and deliver her to the docks, to the same men Noah and I had delivered the Ferrari to.

"According to Noah, it should be a piece of cake," Edmund told me, and I pictured him sweating through his expensive suit.

"Then let Noah do it," I growled, mainly because I wanted to hear the threat from him, not this thinly veiled shit.

Instead, Edmund told me in his most reasonable tone, "Rush, I'd hate to have to call over to the police station and report what you've been doing. You and Noah could go back to jail."

"And you'd be reporting yourself," I pointed out, although really, it was my word against his. Thief against thief. We'd both go down.

"Maybe. But I'm sure that drag racing isn't part of your parole."

"I'm not on parole," I said through gritted teeth.

"And I've got video of you racing a stolen car." Edmund's smugness made me cold.

"I'm assuming that when I give you the car, I'll get the tape?" And Noah.

"Let's just say I'm keeping it for insurance purposes."

Motherfucker. "I want the tape after this job. Noah and I are done."

"You're done when I say you're done, Rush. You've got a sweet deal—what's the problem?"

I hung up before I answered that. Mainly because I couldn't—beyond the fact that he was threatening Noah (and I wasn't even fully convinced of that), it *was* a sweet deal, something I would've jumped at in the old days. And it wasn't just the risk of jail time leading to the sick pit in my stomach. It was being held hostage. It was the lack of freedom.

Stealing was freedom. Being forced to steal, not so much. I resented the fuck out of Edmund for it. And I thought about all the ways I'd fuck him over when this was done, including making a plan to steal every car in his garage and send them off the pier to watch his insurance premium bury him and his high-class clients destroy him.

"Goddammit, Noah," I muttered. "You'd think you'd be able to see through complete assholes in suits by now." But Noah was always looking to legitimize stealing. For him, doing it for a guy in a suit was better than doing it for fun, for himself.

I never needed that validation.

I called Noah's phone and, unsurprisingly, got no answer except a *voice mail full* message.

So I texted.

Nothing.

I was hoping to at least confirm that one of Edmund's goons had him, because this shit was something Edmund could easily make up. But I couldn't risk Noah—even though my gut told me that he was fine, that this was some kind of goddamned ruse. A lesson. A power play. And I never reacted well to that shit. But I couldn't be sure Noah was actually safe, and stealing a car to save him shouldn't be a hardship.

No, it was a justification. Because even though I'd been resisting the lure, the other night's boost had heightened that familiar, low-level buzz, the one that kept me on alert for any muscle car within a thirty-mile radius that I could borrow, just for the hell of it.

I called Linc. After five rings, he picked up, his voice full of sleep. "Hey Rush—what's going on? Looking to break any more windows? I'm in."

Of course he was. Linc loved a good bar fight, more than I did, but I wasn't in the mood for his laid-back shit. "Fuck off, Linc. This is all your fault."

Of course, Linc knew what I was talking about. "You guys always need someone to blame. Go ahead, I'll shoulder it."

Linc would too, even when it wasn't his fault. Granted, ninety percent of the time it was, but even so, there wasn't a malicious bone in his body. Linc was all about good times—although he'd be there for you in the bad. He didn't abandon people going through tough times, but if he had any himself, he didn't show it.

"You really think he's been kidnapped?" Linc asked. "Because this is just like Noah."

"Actually, this is just like you," I pointed out.

"Oh. Yeah. That's true," Linc said thoughtfully. "You're doing it, right?"

"No question. But keep calling him."

"I'll do you one better. I'll drive in."

That wasn't a bad idea. "Why don't you hang at the docks? That's where I'll drop the car. Maybe they're holding him there. If they're holding him at all."

"I'll be there." Linc lived an hour from Shades—and he'd been there five months. He said that was the longest he'd ever stayed anywhere, and I figured it was for me and Noah. As irresponsible as Linc could be, from our first day of boot camp, he'd somehow become responsible for us. For me, especially.

Talk about the blind leading the blind.

In the end, I approached it the way I would any job. If I thought too much about what was possibly at stake—like Noah's life, my freedom—I'd get all fucked up. I had some kind of uneasy feeling overriding everything—Linc would call it hinky—which meant it'd be that much tougher anyway. If Noah's life didn't possibly hang in the balance, I'd walk away. Because the uneasiness was replacing the adrenaline high with something I'd never felt before. It didn't matter that I couldn't put my finger on it. What mattered, Al would have told me, was that something felt wrong, and that I should always walk away when that happened.

Al was always goddamned right, but this time, I couldn't let it matter.

I cabbed it to the wedding hall. I'd dressed like one of the valets, so I blended in easily. I parked a few cars, slipped the keys for the Chevelle into my pocket, and when the wedding was in full swing and over half our crew went to grab dinner—and the others, smokes—I left.

She was big and mean and beautiful, sitting on her haunches, pure American muscle with her nose-to-tail white stripes and gleaming blue paint, taking my breath away.

"You'll like this," I assured her as I ran my hand along the bumper, introducing myself. It was the one superstition I wouldn't give up. It had also been Al's and he'd tried to get me to stop, convinced that wasting those few seconds would be what got him caught.

In the end, it hadn't been a matter of a few seconds at all. Even if it had been, I wasn't about to stop.

Sometimes, jobs were so easy they were almost disappointing. I'd opened the back gates earlier, and now an hour later, no one had noticed or closed them. All I had to do was get her down the short block and onto the highway—such easy access for a car thief.

I sat behind the wheel for longer than I should've, tempting fate and everything else.

"We're moving to Florida," I said out loud, practicing my speech to Noah. "New names. New jobs. We start over."

I gripped the wheel.

And Ryker?

Why did the thought of leaving him behind make my head hurt? There was plenty of good sex in Florida. Bikers too. I could fuck my way through Bike Week to get this kink out of my system.

Damn Ryker for taking over my mind again.

The Chevelle growled at me during start-up like a lion disturbed from its sleep. I was convinced they'd be able to hear that roar over the DJ's music. That shook me enough to slide her into gear, pedal through the floorboards, and let all that goddamned angry muscle take me away.

This was as close as it got to riding Ryker. The g-forces kept me glued to the seat, the vibrations jarring me out of my comfort zone.

Ryker.

I eased onto the brakes.

And realized that there were none.

At the same time, my phone dinged. A text. From Noah.

Lost my phone. Dude, what's going on?

I closed my eyes as the Chevelle hurtled through the darkness, wondered if she was aware of her fate, wondering if this big, mean, beautiful baby was looking to me to save her.

How the hell could I be expected to save her, when I'd never been able to save anything.

Anyone.

Definitely not myself.

Dude, what's going on . . .

I passed the exit for the docks, because there was no way to make that without a total crash and burn. There might be no way to avoid that, but I was going to ride this as long as I could.

I turned on the radio because fuck it, I wasn't going to die without music.

"Casey Jones" came on, like a beacon to me, a message, and maybe it was a coincidence.

It didn't matter. It was enough. I was convinced I needed to do whatever I could to save myself.

CHAPTER 6

NEXT TIME YOU SEE ME

I stripped out of the scrubs the hospital had given me to go home in, since my clothes had basically been destroyed, and took a hot shower even though in places it felt like needles dancing on my skin. I cursed at the sting, but I didn't move, not until I didn't smell like antiseptic and blood.

I'd also been cursing myself left, right, and sideways ever since I stumbled away from the wreck. I should've known better than to trust Edmund.

Feeling semihuman, mainly because the two pain pills I popped when I got home had started to work, I avoided the bathroom mirror and instead grabbed a towel and patted dry, careful around the bruises that would be there a long time. I also took the tape off the stitches—Gretchen had put it there for me before I'd left so I could shower. Then I wrapped the towel around my waist and stilled.

Ryker was *here*. Broad daylight. And he'd seen everything I'd avoided looking at in the mirror.

I blinked and wondered if maybe I'd hit my head harder than I'd thought. Or maybe the pills were making me hallucinate.

"If you hit your head that hard, you should still be in the goddamned hospital."

So I'd spoken out loud. And the mirage was speaking back, which didn't help me to know if this was real. "Nah. Can't be."

He grabbed my biceps to steady me as I tried to push by him out of the bathroom, and I stopped and stared. Fuck yeah, he was real. And bigger than I'd remembered. I wasn't small, but the guy was at least six foot four, muscled as hell, and covered in tattoos. And scars under the tattoos. I could feel them when I held him.

I couldn't remember the last time I'd held him. Hours? Days? My cock had zero problems with memory, though. Like a heat-seeking missile . . .

"Sean, how fucking hard did you hit your head?" he demanded.

"Have I been saying everything out loud? Because I meant to keep it in here." I pointed to my head. Tried to, but got somewhere around my neck. He clenched his jaw and attempted to guide me to the bedroom, and that's when my memory and sense of reality snapped into place. Because I knew what it meant when Ryker came here.

"You can go." My voice was hoarse as I backed away. He didn't argue, but he didn't move either. "I can't fuck tonight, so you can go."

Again, nothing.

I tried one more time. "At least you'll save money on the flowers."

This time, Ryker cursed low under his breath and came forward. How the guy moved so quietly in those heavy black boots amazed me. Which annoyed me, because I didn't want to be amazed by anything he did.

He was staring at the mess of bruises and cuts. I'd been damned lucky.

"Skilled," he corrected. "Not lucky."

Shit. I guess this speaking out loud thing was still happening. "Great. Like I said, I'm not up to fucking, so you can head out. I'm sure you've got half a dozen other houses you can break into."

Again with the swearing under his breath. He wasn't moving to leave, and I was sore and tired, and especially tired of the once-over. I missed the usual heat in his eyes when he looked at me, and I sure as hell didn't want his goddamned pity.

I'd officially entered ridiculous territory. Especially when he cupped a hand around the back of my neck and took a fresh towel to run along my hair to take it from soaked to merely damp, and my cock tented the towel. Traitor.

Damn him. I pushed past him into the bedroom.

And he followed.

I stood in place, not turning around. "I told you, no."

"I heard what you said." Ryker was literally the meaning of *on my six*, his breath warm, fanning the back of my neck. "Made a mistake."

"Yeah, made a mistake by coming here when I wasn't up to fucking. The whole thing was a mistake." I'd tensed, but only noticed it when his hands skimmed my bare shoulders. "I said—"

"I heard what you said. Now shut the hell up." His hand cupped the back of my neck, the other, my shoulder. "Get into the bed."

Did the guy get off on screwing a beaten man? I opened my mouth to reiterate my point for what felt like the hundredth time when he said, "And if you imply one more time that I only come here to fuck you—"

"Why else do you?"

Christ, I sounded bitter. And like a woman. Maybe it was all the roses.

Ryker sighed, murmured, "Yeah, I fucked up good," and steered me to the bed.

It didn't matter anymore. With the pain pills working, King Kong could take a walk in my bed and I wouldn't care. Although Ryker was like King Kong to me . . .

"Thanks for that compliment," he said with a small grin.

"Shut up," I muttered, but more to myself than him. Because I really needed to shut up. Which I couldn't seem to do. "Actual talking during the fucking . . . and now seeing him in the daylight. Gotta be a fucking hallucination."

"We talk during sex."

"No, I yell and curse a lot. Mainly in combinations of your name mixed with God's and some cursing," I told him. He bit back a laugh. "That is not funny. Dammit."

Ryker pulled the covers up around me as I told myself to shut up—out loud, no doubt. Then he fixed the pillows.

"You'd make a good nurse," I told him sleepily, and he just stared at me.

Guess he wasn't used to anyone talking to him like that.

"If I was a medical professional, I wouldn't have let you leave the hospital in this condition," he told me.

But I'd have gone stir-crazy, and I'd left with promises to the nurse that I'd stay home and rest, and not do anything crazy.

Yeah, not crazy like letting some guy fuck you and send you roses without ever introducing himself.

Not formally, anyway.

"Didn't think you were big on formal, Sean."

Ryker's drawl. Fuck, was I *still* babbling out loud? Hated these drugs. Hated them. "And," he continued, "I did introduce myself. But you'd had a lot of tequila. I guess I shouldn't have expected you to remember."

"I remember," I protested. "Some of the things." Like the way he'd always fuck me and leave, and yeah, I wasn't in the mood for that shit. "Look, can you just go?"

And this time, he did.

Got what I'd asked for, so why did I feel miserable? I pulled the covers up more, curled on my side. And then he walked back in carrying a soda.

"I ordered Chinese," he said when the doorbell rang seconds later.

"Make yourself at home," I said as sarcastically as possible, and he glowered. Left again, and came back with a tray of cartons and bowls.

All my favorites.

Or a good guess.

But I had a strong feeling nothing Ryker did was by chance.

He took his boots off. They fell with a slam to the floor, and fuck me, I tried not to jump at the loud sound, but I must've. Always did shit like that when I came back from anything combat-related.

He was next to me in a second, hand on my shoulder, telling me that it was all okay. It wasn't, and it felt too good to be comforted. I didn't want to get used to that.

He ran a hand through my hair. Studied my face and reiterated, "I made a mistake."

"You got the food right," I offered and yeah, the drugs were working. He must've known, because his expression softened. And I figured now was a good time to share that, "I, uh, sometimes have reactions to the pills."

His eyes narrowed. "What kind of reaction?"

"I stop breathing. Just for a few seconds. When I'm sleeping. I mean, I always start again, but Noah . . ." I trailed off.

Noah. Linc. My phone. There were reasons why they weren't here, but fuck if I could remember now.

"Sean, I'm staying."

"Noah—"

"I'll deal with Noah when he comes."

Ah hell, those two could fight it out. I ate the noodles and egg rolls and drifted off into a good, drugged, full-stomached sleep in which I dreamed about Ryker's mouth on my skin, his fingers doing that skilled thing that made me shoot fireworks, and moaning his name.

I woke to shouting and an empty bed. And not a single goddamned rose to be found.

CHAPTER 7

SICK AND TIRED

It took me a few minutes to surface from the pain pills and realize that Ryker and Noah were fighting. I dragged myself out of bed but didn't get much farther as the searing pain in my side jolted me into the postwreck reality.

I hadn't had much time to let myself think about what happened. If I hadn't been trained to crash well, I wouldn't have walked away, leaving the Chevelle hurt but not totaled. And if I hadn't had Army training, I wouldn't have made it out of the car. But as I sat there, dazed, the car half off the road, I'd heard my drill sergeant in my head ordering, "Get the fuck up, Rush." And I got up and out, and started walking.

I'd had plenty of motor vehicle–related accidents, but this *wasn't* an accident. Someone had cut the brakes—all the brakes—in anticipation of the car being boosted. If I didn't know how to drive the shit out of a fast car and handle it correctly, I'd be dead.

My phone had been crushed in the wreck—I'd taken it with me anyway, kept the SIM card and ditched the rest. When I didn't show at the docks, Linc and Noah and Edmund and whatever mafia was waiting for the car would do whatever they'd do. I'd stumbled off the closest exit ramp, and maybe Al was looking down on me, because the exit was near a train station. From there, I'd grabbed a cab to take me to the hospital—the driver heard the sirens, saw my condition and said, "My baby brother's doin' time for stealing," which I took as code for, *The police won't hear about you from me.*

He dropped me outside the ER. I'd called Linc from a payphone. He'd found the crash site by that point, but I refused to tell him where I was. Mainly because Noah was with him, and fuck that.

Had I told Ryker any of this? It didn't matter, because, as I manned up, held my breath against the pain, and made it to the opened bedroom door, he was telling Noah to "get the fuck out" in no uncertain terms, and I agreed with the sentiment.

Then he added, "Where the fuck have you been? Because you haven't been to see your friend."

"Right," I said out loud to no one. Because I'd been at a hospital three towns over from where the wreck had happened, where I knew a girl I'd gone to high school with was now an ER nurse. I had insurance, so that wasn't an issue, except I knew it could be traced—and I needed to lie low. Once Gretchen got me checked out by a doctor, I'd discovered that I had a concussion, sprained wrist, bruised ribs, and lots of other contusions to go along with the aches and pains. And then he'd wanted to know if I had someone to call. Gretchen saved me from his scrutiny, but even so, I'd had the chance to call Noah or Linc again, but I didn't. Half of it was the pain daze and the other half was uncertainty. I couldn't pick that all apart, and I hadn't bothered trying.

"I'm here to see him now," Noah was telling Ryker. "I've been looking for him."

"I'm taking care of him. He's not up for visitors." Ryker's voice held that no-nonsense edge, coupled with a growl.

"I'm his best friend," Noah challenged. "And you're nothing more than a self-appointed bodyguard who shows up whenever the fuck he feels like it."

Ryker remained unperturbed. "Better bodyguard than you are for your supposed friend."

"I don't fuck him and leave."

"I don't fuck him over and leave."

"Good one," I muttered from my spying position. But I did want to know where the hell Noah had been without his phone. I knew he and Linc had probably been going crazy looking for me while Gretchen kept me in the ER for about six hours, most of which involved me trying to sleep and failing. She'd sent me off with strict instructions for lots of rest, along with pain meds and a wrap for my ribs. And a sleep aid, since every time I closed my eyes, I flashed back to Iraq.

Christ. I leaned my forehead against the doorjamb as a wave of dizziness sifted through me, and just tried to breathe as Noah and

Ryker continued to argue, their voices like tomahawks pounding a drum that was my skull.

"What the fuck business are you getting Sean involved in?" Ryker demanded.

"He likes to be called Rush. Not that you'd know shit like that. He's nothing to you but a convenient lay," Noah said now, and I bristled. Because that wasn't true. There was more than fucking and roses and hell, it was just more shit I'd forgotten in my denial. There was the music he left for me—loaded onto my iPod. The way he checked me over for injury when I'd still been in the Army, subtly, sure, but he'd done it. All the while, I'd pushed that down, pretended it didn't mean anything, just like the roses didn't.

But they did. It all did.

Noah wasn't stopping to let Ryker respond. "And none of this is your business, because I don't report to Havoc." Noah's words were snarled, the anger directed at Ryker—or more accurately, at me because of Ryker. For Noah, bringing Ryker around was some kind of betrayal.

Like the kind where your friend does a job to save your life, and you were too busy to think that maybe someone stole your phone on purpose.

I swore I heard Ryker growl. Jesus, this was bad. Noah could fight, but I knew from up close and personal ways that Ryker could take him easily.

And of course, despite all my aches and pains, I got hard thinking about it.

"And you *are* going to fucking report to me when you're talking him into doing shit that almost got him killed," Ryker said.

"Rush's a big boy. I don't have to talk him into anything. And I'm betting you do a ton of shit that's outside the law. You're worse for him than I could ever be."

"Jesus, Noah," I muttered, fisting my hand against the doorframe.

"You almost got him killed and walked away, scot-free. He took a job for you. And then he got himself to the hospital and home, and where the fuck were you?" Ryker's voice was controlled and calm.

I grabbed the doorjamb and waited for Noah's response, which was, "I lost my goddamned phone. I was on a job. Rush knew I was on a job." Noah said it so convincingly, I almost believed him.

Fuck. I exhaled painfully. Because no, "I goddamned didn't, and you know it."

My words were low. But, as if Ryker heard me, he issued Noah a final ultimatum. "Get out of here. Don't get him involved in another one of your jobs or you'll regret it."

"Is that a threat?"

"Take it as such, and take it seriously."

"I've known Rush for over twelve years. You've known him for a matter of months. No, I take that back—you don't know him, you *fuck* him."

I heard a crash. A semihowl from Noah followed, and then Ryker's low voice vibrated through me. "I know Sean better than you ever could."

And then, there was the slam of a door, followed by silence. Whether Noah left on his own accord or Ryker tossed him out, I didn't know or care at the moment, although once the painkillers wore off, I was pretty sure I would.

Ryker came in and caught me before I made it back to bed. Then again, I hadn't tried really hard not to be seen.

He glanced at me, raised his brows. "Hear what you wanted to?"

"Not especially." I white-knuckled it back to bed, but I would've refused help if he'd offered. Which he didn't. Although I swore I heard him call me a "motherfucking stubborn bastard" under his breath while he waited for me to get into bed. And then he fixed my pillows and the blanket, and I let him. Because I'd accomplished a day's work by walking ten paces back and forth.

"Take this, Sean."

I didn't argue about the pain pills. I hated them, but I wasn't a martyr. I gulped them down and lay back against the pillows, my brain spinning, still trying to figure out why the fuck Noah had lied about me knowing he was on a job. Why he'd been safe, walking away from his job last night without a scratch, and I'd barely limped to safety, all fucked up.

"What's Noah into?" Ryker asked finally.

I didn't like actually saying what I did out loud—part covering my ass but mainly a superstition. "Same thing as me."

Ryker jerked back, stared at me. "No, babe, not the same thing at all, because he looks perfectly fine and you look like you went ten rounds with a wall."

"I took the job to help him out."

"You weren't on the same job—understand?"

I got it, although I wish to hell I didn't. I didn't believe Noah would've knowingly set me up, but something had happened . . . and he had to have realized it when I called Linc about the crash.

"How long've you known Noah?"

"Feels like forever." And right now, not in a good way.

"You got instincts?"

"Fuck you, Ryker. Noah's been in my life for a long time and he's never deserted me, so that trumps instinct every time."

"He's deserted you now. And you're too loyal."

"Yeah, I am. Too bad you can't say the same."

His mouth quirked. "You jealous, babe? Think I'm not loyal to you in some way?"

I snorted. But the answer was yes. To both.

"Yeah, you're jealous."

"Keep wishing that."

"I don't have to wish." He leaned forward, so his forehead was nearly touching mine. "For the record, I'm not fucking anyone else. Neither are you."

I didn't know if he was asking or telling on that last part, but my money was on *telling*. And he'd walked out of the room before I could shoot back a smart answer. Which was good, since the pain pills were making me not so smart. I closed my eyes instead, and felt the stupid smile on my face.

For the record, I'm not fucking anyone else.

I must've slept again, because I woke to the smell of food and my stomach growling. Ryker was there with a tray.

"Definitely a good nurse," I said, just to piss him off, because he was revealing things about the people in my life that I didn't want to know.

Halfway through the soup, I was tired. So Ryker fucking *fed* me. I let him, because I was hungry. I swear, if I could've let him fuck me at that moment, it would've happened.

"Thanks," I managed. He gave a half grin, had to know what I was thinking, then picked up the tray and started to walk out of the room with it.

Before I could stop myself, I blurted out, "The brakes in the car were cut."

He turned around. Put the tray down on top of the dresser and came back to the bed.

"And yeah, I'm sure," I told him, when all he did was study me.

He continued to do so, and I shifted until he finally said, "And you don't think there's a target right between your eyes?"

"There's always competition in the imports market. Guess Edmund stepped on someone's toes."

"Jesus, Sean. I figured . . ."

"What?" I prompted when he didn't continue.

He looked at me with those dark eyes that missed nothing. "I didn't take you for naive."

I bristled. "Trust me, that's not a problem of mine."

Ryker considered that, then asked, "What kind of hold does Noah have over you?"

"He doesn't." That wasn't exactly the truth, but I refused to get into it now. I was avoiding all of it, refusing to center in on what really happened, changing the subject. "Did you know the Hangmen were into stealing cars?"

"What makes you think that?"

"I met Casey at a drag race."

"*Met* him?"

I sat back, enjoying Ryker's seeming jealousy for about two seconds. "He told me to get in touch. You know, about cars."

Ryker gave a slow, disapproving shake of his head. "Before or after you won?"

"How do you know I won?"

"Sean . . ."

Jesus, warnings from him equaled a hard dick. Immediately. "Before."

"Not about the car. That's a bonus for him now." It was Ryker's turn to sit back. "You're in some dangerous territory."

"Tell me about it." I stared at him pointedly.

His brows raised. "You like my danger though, Sean."

I couldn't deny it. But this shit with Noah . . . "You really think Noah's in over his head?"

Ryker nodded. "He's involved in bad shit. He can't protect himself or his friends."

Ryker's cut lay casually across my chair. The Havoc guys were like legends, rarely seen, but once they were, they lived up to their rep . . . and everyone else lived with the consequences. Ryker could protect himself and his friends, and if he considered me a friend, just what would be the cost of that protection? Was Noah now the one in real danger? And was I going to have to choose between Ryker and Noah?

I glanced down at the rose tattooed on the back of his hand, the stems disappearing up his sleeve. It'd been there all along . . . another thing I'd missed. Or noticed and blocked out on purpose.

What else was I missing?

CHAPTER 8

THE WICKED MESSENGER

I slept and woke and slept for what seemed like years, but each time I woke up, instead of roses, Ryker was still there. Which meant he was also there two days after the accident to let McKibbins in for an unexpected visit.

For the first time since the wreck, I was clearer. The pain was lessening, and I was sitting at the kitchen table, feeling semihuman again and dealing with the new cell phone that Ryker had gotten me (through my plan, though, because I had insurance on the damned thing so it's not like I was a kept man), when the doorbell rang. Ryker gave me his best *stay put* look and I rolled my eyes at him and then he went to answer it.

"Babe, it's the police. Officer McKibbins. Should I let him in?"

I was still caught on the *babe* part, kind of reveling in that until the *McKibbins* part totally fucking ruined it, especially when I heard him bitch at Ryker, "I'm coming in," which probably meant official business.

I was now actively thinking about taking more pain pills, because getting through this visit sober was going to be a bitch. He had to know about the accident—or he suspected. And even if I'd had on long-sleeves, which I didn't, there was no way to hide the bruises on my face.

McKibbins walked into the kitchen—in full uniform blues—like he owned the place. Ryker was right behind him, and stopped in the doorway, eyeing McKibbins warily.

I didn't bother to get up. "Always a pleasure, Officer McKibbins. So glad you've been keeping current on my address."

The man who'd known me since I was ten didn't crack a smile. "When did you get out of the service?"

Ah man, we were going to start here? "Like you don't know?"

"Sean Rush, answer the damned question," he snarled and Ryker moved around the table, leaving plenty of space between himself and McKibbins, to stand behind me, unmistakably protective with his hand on the back of my chair. I felt the heat from his body close to mine.

I wanted to tell him that this shit with McKibbins was old news, that this was actually a pretty damned civil exchange. Not only had McKibbins's father arrested mine, but McKibbins had always hated me for getting his baby brother in trouble, hated me more for Billy's death our first week in the Sandbox.

I guess I couldn't blame him. But I did, because I'd never had to talk Billy into anything. The guy'd been a juvenile delinquent from birth, way worse than me, and having a family full of cops did something to him, made him want to rebel against anything resembling authority.

Billy only chose the Army to spite his family. Because of his connections, he'd had an opportunity for some kind of daytime reform school / nighttime house arrest deal. He'd actually been ready to choose jail, he'd told me, but he hadn't wanted to leave me or Noah, and we'd been forced to enlist when our sentences were handed down.

I stared at McKibbins. He looked nothing like Billy at all—there was none of that casually handsomeness, and none of the goddamned joy the kid had been born with. "I've been home for three months."

"And what've you been filling your time with?"

I stretched, trying to appear calm and casual, but fuck, moving meant wincing. Still, I managed, "Reading. Journaling. Getting in touch with my inner self."

McKibbins's face got nice and red, just the way I remembered it looking, and hell, he was lucky I didn't tell him that he wasn't my goddamned parole officer. Because I wasn't on parole. But then he said, "You're such a fucking wiseass. Don't know how to help yourself." That much was true. And then he crossed his arms and got into why he was really here. "You look like you've been in an accident."

Ryker snorted. "I rode him too hard."

McKibbins blinked at me, then turned to Ryker, while I gave Ryker a brief *what the fuck* expression of my own. But Ryker continued, "He was fixing my bike and I wanted him to take it for a test run. He pushed the throttle too hard and wiped out. He's more used to cars these days."

"That he is," McKibbins managed without a trace of irony. "And I guess I'm supposed to take the word of a known gang member."

"Havoc's a club. But you know that." Ryker reached in his pocket, and McKibbins tensed, his hand going to his holster. "Shit," Ryker muttered. "I'm grabbing my phone, okay?"

Slowly, he drew his hand out of his pocket, holding his cell phone. "I've got pictures of the accident."

"You just happen to have evidence of the crash?"

"So I can send them to insurance." Ryker smiled innocently and showed McKibbins a picture that made him glare. "For the record, stubborn over there looks worse in person than my poor bike."

"When did this happen?" McKibbins demanded of me, but Ryker broke in, saying, "Tuesday," with the ease of someone who lied regularly, often, and well.

Hell, was he lying to me?

I shook that off in favor of the current standoff. I even pulled myself out of the seat, slowly. Painfully. I wasn't sure what I'd do if they started fighting, but I'd have to do something.

Finally, McKibbins spoke, his tone ugly when he told me, "Glad you have a new patsy to stand up for you."

Instead of growling or getting pissed, Ryker just gave a short laugh and remained at ease. I admired him for that, but I couldn't laugh it off. With that one statement, McKibbins got to me, easily and effectively, and I knew it showed on my face because his expression was triumphant.

"He's done it before," McKibbins continued, making sure to shove the knife in deeper and twist it. "He ends up killing his so-called friends who protect him. In this case, might be a blessing."

"Get the fuck out of my house," I snarled. Must've started to lunge at him without noticing, because Ryker's hand was now on my shoulder, holding me in place. But I was beyond the pain. I was all anger now.

"I think you should leave," Ryker suggested to McKibbins, his tone still placid. McKibbins had actually taken a few steps back when

I'd moved toward him, and his hand had gone to his holster again. Like he was just looking for an excuse.

My gut churned—rage and guilt a massively awful combination. I twisted away from Ryker—I don't know if he let me or if I surprised him with my strength or if he'd been holding me loosely because of the injury. I don't know how close I got to McKibbins, if I made contact or not—I suspected not because I'd have been in cuffs in his car. But I was moving. Fighting Ryker's hold.

And I didn't know when McKibbins left or if he said anything else because the sound inside my head was an angry dull roar. When I was able to think—and see and talk clearly without spitting out curses—I found myself holding on to Ryker, my forehead pressed to his chest, clutching a fistful of his T-shirt.

I blinked, then breathed in the scent of him. Goddamn, he always smelled so fucking good.

"Thanks," he murmured.

"Gotta stop speaking out loud like that."

"I don't mind it."

"Figured," I muttered. He didn't press me to look up or let go of him. In fact, his arm remained around my lower back. Finally, I lifted my head to meet his eyes. "Thanks."

"Anytime, Sean." A pause. "He seems to know you pretty well."

"Seems like a lifetime ago. Billy and I stole cars together before we went into the Army. Like you heard, his family thinks it was all my fault, that Billy was on the straight and narrow until I came along." I spoke like it was rote to say, like the feeling wasn't coursing through me. The whole thing was like a fucking nightmare I couldn't wake up from.

"Ah, Sean." His hand ran roughly through my hair.

All the memories of that time were sifting, rolling together, threatening to catch me up and take me under. I didn't want that. "I can't go there right now," I said, more to myself than to him, but he still answered me.

"He'll be back."

McKibbins definitely would be. He'd be checking my story and Ryker's for any cracks. But right now, I was more interested in Ryker's story itself. "How'd you set up an alibi for me?"

He didn't answer that, telling me instead, "Just stick with the story and you'll be fine. Happened on Havoc's property."

"I've never been to Havoc's compound."

"I've got a list of guys who saw you have your accident on the bike."

Fuck, he was serious. I tried a different approach. "Pretty sure I left blood in the car."

"Pretty sure that information won't pan out."

"Jesus." Apparently, Ryker was a better criminal than I was. He'd tracked down the car after the crash . . . and he was here, after the accident. And maybe, just maybe, Ryker being here when I got home from the hospital wasn't an accident at all. "Jesus, you've been watching me."

"Yes."

"Just like McKibbins."

The words were barely out of my mouth before I found myself pressed between Ryker and the wall, not hard enough to hurt, but hard enough for me to know I wasn't getting away easily. "You know better than that," he growled.

"No, actually, I don't." Christ, I was irritable. I blamed the pain and the meds. The lack of sex. Being this close to the only man I wanted to have sex with and not being able to have sex with him. "Ryker, I'm twenty-fucking-four years old—"

"And you almost died the other night."

"Not the first time and I'm sure it won't be the last," I told him as calmly as I could manage, but he didn't react. At least not how I thought he would. Instead of anger, his eyes held a compassion that made my throat tighten. "I can take care of myself. I've been doing it for a hell of a long time."

"This hit you hard. Up till now, you've been in enough crashes and close calls, seen enough shit on the battlefield and walked away in one piece, to think you're invincible." He paused, rubbed my cheek with his tattooed knuckles. "I want to keep you that way."

"Why's that?" I asked before I could stop myself. Because I was pissed. Pissed that he was being nice. Pissed that he wouldn't let me pick this goddamned fight.

"Like I haven't been showing you that for eight months?"

I blinked, because we'd been here before. It was maybe the third time he'd broken into my place. I hadn't seen him for three months because I hadn't been home. But there'd been a firefight and a bombing and my unit had seen a lot of action. All of us limped to a hospital in Germany and then back to the States, and I'd been put on a couple weeks medical leave to heal broken ribs and a sprained elbow.

I'd been pissed then too. Especially when he'd come in and tried to treat me like I was made of glass. I'd pushed then too—without words—and we'd ended up fucking like it was a fight. He'd held me down for most of it, mainly so I wouldn't hurt myself.

Afterwards, when he'd rolled away from me, I'd muttered into the dark, "Don't fucking need to be taken care of."

In seconds, I'd been lifted and pinned to the wall and Jesus Christ, like he'd taken my words as some kind of dare, he'd stayed for hours more and he'd definitely taken care of me. I just hadn't put it together like that . . . until right now.

And right now, he was watching me as I was lost in remembering. Nodding slowly as I focused back on him. "Whatever you're thinking about is taking the anger out of your eyes, babe. You need reminding. When you're better, I'll remind you. Fuck you on every available flat surface. And the not-so-flat ones."

"You want to take care of me."

"And?"

"You're talking about fucking me, which is different from taking care of me. And I don't need to be taken care of." Beyond the past seventy-two hours. But I wasn't going to argue about the fucking because hey, needed and wanted.

His knee pressed my cock through my sweats. "You realize your dick gets harder every time I talk about taking care of you?"

"You need to let me the fuck down," I growled.

Instead of complying, he tilted his head, examining me. "You'd get twitchy when you first came home from combat, no?"

His eyes bore into mine, and I didn't want him knowing shit like that about me. I didn't want anyone knowing anything about me, but he wasn't going to let the subject drop.

"Sometimes," I admitted.

"And that didn't stop when you got out for good." I didn't confirm or deny. "I help with that, by fucking you so hard you can't see straight, think straight, or walk straight. Till you're holding on to me for dear life, yelling so loud the neighbors know my name. That's taking care of you." The shudder went from the bottom of my spine and spread everywhere. And he noticed. Nodded slowly. "Yeah, my baby liked that."

"I'm going to lose my mind with you."

"Gonna like it though."

I had. I did. "What's in it for you?"

"You, Sean," he said, and I got that tight feeling in my throat again, because fuck, he really meant that. "I'd never do anything to get you in trouble. That's first."

I stared into his dark eyes, managed, "Good for you. I'll get you a medal."

His mouth twitched. "Don't need one. Got you."

"Again, you don't have me," I said irritably, mainly to hide the fact that yeah, he most definitely did have me.

"You woke me up. Getting me all domestic and shit."

I rolled my eyes. "Last time I looked, I didn't have a pussy, so cut all the romantic shit."

"Babe, if that's romance to you, you've been with guys who've been doing it wrong. Really goddamned wrong."

Okay, fine, I liked being fucked by him, and if he wanted to consider that taking care of me, I wasn't arguing. But I wasn't telling him that either. "You've seriously been watching me this whole time?"

He nodded. "Not just me. You would've noticed."

He was right. My body responded to him whenever he was in close proximity. Which meant . . . "You *were* at the race the other night." He smiled. I took it as a yes. "I don't get it—you're bikers, not secret agents."

"We all have our special talents."

He wasn't moving, wasn't letting me down, kept my weight balanced against his and the wall, making my cock hard and my body ache for him. But fuck, I wasn't giving in. I might not be able to move, but I wasn't losing this round. "So what else did you learn over the last eight months?"

Ryker stared at me, his dark eyes like endless depths. "You go out a lot."

"Excellent spy work."

He seemed thoroughly unimpressed with my wiseassedness, and somehow amused by it at the same time. His mouth quirked up at the corner. "You get hit on a lot."

I nodded my acknowledgment.

"And you flirt."

Again, I nodded, realizing that maybe I wasn't going to win this one.

"And then you leave."

"Can't sleep on a bar," I pointed out.

"You leave alone."

I shifted and his knee rocked against my cock and balls.

I might've whimpered.

He definitely might've noticed.

"Why not bring someone home?" he asked.

"Didn't want to," I muttered.

"Because your bed was already crowded." He smirked. "Of course, if you were worried I'd crash your party, you could've gone to their place. Or a hotel."

I closed my eyes, the only defense mechanism I could think of at the moment. Mainly because he continued rubbing my crotch with his knee, and I needed to come.

"You push people away," Ryker continued.

"You don't even need me here for this." I wanted to point out that I wasn't pushing him away at the present moment—that, if anything, I wanted him closer. But that would weaken my position even more.

Ryker ignored me. "But you flirt, lead them on. You tried to pull that shit with me too. That first night when you propositioned me."

I frantically sought out that memory and once again, failed to bring it to the forefront. I opened my eyes and asked, "That first night you broke into my bedroom and fucked me?"

"While you yelled out my name? Yes, that one," Ryker said casually. "But suppose I'd taken you to the backroom?"

His knee stopped and I groaned. "Did you even try?"

"No. Because you would've blown me off afterwards. If we'd even gotten that far."

My eyes narrowed. "You were spying on me in backrooms? How long was the surveillance going on for?"

"As long as it needed to."

And all because I'd propositioned him? Dammit—I'd started this whole thing. "Let me the fuck down." I shoved at him. He stared at me, then let me down, making it clear that he was letting me go rather than me getting away from him. Asshole. "You can't do this. Can't come in here and try to run my fucking life."

"Not what I'm doing, babe."

"Really? Spying on me?"

"Keeping an eye out for you. And good thing I was, yes?"

"No. Because I got myself to the hospital."

Ryker swallowed. Hard. My words were an accusation to him too, and no matter how subtle, he'd caught it. "Where was your best friend while all this was happening, Sean?"

"He lost his phone. I called Linc, who was with Noah, and told him about the accident and then I didn't call either of them back."

"So you're going to shoulder the blame for this?"

I ignored that—because why was he right all the time, dammit—and said, "It's not your goddamned right to kick my friends out of my house, no matter how fucking pissed I might be at them."

His tone was controlled when he answered. "It's my goddamned right when you're involved. Because I'm goddamned involved in all of this."

"You put yourself in the middle. I didn't ask you to alibi me for McKibbins. I don't need to owe anyone shit."

"I'm not just anyone, Sean."

His voice had gotten low and dangerous, his expression tight, and I didn't care. I was pissed at everything, including and especially myself, and I'd keep pushing. Mainly because he was right—he wasn't just anyone, and I'd been too wrapped up to truly notice that. And I wanted him to get pissed, to lose control, because calm, cool, and collected screamed indifference to me. "What I do with my time's my business, unless you're planning on jumping to McKibbins's side of the street and making a citizen's arrest."

"I'm involved, Sean, because you got me involved."

"*I* got you involved?"

"Edmund's a low-level player in the car theft game with ties to different mafias. And he's using you."

"I got paid. I was helping Noah get out." And I'd enjoyed the fuck out of it until I'd almost died. And even *that* hadn't taken away the need to steal. What the fuck was wrong with me?

"I'm not talking about payment."

I stared at him, finally going back to the subject I'd been avoiding. "So the brakes being cut—was that a message to Edmund?"

"A message from him, actually. To you," he added, like it was necessary to emphasize it. And fuck, it had been, because I didn't want to see it.

But it was right in front of my face, and still, I was ducking and weaving.

"You're saying Edmund tried to kill me? Because that's a stretch."

Ryker stared at me, leveling the fuck out of me with his gaze before hitting me with, "Do you think Noah has been stupid enough to mention your involvement with me?"

CHAPTER 9

GOTTA SERVE SOMEBODY

Shit. I opened my mouth, then closed it. Because Noah would've definitely seen my relationship with Ryker—and Havoc—as something to mention, as an opportunity, even if he didn't quite know what the hell kind of opportunity it was.

I did manage a "Fuck me," then pointed at Ryker when his eyes lit a little. "I didn't mean that literally. Okay, I did, just not right now. Fuck, I'm pissed . . . okay, come here."

He kissed me, hard and fast, and I murmured, "Fuck. Fuck," against his mouth, my mind reeling. "Ryk . . ."

Because he was involved. Because of me. Edmund'd tried to fucking kill me because of Ryker. Which meant somehow Ryker and I could both be targets of his.

My fingers curled into his hair, keeping him close. My entire body was a giant heartbeat, a throbbing, endless need I wanted him to fill. We'd done this dance before, so many times and ways, but right now, I knew what I had to do.

Normally, he kept me too on the edge to protest, even though we both knew damned well that I could. Kept me pleasured and pliant and willing. Kept me yearning. No one could replace Ryker's touch, his tongue, his cock, his hands . . . the man dominated me without really trying, like he knew I'd strike back, buck, and run with an outward show of dominance.

Yeah, he'd gotten me from minute one, it seemed. And now, we managed to get to the bedroom and he was letting me climb him, his big body lying submissive for me. At first, I think it was shock, because really, I'd never actually fought his hold and I'm damned strong. I pushed his wrists up to the headboard and jacked his cock slowly, his jeans open but still on.

He groaned through his teeth.

"You going to keep your hands there?" I asked him.

"That's what you want?"

"Yes."

"Consider it done, Sean."

He grabbed tight to the headboard. I glanced up from sucking his cock and balls and saw the muscles in his forearms straining.

The strange thing was, I didn't want to top him. Not right now, anyway. This was about him being right, and me being angry about that, but accepting it anyway. I grabbed a condom, slid it onto his cock and added some extra lube, then lowered myself onto him without preparing myself. He almost stopped me—I saw it in his eyes—but then he didn't.

I lowered myself—carefully, because that's the only thing that made his jaw unclench and this was supposed to be my goddamned apology. And I had no other way to say it but this way. This and stealing—it was all I knew, and the danger of both was all I needed.

He was so goddamned big, and I took him inside me. Without waiting, I rode him, pressing his chest with my palms, holding him down (and he pretended I could) and fucking him, trying to force his orgasm first—a hoarsely rasped "Fucking hell, Sean" rumbling from deep in his chest.

One goddamned touch from him, and it was like he tamed some wild thing that lived inside of me that was ready and waiting for the right time to strike.

Conventional wisdom stated that the bottom was the one in control. Whoever made that shit up hadn't been fucked by Ryker. Because I was on top, riding him, setting the pace and the only one orchestrating this thing? The dark-haired, dark-eyed man who undid me with a look, never mind his cock.

He smiled, a cat who ate the canary smile, as he flexed his hips, driving himself deeper inside of me. I came, splattering cum on my chest and his belly, and then I fell forward as he kept fucking me.

My lips trailed down his chest. I tweaked his nipples, tugged them between my teeth and his body tensed. I swear he got harder. But I wanted him begging, wanted to channel all our anger into the sex and let it burn there, let it diffuse. Turn it into something amazing and powerful.

"Hold me, Ryker." Maybe I said it out loud. Maybe I didn't. Either way, his arms went around me, holding me tight as I continued to shudder through my orgasm. And then I swear I almost came again when he came, and I shuddered all over again. I was hot and cold, my muscles loose. I was easy right now.

"I like you easy."

"I bet you do."

He laughed. "I'm not talking that kind of easy. I mean this." His arms tightened around me. "Happy. Unguarded. Letting me inside."

We stayed like that, contented, for a while. At one point, he rolled away to clean up and came back with a washcloth for me. And then he got back into bed.

It was light out. I could see him—really see him. For the first time since the accident, when I wasn't in pain or doped up. He was really beautiful. It was easy to miss with the leather and tattoos and the attitude . . . the sharp cheekbones, aquiline nose.

I could see the Indian heritage standing out in stark contrast to a lighter complexion. I traced his lips with my finger, then pressed it into his mouth. He sucked hard, and it jolted through my nervous system. My cock dripped.

"Come on, baby. Come let me suck on you." His voice was a single point, a rasp, the only thing for me to hold on to as I completely lost control.

As if I'd ever had it with him.

I made my way up his body, until I was straddling his head. I grabbed the headboard for support at the same time he grabbed my hips and brought my cock to his mouth. As he stared up at me, he dragged his tongue along the slit and then took my cock into his mouth and sucked. His tongue lapped the broad head, tasting me. I watched, because this was everything I'd missed over the past months by staying in the dark. I'd been worried that turning on the light would break the spell—for both of us, maybe—and would've made this thing end much too soon.

"*You* never turned . . . the light . . . on," I managed.

He pulled back a fraction. "You weren't ready." His warm breath brushed my cock and then he leaned in and took it in his mouth again, sucking with just the right amount of pressure that my mouth dropped and Jesus, it was perfect. The top of my head tightened, preparing to explode. I held the headboard for dear goddamned life as he made my entire body scream for mercy.

I was aware that I was babbling. Most of it sounded incoherent, but I know there was *Ryker*, *God*, and *fuck* in there . . . and he teased me. Brought me to the edge and pulled back until I was covered with sweat and trembling from exhaustion.

I might've stopped breathing when I came. All I know, beyond the pleasure, was Ryker helping me ease away from him, catching me before I fell completely off the side of the bed. He rolled me onto my belly and I lay there, splayed, boneless for him. He took me without mercy, his cock fitting into me, my body hitching for him when he came. And then I came again. Like, what the fuck? It wrung me out, left me helpless. And I didn't care, because Ryker was there with me.

"No more lights off. Ever," I told him. He gave me that sly grin again. "Bastard."

The way he looked at me made the world still. All the noise, the bullshit, stopped cold. He was all I wanted to focus on. Everything else fell away until it was just the beating of my goddamned heart, and he'd snuck in there when I wasn't looking. When I was being too dense to notice, and he'd known it the entire time. Known and waited, semipatiently, until I'd discovered it.

His hand traveled along my side, the way it always did, slid under my arm, then settled, palm open, fingers splayed over my left side, fitting against the slope of my ribcage. He studied his hand and my skin intently, and now I realized he'd been doing that since our second night together.

His hand seemed to fit there, perfectly. I didn't question why he did it. It was one of those things where, if I mentioned it, he might stop doing it.

Once his hand settled into its spot, my eyelids got heavy. His arm slung over me. An anchor. I slept, even though I didn't want to.

When I woke, he was gone.

CHAPTER 10

HEAVEN HELP THE FOOL

Just like the good old days, I'd rolled over and found myself alone. No roses though. Not even coffee.

I sighed. Stared at the ceiling, wondering if we were really going back there. But hell, was there any kind of future to move forward on with a guy from Havoc?

And speaking of assholes, I moved to grab the phone to call Noah for the first time in days, but the doorbell rang before I could dial.

I rolled off the bed and headed to the door, dressed in sweats, pulling on a flannel shirt as I went. Last time I'd looked, my cheek and chest were still covered in colorful bruises that would be slow to fade, and I was sore all over, but I'd stopped taking the painkillers.

I glanced out the side window. No black-and-white. I didn't recognize the car, but I knew it wasn't McKibbins's. Still, when I opened the door and saw the guy I'd raced against last week standing there, I knew it couldn't be good. For one thing, I'd never given him my address. Or my last name. Or any name, for that matter.

For another, even though he looked the same as he had that night, with old jeans, black boots, a ratty T-shirt, and a bandanna wrapped around his head, there was something different about him. The goddamned ATF badge he held out to me. Jethro Holmes.

I frowned. Stared between it and him. Waited.

Finally, he said, "We need to talk."

"A lot of that going around," I said with a smile but stepped aside.

He brushed past me. "I'll just bet."

I closed the door behind him. He'd already made himself comfortable on my couch, his long legs splayed in front of him. "Don't take this the wrong way, but don't you have some kind of official uniform when you come calling with your badge?"

He eyed me. "Seriously? I caught you racing a stolen car and you're questioning my clothing choices?"

I shrugged. "Is that enough to arrest me?"

"Sadly, no." He pointed to his T-shirt. "This shit's vintage."

"Are you pissed because I beat you? You can't pull that, 'I let you win because I'm really ATF' bullshit."

"For the love of Christ." He shook his head, then got serious. "I was supposed to fucking win, asshole. So no, I didn't *let* you do anything. I didn't expect you to be there." Then he sighed, stared up at the ceiling for a second before bringing his gaze down to me. "Rush, there's a lot of shit going down. You're in the middle of it."

"No, I'm not actually. I'm pretty much done."

"That's what they all say."

"This time, I mean it." For him to introduce himself to me meant he was either damned confident I wouldn't spill his secret to the Hangmen . . . or the Hangmen already knew what he was. Either way, it meant there were much bigger fish to fry than me or Noah.

"Noah Carson's trouble," he said, echoing Ryker's sentiment. "Any idea where I can find him?"

"I haven't spoken to him in days." And that was the truth. I hadn't called him—he'd texted a few times, but I'd ignored those too. Until just before Jethro came, I couldn't figure out the level of pissed I was at him, and until I did, I wasn't going there. Nothing to do with the fact that Ryker told me I needed to cut him off.

"Noah's been running with Edmund for a while," Jethro told me. "You're not surprised."

"I was when I first figured it out," I told him. *Fuck.* So maybe Ryker was right about my level of naïveté.

Or maybe Noah and I had been to hell and back together, and I expected more from him than being the last one to know.

Jethro left. He'd been muttering under his breath a lot, especially after I asked him about the Hangmen killing him if they found out who he was. And when he didn't answer that—maybe he thought it was an obvious enough *yes*—I asked, "I don't get it. Are the MCs into stealing cars now?"

"The car I raced wasn't stolen," was the last thing he'd said before leaving me his card with only his name and cell number on it and telling me that I needed to stay away from Noah Carson at all costs.

Which meant I called Noah before Jethro pulled out of the driveway. I now knew the level of pissed I was at him, and it was through the motherfucking roof.

He started with, "Rush, I know you're pissed," forgoing any of the hello bullshit.

And I knew that tone of Noah's. He couldn't fake or hide the true fear in his voice. And he was driving—I could hear the engine, the rhythm of the way he talked in time with his shifting and steering. No one else would've noticed it, but I did.

"Where are you?" I was pulling on boots and grabbing for the keys to my truck.

"Almost to goddamned South Carolina."

"Noah, talk to me."

"I've been trying to talk to you, but that fucking brute's been threatening me. Linc and I've been worried sick since you called about the accident. And now I'm in the middle of a job, so it's not a good time."

Dammit, no matter how pissed I was, how much I needed to know, this *wasn't* the time. Whether what was happening to him now was tied into my accident or not, it was most definitely tied into Edmund. Which meant Noah still needed my help. "Are the cops after you?"

"No. Some other asshole who claims I cut in on his deal. No idea what he's talking about, but he and two other jacked-up dudes are following me. I can't lose them, and I've got to bring this to the docks, to Carlton, the same guy from the other night. I figured I'd try to hide the car until tomorrow night, when the coast is clear."

"Yeah, brilliant."

"I didn't plan this shit. I've got another car to grab before midnight."

I checked my watch. "Not happening, brother."

"Fuck. Never get back to Hiland before then." I heard him slam the steering wheel with his palm. My hand was on the doorknob still. Hiland Park was an hour from here, a ritzy suburb, mostly gated communities.

"What's waiting for you?"

"A sweet '67 Corvette."

"You know that's not my favorite," I bitched, even as I left the house, got into my truck, and started driving in the general direction of Hiland. I'd have Noah pick my truck up tomorrow from Hiland after it was all over.

"You still there?" Noah asked finally.

I turned onto the highway. "Yep."

"Are you feeling better?"

"Better than I look." He blew out a sharp breath, but before he could launch into an apology, which I knew was coming next, I asked, "Did you tell Edmund about me and Ryker?"

"I didn't know there was a 'you and Ryker,'" he said irritably.

"Don't play dumb, Noah."

"Fucking asshole threw me out of your place, Rush."

"You pissed him off. You pissed me off too."

"Yeah, okay, I deserved that." He sighed. "And all right, fine. I might've mentioned about you and Ryker to Edmund after that first job we did for him."

"The first job *I* did for him. You've been working for him for a while." Because yeah, I'd seen the newspaper articles about the car thefts that had just happened to coincide with our leaves. I'd long suspected it was him. "So you just blurted out my sex life to Edmund out of the blue?"

"Edmund's been worried because the MCs have been blocking his dock access. He doesn't know why, just says they don't like anyone doing things in what they consider their territory."

"Wouldn't it make more sense that it's the Hangmen involved in that shit, since they were at the race?"

"Maybe. Edmund says all the MCs like to throw their weight around, always want a cut of shit they did none of the work on. So I just mentioned that getting through the docks shouldn't be a problem for you, because you had an in."

I groaned. "Don't you think that might've made Edmund see me as a liability instead?"

There was a pause and then, "You can't think Edmund caused that crash?"

"He called me and said he couldn't get in touch with you."

"I left my phone at the shop."

"You never do that, Noah."

"I was in a hurry—it was a last minute job."

"Edmund implied he'd hurt you if I didn't do your job."

"Fuck. Edmund lost a ton of money. He's pissed, Rush. He thinks the MC sabotaged his car. That somehow, we've caused an MC war."

"That's ridiculous."

"So is cutting the brakes on a car you needed to deliver on," he pointed out. "Ryker's really got you turned around."

"Whoever cut the brakes knew that car was going to be stolen."

"But they wouldn't know you'd be the one stealing it, Rush."

"Unless Edmund told them, since he goddamned knew."

Noah paused. "Maybe Ryker let that out."

"Ryker didn't know anything about it." But I started thinking about what Ryker said, about how he'd had his guys watching me. In which case . . . would they have known what I was planning? They weren't wiretapping my conversations though. Following me was different than spying on me to know my next moves.

"You're really hung up on him."

I countered with, "He's been with me through my recovery."

"Ouch," Noah said plaintively, followed by a string of curses, the squeal of tires on asphalt. I was doing ninety, a straight shot up on the semideserted highway, so I waited until he said, "That was close. Think I lost them. Look, after the accident, I told Edmund you didn't want to do these jobs, and he agreed not to call you again. So that's done. And dude, Ryker's MC. He's the fuck-you-and-leave-you type."

"And you know this how? Because I didn't realize you'd fucked your way through Havoc."

Noah's tone softened. "Rush, come on. I just think you're putting too much into this. He's having fun. He liked the chase, but once he caught you . . ."

No more flowers.

Noah continued, "I think you're confusing sex and love, Rush, and you're the last person who should be. You've never trusted very easily, so why now, with him? I mean, look, you're talking Havoc here. Even for you, that's extreme."

I stared at the open road and, for the first time, fully realized that maybe I couldn't trust my best friend. I hated him for that, wanted to hate Ryker more for opening my eyes to it, but I couldn't. He'd been trying to protect me.

But I couldn't discount what Noah was saying either. "Ryker knows things about me."

"Like what? Sex things?"

"Beyond sex things." Although he knew those really well too. And he made me realize there were things I actually did like.

Like bottoming. For him. "You know, about Dad. Billy. My record."

Noah huffed. "So that makes him Prince Charming?"

"Little bit, yeah."

"You need to get your head out of his ass, Rush. We've got shit to do."

"Like what? You said it was a one-time thing. That if we wanted more, we picked, but if we wanted to be done, that'd be it."

"And we both knew it wouldn't stay that way." He paused. "Billy'd love this."

He meant that. It was a nonmanipulative, purely truthful statement, said wistfully. We both missed our friend. Our partner in crime.

Noah and Billy liked to steal. They only specialized because that was my thing. Because I didn't like the idea of breaking in and invading someone else's space, no matter how wealthy they were. It wasn't what I did.

I'm sure Noah and Billy had done runs without me. I'm sure Noah felt that urge still. But we were back in the car game now, and there was safety in doing things together. I was also beginning to realize just how locked into this Noah was—and me, by extension—because of Edmund.

There wasn't time to worry about who was after Noah. He owed Edmund a car and even though Edmund was the one who'd fucked up the last job, dammit, I hadn't even thought twice about helping Noah. But inside, I was torn somewhere between *Ryker wouldn't want me to do this* and *I don't take orders from anyone*, and I was pissed that I was torn. Because Ryker wasn't here, for all his talk. And I had no real way to reach him either.

"Why didn't you tell me about this sooner?" I demanded. "You're in so fucking deep, Noah, and now so am I."

"I was protecting you."

"Yeah? How's that?"

Noah sighed. "You were trying to stay out of trouble. I was too, but I couldn't handle it. I figured . . . I wouldn't tempt you. But I was scouting out jobs for both of us. Finding ways we could do what we wanted to do without getting into trouble."

Noah's twisted logic made perfect sense to me. More so when he said, "You're always taking care of me. Like you always took care of Billy. I wanted to do the same for you."

The guilt lodged itself in my throat, because he was so sincere when he said that I always took care of Billy. In my estimation, I'd gotten him killed because I hadn't been able to stop him from doing exactly what Noah was doing—putting himself in the line of fire for me.

Which was exactly what Ryker was doing too.

I couldn't take any more blood on my conscience. "Where are you now?"

"Crossing the state line."

"And they're still following?"

"Yeah. I just hope the rest of their gang's not doubling back to steal the other car I need."

"What's the address—I'll try to find you the shortest route," I lied. He rattled it off. "I'm on it."

"Rush—"

I hung up before he could say anything else.

CHAPTER 11

BABY WHAT YOU WANT ME TO DO

According to Noah, the Corvette was half a mile from the 3-D movie theater, at a private house in a gated community. I parked in the massive movie theater lot, bought a ticket, went inside the actual theater with popcorn and a soda and came out the back emergency exit once the movie started. It was ten forty-five. I walked to the house, casually, like I belonged in the area, and no one looked at me twice.

Someone was watching over me, because no one was home, and because they counted on the gated community keeping riffraff like me out, their garage wasn't locked, and nothing was armed. I ran my hand along the bumper, introducing myself to her. She was in decent shape, but she'd been ridden a lot and no doubt her gears were stripped. And, I noticed, she was goddamned open.

No respect. I probably could've gone inside to find the keys so I didn't have to take her column apart, but I didn't have the time. I disabled the tracking chip and the GPS and guided her carefully down the road and took the most secluded way possible back to the docks.

It had taken me under three minutes to lift her. No one else seemed to be aware that she was part of the deal for Noah and Edmund, so I didn't have to do the evade-and-escape thing the way Noah was. When I checked my phone, I saw he'd called me a million times. I didn't text him back, because if Edmund really wanted me gone, I wasn't giving him my whereabouts as extra ammunition. And hopefully Noah didn't mention to Edmund that he'd given me the address.

For a moment, I thought about just going—taking her down to Florida. I could pick up Noah and we'd go together. Except Noah had no interest in starting over. He was living in the past and I was caught somewhere between present and future.

I pulled the car into a secluded spot a couple of blocks away from the dock, pocketed the registration and snapped a picture of the car before walking over to the north side.

There were always people hanging around the docks. It was difficult to tell who was legitimate and who wasn't because everyone was seedy looking. Tonight, it was more crowded than normal. Lots of shipments going out, but no police and customs agents around at this time of night. I spotted the container that we'd brought the last car to. Same guys too—Carlton, the one Noah mentioned, plus two other big guys. But Carlton frowned when he saw me. Maybe because I wasn't dead?

"Noah got held up," I told him. "I've got one." I held up the registration in one hand and my phone with the picture and he looked at both.

"Deal was for two." He glanced up and down the area, suddenly antsy.

"Fine. I'll sell it someplace else." As soon as I turned, I felt the change in air. Forced myself not to turn around until the last possible second. When I did swing around to face the two men who'd been standing next to Carlton, I caught one of them solidly in the diaphragm. He doubled over, out of commission for a while, leaving me to deal with the giant bald man who sneered and grabbed me by the throat.

I chopped his arm and he let go. A couple of quick, well-placed movements brought him down. Another thing I'd learned from hanging out with those Special Forces guys—economy of movement was imperative. Never use six moves when two will do. Also, know your strength. If you can kill with your bare hands, you have to know how and when to hold back.

When he went down, I walked over to Carlton. "Car or no?"

He sneered. "Give me the goddamned car. No money until Noah shows."

"How about half, asshole. Because you'll still sell this one."

I guess he figured he wouldn't get rid of me. He paid me and I checked the money, then gave him the directions to find the car and walked away. Unless I wanted to pass the men I'd taken down again, I'd have to take the long way down the docks.

Obviously, Noah playing my wingman wasn't happening, so I was prepared to walk home.

I made it halfway through the big field that separated the docks from the rest of society when I heard the bikes. In seconds, I was surrounded. Which meant whatever was happening was part of a setup. Had to be, because I never fucking got caught, and unless Noah actually *had* been stupid enough to tell Edmund I was helping him . . .

It took me ten seconds to realize two things: the guys surrounding me were Havoc, and they hadn't caught me as much as saved my ass, since Carlton's goons were coming back for me. Or at least trying to, and currently being held by two large, black leather–wearing Havoc guys.

I turned around to face the MC guys and in no way was I prepared to see Ryker, standing calmly next to his big black bike, waiting. For me. And while there was patience in his stance, there was none in his expression when he said, "You're hurt."

"I'm fine," I told him through clenched teeth. Because I was sore and fighting hadn't helped but I'd handled it, dammit. "What's going to happen to those two guys?"

"Let me worry about that," Ryker told me. Hell, I would—the fewer of Edmund's guys around, the better.

Ryker wasn't coming toward me. I could stand in the middle like an idiot or move closer so everyone didn't hear our conversation. So I did. The other MC members backed off a little, giving us space, which was good. Or bad, maybe. I wasn't sure yet. Who the hell knew what Ryker told them about me? About who I was? Some random car thief he was helping, probably.

"Why were you on the docks?" I asked, and Ryker stared at me, then raised his brows. "No fucking way are you here for me."

"If we weren't here already, it goddamned would've been because of you," he informed me. "I told you that you'd need to lay low for a while not ten hours ago."

"You left." It came out of my mouth before I could stop it, and he looked confused.

"What are you talking about?"

"I woke up. You were gone."

"I told you I'd had somebody on you."

"Yeah but . . ." Christ, I was not this needy. *Pull it together, Rush.* I'd just boosted a significant chunk of change in car and parts. I'd defended my country. I didn't need to be fucking taken care of. I didn't need a relationship, no matter how badly I suddenly thought I wanted one. "I don't want to need you."

Ryker tilted his head to the side, frowning slightly. "Is it really so bad?"

When you leave, and I don't know what the fuck to do? Yeah. And I was pretty sure I didn't say that last part out loud, but the way he looked at me . . . dammit, I didn't have to say anything.

"You're fucking up my meeting, Sean. Badly."

He looked different. I'd seen him in his leathers before, but in a much different context. Here, he was primed and ready for some kind of meeting or brawl or whatever the fuck, and he wanted me the hell out of there.

"I can't do this." I motioned between us. "Whatever it is, I can't do it."

"Why's that?"

"For one thing, I'm not good at being controlled, being told what to do. And this? You're telling me I'm fucking up your business. I'm not going to sit at home not doing anything because it might fuck with your business."

Ryker swore. "You're going to have to."

"And if I won't, what? You'll be done with me? Done pulling my ass from the fire?"

"You want me to do that, Sean? Why? Because that would make it easy on you?"

"Yes."

Ryker shook his head, huffed out a breath, his anger dissipating in front of my eyes. Mine didn't, but he didn't seem to expect it to. His arms were crossed though, and his body language was serious.

I pushed my luck. "I didn't ask for this. I'll get the fuck out of here. I get how things work in your world."

"What do you know about my world?" Ryker demanded.

"Enough to know I could ruin your image if your club knew about us," I muttered. God, I was a fucking brat, because he'd told me I was in the middle of his work—nothing about being embarrassed to be around me—but I took it there anyway. Because I was pretty damned certain gay bikers weren't a thing.

Once I'd said it, I couldn't take it back, so I just turned and walked away.

Before I could get farther than two steps, his heavy hand was on the back of my neck, his other arm spinning me around so not only was I facing him again, but I was pressed against his body.

There was dead silence all around us.

Then he leaned in and kissed the shit out of me, one of those tongue-fucking, *I'm going to fuck you blind* promises of a kiss kisses.

I surged against him, because my body always turned goddamned traitor for Ryker, and he chuckled into my mouth when I groaned.

Then he pulled back, his eyes dark and serious. "Got it, Sean? I don't give a fuck who knows you're mine, but I do give a fuck when you disrespect me by not fucking listening to me in front of my club. Clear?"

It was. But I was stuck on the *mine* thing, especially when he said, "Let's go," straddled his bike and jerked his head toward the back. Like I was supposed to get on behind him. Like he hadn't heard a goddamned word I said about not being able to sit at home and not wanting to worry about fucking up his business. He was ignoring my whole *we can't do this* speech.

But my car was an hour away, and I had no other way out of here. I couldn't hang out at the docks alone after this display, and it's not like there were waiting cabs.

I was trapped, but hell, that's not the reason I was considering getting on his bike.

Around us, the other bikers were still silent. I felt like an idiot, and, as if he knew, he cupped my chin and winked at me, then smiled.

But I couldn't. Still, I kept my voice down so no one could hear when I told him, "I'm not riding in the bitch seat."

He was trying not to grin, but failing. "Why not?"

"I know exactly what it means when you ride on the back of a guy's bike."

"Really?"

"It means you fucking own me, Ryker."

"Don't I?"

His words were a low rumble that shot straight to my dick and holy fuck . . . I had no answer. Well, obviously I did, but I refused to put voice to it.

I was out—that wasn't the issue. And obviously being out wasn't an issue for him either. But the MC shit, we'd never talked about it, what it meant for us. All these men knew about our relationship, knew he was looking out for me. Knew he considered me his.

I swear I had to remind myself to breathe.

"Get on the bike, Sean."

This time, Ryker's tone left no room for argument. If anything, it made me harder. I stopped thinking—par for the course when I was around Ryker—and I got on the bike behind him.

PASSENGER

Ryker's bike was sleek and silent. He powered through the darkness, and I leaned into the curves with him. I'd ridden before, bought a bike when I was sixteen, but I'd given it up quickly, because a car thief who rode a motorcycle was too damned visible.

Now, I wondered why I had given it up so easily. The ride was awesome, the freedom a blast of energy. Or maybe that was because I'd cheated death, at this point, more times than I cared to count.

I lost track of how long we were on the road, because really, what the hell did it matter? I had nowhere to be, no job, no one to report to. No one except the man sitting in front of me, if I was to believe what he said.

I know *he* thoroughly believed it.

Eventually, he pulled off the road and guided the bike uphill along a narrow path, going deeper into the woods. Finally, he stopped in a clearing that was off even that path, shielded and private, although there was light filtering softly into the area.

"Where are we?" I asked as I got off the bike and took off the borrowed helmet.

"Havoc land." He did the same, then tugged me to him. He was hard, so that was a consolation, like I might have a bit of control in this situation. "You're staying with me."

"I don't think those guys from the docks will bother me anymore."

"Wasn't a question."

I stared at him, starting to wonder if it was worth arguing over. But he wasn't even going to let me get that far, because he was guiding my head to his chest, cradling it. I hadn't even realized the tension making it pound. Whether the pain was physical or emotional, I couldn't pull them apart.

"'S'all right, Sean. I'll take care of everything."

"I can take care of myself." My broken record.

"You don't have to." And that was his. His hand was big and warm as his fingertips rubbed my scalp, then moved to my neck. His cock was rigid against mine through our jeans. I just closed my eyes and tried to imagine being taken care of all the goddamned time. "But you do have to start listening."

"I'm not a goddamned dog you're teaching to heel." I pushed back, but his arms banded like steel around me. "And I'm not fucking you so . . ."

Ryker rolled his hips against mine, said, "Ah, sugar, don't be like that."

Shit. He used the drawl that went up and down my spine like his touch. The sex drawl. "Ryker . . ."

"Yeah, that's the sound." He wasn't making fun of me at all. If I wasn't reading that wrong, I'd think he was . . . *worried* about me. Like, beyond the possessive crap. "I wasn't there when you had your accident. I should've been. You should've had my number in your phone. I should've been your first call. Beyond that, I should've been keeping a better eye on you, so you didn't get into that position in the first place. You should've been able to come to me the second Edmund called you."

The guilt in his voice was so apparent, I ached. I put a hand on his chest, keeping our bodies separate for a moment so I could think. "None of that's your fault, Ryker. I don't blame you for it. I'm really okay. I can take care of myself."

"I know you can. But suppose I want to do it?"

"Why?"

"Sean, you really still have to ask?"

"Obviously, yes."

He pushed my hand away and turned me around, pulled me so my back was to his chest. Licked the spot behind my ear as his hand went to my zipper. "How about I show, then tell?"

"I can't argue with that."

"Good. See, I'm really a reasonable guy."

I laughed. "Next you'll tell me that you don't bite."

"Oh, I definitely bite. I've been tame so far."

"Tame?" I managed as he pulled my jeans open and down, and his hand circled my cock. My breath hitched, and he chuckled against my skin, stroking me, running a finger between my ass cheeks, fingering me open. My jeans were around my ankles. My hands were on the heavy leather seat of the bike. "Ryker . . ."

"Got you," he said as his free hand trailed along my hip.

"I don't know . . ."

"I do."

His tongue ran down my spine. He sank to his knees behind me. Spread me. Ran his tongue down my ass crack, then buried his face in my ass, rimming me. That had been pretty new to me before Ryker started invading my bed, but he seemed to love it. His tongue circled my hole, and then he speared it, fucked me with it, thrusting in and out as I struggled to hang on to any last shred of dignity I had before I whimpered his name.

Ryker had complete control. The one thing I never told him to do was stop, because I didn't want that at all.

It wasn't any kind of race to the finish, because no matter how fast, how intense things were between us, Ryker always kept me skating that edge until I couldn't stand it. I was holding on to the bike so hard my hands would ache in the morning. He held me so tightly I'd have bruises, and I wanted that.

He'd pushed me past any boundaries I'd set for myself before, and it didn't appear that he planned on stopping.

I wanted to grab my cock, but I needed to hang on. "Ryk, come on, touch me."

I jutted my hips forward, looking desperately for any kind of friction. He buried his tongue deeper inside of me, and I groaned into the darkness, begging. "Please. Come on, fuck my cock. I need . . ."

He put me out of my misery, winding an arm around to jack me in time with his tongue, making the orgasm a hard, blissful blast.

After I came all over his seat, he was up, entering me from behind, driving me onto my toes.

"Sean," Ryker murmured against my neck, and for a long moment, we were still. Staring at the sky. And then he fucked me over his bike, hard and fast, until I cried out his name, and he bit the back of my neck and then sucked it as he came, his entire body shuddering against mine.

We stayed like that for a while, the cool air like heaven on my skin. Everything was calm around us—I was finally calm. And I saw no reason not to go with him to Havoc. Because even though he acted like I didn't have a goddamned choice, I did, and I guess I'd just made it.

And even though Ryker hadn't asked me for an explanation about tonight's theft, I couldn't help but give one. "Noah was in trouble. I couldn't leave him hanging."

"He left you."

Well, not really, but hell, I was too tired to explain it all. I simply said, "That's not the way I am, Ryker."

He put his face between my shoulders, his arms tightening around me. "I know. But this is going to kill you, babe. One way or another."

I swallowed hard, but didn't respond. Because I'd been thinking the same thing for as long as I'd been in this shit. But once I'd gotten sucked in, there wasn't much I could do about it—I was good at it. I liked it. And it allowed me to keep running, from everyone and everything.

Ryker was someone I couldn't run from—at least not for the past eight months—because he always found me. Because I wasn't in control. And for the first time in my life, it was a fucking relief.

CHAPTER 13

CAN'T COME DOWN

We got back on the bike and rode the last mile to Ryker's place. I couldn't get a sense of the compound in the dark, and when he ushered me inside his house, he said, "I'll show you around in the morning."

I stared around at the open floor plan—the first floor had a fireplace, and thanks to the spotlight off the back porch, a great view of land. A killer kitchen. I looked up and saw the second floor. The whole place was modern mixed with rustic. It was huge, capable, and surprising, just like the man himself.

He offered me a beer. I asked for a soda instead. He glanced at me and gave me a soda and Advil. I didn't bother pretending I didn't need them. As I drank the sugary drink, Ryker brought over a couple of sandwiches, and I ate as he made a few calls. He didn't try to hide what he was saying, but honestly, it had to be some kind of code, because I had no idea what he was talking about.

I thought about Bertha's, where we'd first met. The bar was mainly an after-hours club, and it was in the middle of buttfuck nowhere, kind of like this compound. And since Bertha's was rumored to be owned by Havoc, it was constantly packed with women (and men) hoping to catch a glimpse of a real, live Havoc biker. They were like celebrities at this point, more so than any other MC I'd ever come across. There was just a level of secrecy about them, and their mystique had been built on that.

That, plus the danger, plus Ryker, all equaled a major fucking turn-on for me.

Which he also fucking knew.

"You know too much," I grumbled, not expecting him to answer.

"Which is something that never bothers you when I'm fucking you," he pointed out. He put his phone down and asked, "Nightmares this week?"

"You tell me, Superman."

"At least two. You'll sleep better tonight."

He was right. On both counts. "It's really all right that I'm here?"

"You're with me. That makes it all right."

I studied him. He'd taken his cut off. The black T-shirt he wore pulled tight across his chest and the tattoos stood out under the lights. "Your MC really doesn't care that you're gay? Because I'm just not seeing gay and biker going together."

"No one saw gay and soldier together either," he said. "Just as easy to be a gay outlaw as it is to be a straight one. Besides, MC world's no place for a woman."

"That doesn't stop them."

"Everyone likes bad boys."

I smiled at the truth in that. "I just wouldn't have expected an MC to be that enlightened."

"Some are, some aren't. But I grew up in this—guys know what I can do. Nothing to do with who I fuck and besides, anyone who's got an issue with it has to come to me."

And since he was built like a brick motherfucking wall . . . "That's cool."

"If you can't trust your brothers, who can you trust?" he asked and my gut twisted, because right now I wasn't sure if I could trust my best friend, never mind myself.

According to Ryker, I never should've in the first place. "You have any active duty MC members?"

He nodded. "They don't live on the compound, though."

His hands slid over my shoulders. He rubbed, his fingertips digging in enough for a powerful massage. I was, of course, putty in his hands. Jesus, I melted for this guy. If he'd bent me over his bike in front of those guys earlier, I'd have let him.

So what did that say about me?

"No way," he said.

"No way what?"

"If you're thinking this hard, I didn't fuck you well enough. Gotta start over."

"Dammit, I like it when you take control."

"Babe, I could've told you that from the first night we met."

"Why didn't you?"

"This is seriously news to you?"

He was still massaging my shoulders. I hung my head down and thought about that very first night we'd met. I'd only started drinking because I was nervous as hell after propositioning him. In fact, I'd done a couple of shots before propositioning too, to get up the nerve to even talk to him, especially after not being able to get his attention at all.

Women circled him, but I'd known he wasn't into them. Finally, I'd slid next to him where he stood, against one of the columns and told him, "The backroom's pretty quiet."

He'd stared at me, his dark eyes fixing on mine, and it was like he could see right through me. It was either the best thing I'd ever done, or my greatest mistake. Either way, I wasn't backing down.

"What's your name?"

"Sean Rush. Everyone calls me Rush."

"I don't hook up with drunk guys, Sean."

"I'm not drunk yet," I'd told him, walked a straight line, and touched my finger to his nose to prove it, because there was a fine line between wiseass and flirting and I'd always been comfortable jumping back and forth over it. "I'm planning on drinking tonight, but I'm giving you my consent now."

Ryker raised his brows. "Your consent?"

"Yeah. I'm not sure if you'll take me up on it."

"Why's that?"

"Big bad Havoc biker probably has his pick of men. So I'll play hard to get."

"Consenting ahead of time isn't playing hard to get," he'd told me.

"It is if you don't know where to find me later."

Now, his chuckle rumbled through me. "You're thinking about that first night. You remember biting me?"

I did. Right before I walked away, I'd nipped his neck along his collarbone.

"Yeah, you bit me, then did that gorgeous strut thing you do." He leaned in then, nipped me on the neck, and I shuddered a little. "You watched me over your shoulder after you walked away. And then you gave me that fucking smile. The one that makes you look like you're this innocent thing. And that's when I knew."

"Knew what?"

"That you weren't as cocky as you pretended to be at all. And *that* was more of a turn-on than anything else you could've done." He gave a knowing smirk. "It was also a dare."

He was right. I'd been daring him as much as I'd been daring myself. "From that point on, my memory's fuzzy."

He leaned in, an elbow on the counter, and grinned. "You don't remember dancing for me?"

"Ah . . ." Jesus, he had to be lying, although it totally sounded like something I'd do.

"It was so fucking hot, Sean."

I closed my eyes. Tried to picture it. "I started off on the bar, didn't I?"

"That's such a lucky guess."

"I must've worked my way over to you."

He turned the stool so I faced him. His gaze held mine, and I couldn't look away. "You gave me a lap dance."

No wonder he'd snuck in and fucked me. I'm surprised I hadn't bent myself over the bar and told him to fuck me right then and . . . "I didn't tell you to fuck me on the bar, did I?"

He gave me a smirky smile, and I groaned, buried my face in my hands.

"I wouldn't have done it. Although I wanted to take you right there. That would've been fucking hot. Taking you, showing everyone you were mine."

Well, yeah, that was hot. Really hot.

"If I'd told you to bend over for me, you would've," he murmured. "You told me as much when you were dancing."

I bit out a curse. His eyes were dark with lust.

"So yeah, you intrigued me enough to take you up on your invite and follow you inside. But after I crawled into your bed, spent time there listening to the way you let go when you fucked . . . I knew I was the one who was screwed."

He actually looked a little pissed by that. Ryker didn't lose control—not easily. We were a lot alike.

"Sorry I messed up your life."

He grunted. "You'll make it up to me."

"How's that?"

The grin that spread along his face made me squirm. It was fucking indecent when he did that. "Lap dance."

My first instinct was to tell him to go fuck himself, but my cock? Seemed to motherfucking love the idea. "I need booze."

He went into another room and came back with a bottle of tequila and two shot glasses. In the background, the low drumbeat of one of his favorite songs played.

Turn on your love light . . .

I slammed back two shots. Went a little slower on the third. It'd been a while since I'd had anything to drink—nearly eight fucking months, so it hit me decently hard. By the fourth shot, I was loosening up. Which was always a dangerous proposition since the words *Sean* and *inhibitions* were never within a million-mile radius of each other anyway.

Ryker did a couple of shots too. He'd moved over to a big comfortable leather recliner. The lights dimmed. I closed my eyes and I was back in the bar, needing so badly for Ryker to notice me.

I hadn't known exactly why back then. I knew now, and it still made me shaky. I leaned over and grabbed the back of his chair, penning him in, my legs straddling his. He watched me as I danced, sparking flashes of memory.

He'd looked at me the same way back then. Like he'd owned me from day goddamned one.

When the song ended, I moved away, took another drink.

Ryker's voice rumbled, "Come here, Sean."

I was freaking out inside, but I obeyed. Like, what the fuck, did he hypnotize me with his voice or something? Ryker stood, tugged a hand through my hair and then put a hand on my shoulder to push me to my knees. From there, I knew what to do, what I wanted. But he gripped my hair tighter. Normally, anything he did was a turn-on but tonight . . . tonight this was triggering something I hadn't felt in a long time. Maybe it was the alcohol or the stress of what was happening with Noah. The fact that I was at Havoc, which meant things were really out of my control.

Ryker murmured, "So pretty down there. Put your mouth on me, baby. Want to see that. Want to take a picture of it, tape it so I can watch it anytime I want."

The panic rose inside of me. I tried to fight it, though, because Ryker had never asked me for anything. Until he'd started asking me to separate from Noah.

With my face in his crotch, his hand carding my hair, I tried to push it all out of my mind. But I couldn't.

I went to get up, but Ryker was faster. If he'd tried to hold me down, I would've fought him. Instead, he sank to his knees and faced me.

"Don't," he said—I didn't know what I wasn't supposed to have done. Fight? Pull away? Ignore his orders? "What the hell just happened?"

"Nothing." My voice sounded hollow. I'd given him blowjobs before—many times before—and I'd never had this reaction. Then again, a lot of shit was coming out in the open for me, a lot of memories surfacing that were better off dead and buried.

"Sean, you gotta trust me. Because if you don't . . ."

"I'll get hurt," I said numbly. "You know how many times I heard that in my life?"

"No. Why not tell me?"

"I don't think so."

Ryker swallowed hard and said, "Okay, Sean. Why don't you take the bed, and I'll stay out here."

I hated the way he sounded—hurt. Upset. Pissed. But I didn't tell him that, and it didn't stop me from getting up and moving up the stairs to the bedroom. I shut the door and sat against it for a long time. Finally, I grabbed a blanket and pillow off the bed, and I curled up in front of the locked door and drifted in and out.

I wasn't sure who I hated more—him for not begging to come in or me for not calling for him.

CHAPTER 14

FEEL LIKE A STRANGER

In the morning, I showered, trying to wash away last night's failure. The hot water sluiced over me, easing my hangover just slightly. When I dressed and went downstairs, I found myself alone. But there was a *Be right back* note with the time on it, and breakfast waiting under the cover of a tray so it stayed warm.

I poured coffee. Piled some food on a plate, because I knew eating would make me feel better. And I ventured outside to the big covered porch, so I could watch the comings and goings of Havoc while I ate.

The compound was miles wide. If I squinted and angled my head just right, I could see a large building in the center that was probably the main clubhouse. I suspected that the trees were buffers for other houses built all around the clubhouse.

It was quiet and calm, the roar of Harleys muffled by the hills. But I could still hear the bikes coming and going. And when Ryker's roared up his driveway, the nervousness faded, replaced by the familiar lust and longing.

He wasn't wearing a helmet, just jeans and a long-sleeved thermal T-shirt—dark gray—pushed up to the elbows. I stared at the rose on his hand, and the others snaking along his arms, because that red ink stood out among the mostly grayscale and darker colors. I was still looking at it when he came onto the porch and settled into the chair next to me. He leaned forward, put a hand on my thigh.

"Glad you're eating. Did you sleep?"

Had he not checked on me at all? Did he really give me that kind of space? "Yeah."

"You sound better."

"It was a long day," I said.

He ran a hand along the back of my neck, pressed a kiss below my ear, and I was hard instantly. So, yeah, no permanent damage done to my body's reaction to him. "Yeah, it was. Today will be better."

"You're going to show me around this place?"

"I am."

"So it's not super top secret?"

"Well, it is. For you, I made an exception. Most of Havoc already knows you anyway."

"You mean, after last night?"

"No."

"Because you had them follow me for the past eight months?"

"Sean, you don't think you have a rep?"

"Not like that." Jesus. I ran my hands through my hair and stared at the big man who most definitely had a rep.

"I knew about you before you went into the Army."

I tried to process that, then decided it was better I didn't. For now, at least. "What exactly does Havoc do?"

"We ride." I rolled my eyes, and he added, "Porn."

My stomach tightened, and the shitty, panicked feelings I'd had last night threatened again. I pushed them down, not sure how long that'd last. "Why porn?"

"It's legal. We've got major productions. Some webcam stuff. Lots of our stars come vetted from this guy named Tenn. His brother's a Viper."

"Sex and fast bikes."

"Best things in life. Both legal."

"Except when the bikes are stolen."

"If they're stolen," Ryker corrected. "We also have Bertha's. Gypsy's Bail Bonds is his own business and it's housed in town, but it's backed by Havoc. We don't run drugs or guns. And we've never let ourselves be managed by anyone but ourselves."

I pretended not to notice he hadn't answered the original question about why porn. "And you're all perfect angels too. I bet you help out in soup kitchens on your days off."

Ryker snorted. "I'm not going to pretend we haven't done some bad shit, but only if it's warranted. We don't start it, but we'll finish it if someone fucks with us or with what's ours. Our guys are rough. Some've done time. Some will fuck up beyond the club being able to save them."

"Anything else?"

"We also provide protection," he said. "Sometimes for individuals or bands. Sometimes for other things."

Everything Ryker said, beyond the porn, was murky. Spread out. Nothing you could put your finger on, pin them down on. And I assumed that was the point. They didn't want anyone knowing their business, because that would mean they couldn't do their business well. Havoc operated very much like the military in that regard.

And the compound was busy. Like a minitown. There were two restaurants that were apparently just open for the Havoc members and their guests, and a garage that I figured was only for Havoc vehicles.

We got halfway across the compound, Ryker waving at groups of people sitting on their porches or hanging out at the garage or outside the small restaurant, when I noticed a man walking through the compound. He commanded attention. Tall. Lanky but well built. Long dark hair tied back from his face. Tanned golden with bright blue eyes—probably the first thing you'd notice about him. They forced you to home in, concentrate. Mesmerizing.

"That's the president of Havoc," Ryker told me. "Name's Samuel Sweeting. Aka Sweet."

Sweet had a lollipop in his mouth, the stick hanging out the corner. He grinned, patting men on the back as he passed them.

"Is he married?"

"Sweet? He's a player, born and bred. Never wanting for company."

And despite all that, the loneliness coming off the guy was palpable. At least to me, and especially when his hawk-like gaze settled on me. For a long moment, he stared, and then he turned his attention to Ryker, motioning for him to come closer.

Ryker nodded in Sweet's direction, then told me, "I'll be back. Look around and stay out of trouble. Is that possible?"

"Of course," I scoffed. Although really, I wasn't sure about that at all. But he went over to Sweet and disappeared, and I continued to walk around, drawn, of course, to the garage.

There was a '99 Aston Martin—cherry red—parked outside the garage. There were three men standing around, staring at it like somehow that would fix it. Give these guys a bike and undoubtedly they could break it down and put it back together blindfolded. But put a cage in front of them, and I swore they stared at it like it was some kind of devil.

I could've asked before barging in, but fuck it. Besides, although she might've been pretty in another life, she'd been beat to hell, and I hated to see cars not cared for. While Noah typically dealt with the bodywork, I cared for the guts. And if the outside looked like hell, the inside was usually worse.

I walked over and rested my hands on the hood reverently. I knew the guys thought I was nuts—mostly true—but I didn't give a fuck.

"Mind if I take a look?" I asked finally.

"Go ahead," one of them said. They were all wearing Havoc cuts. Everywhere I looked was leather and Harleys. This was the only car I saw.

I was aware, as I worked, that those guys had left, that I was the only one around. And I was okay with that. Once I started her up and tuned the transmission and fixed the other myriad small issues, she sounded great.

I looked past the garage and all I saw were hills. Open land. And a small paved road running through it. I looked back at the car and back to the road and wondered if it was suicide. But before I could talk myself out of it, I was putting the car into gear and traveling along those miles of open road as fast as I could take the corners.

When I pulled in post-joyride, miraculously I was still alone. I parked her, hung the keys where I'd found them on the board and headed to find Ryker.

Instead, I got half pulled into the small restaurant I'd seen earlier. A short blonde woman said, "I'm Greta. And it's lunchtime."

"Lunchtime?" I asked, like I'd never heard the term before.

"Yes, sugar. Food. Let's go." She motioned for me to follow, and I stopped arguing. Inside the big room was a table running down the middle of the place, with smaller tables all around it.

"We eat family style on Wednesdays and Sundays," she told me. "Sit. Dig in. Don't be shy."

"You know I'm not . . ."

"Not what?" She studied me. "You're with Ryker, right?"

"Yes."

"Then grab a plate and dig in."

Two of the guys who'd been there when I'd first started to work on the Aston Martin came in. Sat down on either side of me, dwarfing me. Not talking. When they got up, taking their plates with them, I wondered what the hell was going on, but a second later, Ryker sat down next to me.

"Were they bodyguarding me?" I asked him.

"You stole Sweet's car."

"Sweet's car," I echoed. "Shit, not the Aston."

"Uh, yeah."

"I didn't steal. I borrowed," I protested. "I returned it. Is that why those guys were sitting next to me? To hold me here?"

"Pretty much."

"They let me fix the car. What, am I being hazed?" Ryker sighed. "I'll apologize."

"Right. Apologize. Simple as fuck. These guys are looking for an excuse to fuck with you. And you gave it to them."

"'S'what I do," I muttered, looked down at my plate. When I glanced back over at him he was gone.

After I finished eating, I walked back toward Ryker's place. It was one thing to have Greta make me lunch, but another for me to act like I really did belong here. I didn't want to be pissed at Ryker for semideserting me, because hell, I could handle myself anywhere. But Havoc was different—this was his world, and there were rules. Rules I didn't know.

So yeah, I didn't like that vulnerable feeling I had when I didn't have the lay of the land.

Times like this, I realized how much I missed Billy. And now, Noah too.

I was halfway across the compound when I noticed several guys walking in my general direction. And maybe they were heading to Greta's for lunch, or to the clubhouse, but hell, I knew they were coming in my direction.

I kept walking until they were in front of me like a solid brick wall of leather.

"You're Rush," one of them said and I nodded. "You working for Edmund?"

"I was. Things didn't work out." I attempted to just go around them, but the guy who'd asked me the questions moved to stand directly in front of me. His patch was eye level, which meant he was bigger than Ryker. He had some prison tattoos on his face and arms too.

"I don't like him," he said now.

I glanced up at him. "Guess we've got something in common."

His hand went around my throat, holding me but not squeezing. I tried to tamp my temper down, because this could get really fucking bad. "We have nothing in goddamned common. I don't work for lowlifes."

I nodded. Stared at him. Maybe if I just agreed, he'd let go. Or maybe Ryker could just magically fucking appear. Like any time now.

"You still stealing cars?"

"Not at the moment."

"Fuckin' wiseass." He did squeeze my neck, and I tried not to struggle because he'd just get off on that. "What the fuck kind of trouble you bringing to Havoc?"

"You can ask Ryker."

"I'm askin' you."

"You really want . . . to know?" I managed.

He smiled. "Yeah, I really do, *Rush*."

I closed my eyes and pictured what I planned. Just like those Special Forces guys taught me. And then I executed my plan.

The big guy ended up rolling away, howling in pain, which was good. The other two attacked me, wrestled me to the ground, but after a few minutes of fighting, I managed to get one of their necks between my knees while I was holding the guy trying to punch me by the throat.

He got in a couple of shots, until I got annoyed enough to land a solid right hook. His nose spurted blood, but before he could do anything, he was gone. Someone was grabbing at me, attempting to pry my legs off the other guy's neck.

I kept fighting until I realized it was Ryker trying to pull me away. I let him, getting to my feet and surveying what was going on around me.

The biggest guy was up, talking to Sweet and pointing at me. The other two were still kind of rolling around on the ground.

Ryker grabbed my shoulder and shook me to get my attention. "What the fuck, Sean?"

"What the fuck, *Sean*?" I echoed. "How about, 'Are you okay, Sean?' Or 'I'm sorry I ditched you and left you alone on my big bad MC compound, Sean.' Those assholes jumped *me*. I didn't realize that as a guest of yours I was supposed to let myself get rolled by all the inhabitants of Asshole Island."

Ryker's jaw clenched, working overtime. I tugged away from him, because fuck no, I wouldn't take the blame for this.

It was then I noticed Sweet busy giving me the once-over, an angry glare on his face. Then he started to close in on me.

I stood my ground, because fuck that.

"What the fuck are you trying to do?" he demanded.

"Defend. Myself."

"You're a guest of Ryker's. You're making him look bad."

I wanted to tell him that I wasn't going to do anything to hurt Ryker, that I knew, deep down, that he was the one who'd end up hurting me. Havoc equaled family. Ryker's family. Another family that wouldn't accept me.

"Sorry. I'll let them beat the shit out of me for no reason next time. Maybe you should create a handbook for your guests so they know these things."

"You got a smart mouth on you, kid." Sweet tried to corner me, but I sidestepped. I'd let Ryker pin me down, but no one else. My hands fisted, but I knew I couldn't touch him.

"I've got a big fucking problem," Sweet growled. "Get the fuck out of my face before I show you how big it is."

It took everything I had to let him talk to me like that, to walk away. Because even though Noah might be an asshole, he'd never stand around and let anyone talk to me like that. But Ryker? What the fuck was he doing?

I started walking back to his house. Because from there I could at least call a cab and wait at the bottom of the hill. I felt him walking right behind me, because the motherfucker was still silent as hell.

We got to his porch before he grabbed for me and turned me around, but he didn't pin me. I clenched my jaw and my fists, and he stared at me. Finally, he asked, "Are you all right?"

"Yeah, I'm great," I snarled.

"You're bleeding."

"Then why the fuck did you ask if I was all right if you knew I wasn't?" I demanded.

"Calm down and—"

"I'm tired of being calm. Tired of being treated like your bitch by your fellow MCers." I walked away from him. "I'm not staying here anymore."

"The hell you're not."

"You don't fucking own me," I muttered under my breath, unaware of how close he was.

It wasn't until I ended up with my back against the wall, his body pinned to mine that I noticed how upset he looked. "I'll kill them for fucking with you."

And that's when I realized that this was going to be a bigger problem than I'd originally thought. Bigger, and way different.

CHAPTER 15

DON'T MESS UP A GOOD THING

He was still holding me up, but before I could tell him that we both needed to calm the fuck down—that I didn't want to put him in the position where he had to choose between me or his Havoc brothers—a bike backfired in the distance. It echoed through the hills, and I knew, in my rational mind, that's exactly what it was, that's all it was. But everything was jumbling, and when I blinked, I wasn't in Havoc anymore. I was in Iraq and the backfiring was gunfire, and it wasn't stopping.

I don't know how long I stood there frozen, but eventually I became aware of Ryker talking to me. Telling me everything was going to be all right. Touching me . . .

"Don't. Just fucking don't." I pushed at him, hard. Both palms to his chest. He stumbled back, more from surprise than anything.

I don't know when he'd let me down, but my feet were firmly on the deck.

"Sean . . ."

"Don't." It was the only thing I could say. If I attempted anything more, the whole truth would come out. About why last night had me all fucked up and why the porn bothered me. About how I didn't belong here, or anywhere. How all of this was a mistake. How I was coming between Ryker and his MC after less than twenty-four hours in Havoc.

"Let me take you home," he said.

I nodded, not trusting my voice. And I wouldn't ask if it was because he thought that was what I wanted, or if it was what Sweet wanted. Because really, I didn't want to know.

Instead, I climbed into his truck—he didn't even attempt the bike—and he took me home. We didn't speak on the hour-long drive. When we pulled into my driveway, I saw that my truck was back.

Noah had come through on that. Maybe he'd even called, but I hadn't checked my messages.

I walked into the house, aware Ryker was behind me. I wanted him to leave, but the only way to accomplish that was to pretend I was completely fine. I'd done this dance before, with Noah, with Linc, with a therapist or two in Iraq. I knew how to play the game.

There was a rose on the floor next to my bedside table. I hadn't seen it when I woke yesterday afternoon without him—Christ, that seemed like a lifetime ago.

I picked it up and twirled it in between my fingers. The thorns caught on my fingertips, and I was bleeding, but I didn't care.

"The flowers again?" he asked, and God, I felt stupid—again—as stupid as I did when he'd first started sending the roses to me. "You really don't remember anything about that first night?"

I didn't want to remember, because remembering would've forced me to come to terms with the fact that I'd fallen for Ryker, that he hadn't simply been fucking me. No, he'd been wooing me, courting me, playing my own game, turning the tables to beat me at it. And I'd never been so glad to lose in my motherfucking life.

"I remember some things," I admitted. Like his head between my legs, milking me until my balls tightened. Me, shooting so goddamned hard I figured I'd broken something. The first time he'd entered me was maybe the fourth time I'd been fucked in my life and that was saying something, since I'd had a lot of sex. "I don't know why you sent the flowers. I thought you were making fun of me."

I guess I still did. Even after I knew about the rose on his hand and especially after today, when I realized that, despite his threatening to hurt his Havoc brothers, I knew where his loyalties had to lie. Then again, mine kept right on lying with Noah, so I was just as bad.

Ryker frowned. "You came back over to me at the end of the night. You'd been drinking. Dancing. Pulling your usual shit, even after you propositioned me. And then you danced for me. Afterwards, you told me you were leaving, but before you did, you put your arms around my neck."

"Don't tell me." I closed my eyes and willed myself to remember. In a second, I was back inside the bar, my arms around Ryker, and he was teasing me, asking, "Is this you still playing hard to get?"

I was warm inside, from the alcohol, from being this close to Ryker. "Yeah. So don't disappoint me. I'm a romantic at heart."

"That so?"

"What's romance to you?"

"Flowers."

"What kind, Sean?"

"Roses."

"Why's that?"

"The first car I ever stole, there was a Grateful Dead sticker with red roses. When I stole the car, *American Beauty* was playing. Roses—and songs from the Dead—still make me hard."

Now, I said, "I can't believe you . . . fuck." I turned away from him, buried my face in the pillow.

"Sean . . . what's wrong?" His voice was quiet.

"Please just . . . fuck. Just go." My voice was hoarse. I closed my eyes. "I don't want to talk about it."

I didn't want to talk about anything. I didn't want someone—anyone—knowing me that well at all, and the worst part of it was, I'd let him in on it. It was my fucking fault, and I'd fucked everything up. Again.

I felt the mattress shift as he got up, and I thought he'd left. Until he said, "The thorns."

I straightened at the sound of his voice. Stared at my fingertips that had been cut by the thorns moments before. When I dared to turn around, I saw he was at the door.

"I get it, Sean. I get the thorns." Then he was gone, shutting the door behind him. I curled on the mattress, blanket wrapped around me, watching mindless TV until I was bleary. I didn't want to sleep. Couldn't, because I knew the nightmare would come.

The nightmare always started out the same. I was in the car—the '88 Porsche 959—and Billy was next to me. We were going at least ninety, because forcing a car like that to go slower was a goddamned crime. There was some disco crap playing on the radio—Billy loved it and claimed it was from the eighties, so I let that slide.

He pointed to a turnoff, and I followed his direction. When I made the left, past and present melded and there was no more road. Just desert. Miles and miles of sand everywhere, and I looked at Billy, but he was singing along to the radio, not caring.

The car wasn't handling well. I shifted and tried to get her moving, but the sand was trapping the wheels, clogging the engine. Billy refused to close his window and I tasted the sand. It made my eyes gritty.

"Billy, we've got to get the fuck out of here," I told him. "We've been here before. It's not good."

"Rush, relax." He put a hand on my shoulder. "You can turn around if you want, but I don't think you can go back. You're not supposed to go backwards."

I was going to try. Dammit, I was going to try my best. Four months in this godforsaken desert and I'd learned more than I'd ever wanted to know about death and dying. Every day was a new explosion, a new lesson in firearms and hidden mines and roadside bombs.

I put the car in reverse, but it went nowhere. I turned, a wide arc, and realized that the desert behind us had disappeared. Everything had disappeared.

I got out then, tried to stare at the horizon, but the darkness was falling fast.

I heard the shots crack in the darkness. Two of them, sharp and sure, and I yelled at Billy to get down. Until I realized he'd run right in front of me, and the shots had gone straight through him.

He turned around and shrugged. "Can't go back, Rush. Keep moving forward."

I reached for him, but he disappeared. He was gone and in his place was the porn studio, where I'd sucked a dick for money, because I'd been given no other choice. I was on my knees and there was no sand, no Iraq.

No Billy.

I must've been screaming in my sleep, because Ryker was talking to me. Telling me I was okay. Telling me, "Open your fucking eyes."

And that's when I realized he'd never actually left me. "I don't think you're supposed to curse at someone having a nightmare," I muttered when I finally pulled myself out of it. "Besides, I wasn't screaming that loud."

He stared down at me, his face etched in concern. I blew out a shaky breath. He brushed the hair from my forehead. "I'll be right back. You'll be okay for a second?"

"Yeah."

"Good." He never made me feel stupid—that was all me. He never made me feel like anything less than a man, and I wasn't sure how he did it.

I heard the water running, and then he was leading me into the bathroom, putting me in the big tub I never used, and I leaned back against him and I relaxed in the warm water. With his big arms wrapped around me.

It was the first time the intricacies of the roses that wound into his forearms really registered. I traced them with a fingertip and swear I could feel him smiling behind me, that *now he gets it* smile.

Jesus. "Ryk, I . . ."

"Relax, Sean. You had a rough week. Just please put your head back and fucking relax. You deserve it."

No reproach or anger. I turned and somehow curled against him in that tub, and I don't really remember him taking me out, drying me, putting me to bed. I do know that I slept through till morning and when I woke, he was gone, but there was a single red rose by the bedside. A new one. I stared at it and at the heavy brown thorns that someone could easily overlook while reaching for the beauty.

Ryker'd risked all of that, for me. Worked his way around, all the way up to the rose . . . and I'd closed up, refused to fucking open.

I blinked, and I was fifteen again. I'd just escaped that studio where the guy had made me blow him in front of the camera and then threw money at me like I was a fucking dog. I took it, because he fucking owed me. Because I had nothing else to live on. My mom had split the month before—Dad had been in jail for years by that point, and there was nothing left. I was a week away from getting kicked out of the apartment. I'd already been to juvie and gotten out two months later than I was supposed to.

My mom had introduced me to these men who ran the porn studio where she'd worked months earlier, but I'd refused to work with them. I wasn't planning on going back there ever, but I'd been forced to because of the asshole who made the sex tape, so I could beg for it to be taken down. Shaken, hating myself for what I'd had to do, I ran into a group of guys who looked like they were breaking into a car. Instead of calling the police, I'd hidden and watched them expertly pick the lock, pull some wires, and start the car.

I hadn't realized one of the guys had doubled around behind me. It'd been Al. He was coming after me, ready to shut me up, threaten me for what I'd seen, and I'd tried to reason with him. "I don't want to call the police. I want to learn to do that."

"Why's that?"

"I never want to owe anyone anything ever again." My voice must've been so fierce, because his countenance changed. The tough guy look was replaced by something I didn't recognize, and then he shifted back and said, "Then let's go."

"Where?"

"You really want to learn, first rule is to shut up and follow orders."

And I had. I'd gotten into his truck and he'd taken me back to the chop shop. The stolen car was already there and loud music was playing. Guys were drinking and laughing and talking shit. There were women there too, but they weren't part of the ring—they hung out to keep the guys company.

I'd never wanted to fucking owe anyone anything. I'd worked hard at that. And now, I'd fucking blown it because I'd let this shit go too far. Because I owed Ryker.

"I don't want to owe Ryker anything," I said fiercely, like I had to hear the words out loud in order to completely convince myself.

"You don't owe me a damned thing, Sean," Ryker growled, and I wasn't sure when he'd come back. "Don't you dare think of me that way."

I stared up at him. The easy thing to do would've been to say, *I don't* and *Please hold me*, and let it all go. But I couldn't. There was too much stress and need and fear inside of me to do anything but say, "I want you to leave," and actually mean it, more for his own good than for mine.

Because then he didn't have to make a choice between me or his MC guys. I'd made it. And Jesus, I knew I was fucked up when it came to love, but until that moment, I hadn't realized how bad I was at it.

When I looked up again, Ryker was gone. For good, it appeared. No more late-night visits. No more roses. For a solid week, nothing. For a solid week, I tried to get my shit together. And failed.

CHAPTER 16

CHILDHOOD'S END

The nightmares came back every single time I closed my eyes. Not just about Billy and the Army, but Ryker was bringing up some other issues for me. The whole porn thing . . . fuck. I knew Ryker well enough not to believe anyone was being forced but . . .

I shivered. I'd woken in a sweat, and just sat for a while in the dark in bed, the TV flickering, hating that a memory could still have so much power over me. My arms were wrapped around my shins, legs drawn to my chest. The person who I'd want to call—to comfort me—brought this on. So I couldn't call him.

Well, I could, but I'd have to explain, so . . . no.

So then I picked up the phone and dialed the familiar digits.

Noah picked up on the first ring. "Rush, you all right?"

I'd woken him. "Yeah. No."

He sighed. "Dreams?"

I opened my mouth to say yes, but my throat was tight. The panic closed in, its slippery tentacles choking me. Noah spoke to me in that low voice—when I was lucid, I called it his mental patient voice—telling me about the good old days that, at the time, we didn't realize were the good old days.

Running with Billy after he'd annoyed the hell out of his dad.

Sitting in the backseat of our newest acquisition, wondering what the hell to do next.

Joyrides down the highway on a summer's night, when we were all still invincible. Because I was goddamned convinced we'd been, at one point.

"You take on too much, Rush. Because of me. I know that. Always did," Noah was telling me now. I swallowed and forced the panic down like a lion tamer with a whip. Problem was, I was too tired to stay as alert as I needed to be, and the growl of panic was waiting for the right opportunity to bite back in. "Give me twenty. I'll be there. Want me to stay on the line?"

I pulled myself together and said, "No, 's'okay."

"You're not. I'm coming."

I thought about how Ryker probably still had guys watching me. And how Jethro probably did too. And hell, there was still Edmund in the mix. "Go through the back."

Noah snorted. "Yeah, I know I'm wanted."

Twenty minutes later, on the nose, he was in my bedroom. Coffee. Donuts. Smokes. He took one look at me, still shivering, and told me to go take a warm shower.

I did. Came out, got into fresh sweats. Noah had changed my sheets for me.

"When did you get domestic?" I asked.

"When I almost got you killed—twice—and realized what a fuck up I am." He handed me a coffee, and I took it and a chocolate donut while he pressed Play on one of our usual movies—*Red Dawn* (the original). We knew it by heart so it didn't matter if we weren't paying attention. It was background comfort.

"I'm so fucking sorry, Rush. I just . . . I got caught up. I didn't give it much thought when I couldn't find my phone, but I should've. I'd told Edmund you didn't want to play anymore, and he accepted it way too easily. And then he needed me to drop off a customer's car a few hours away. I should've fucking put it together, but I wanted to stay in his good graces, and he was promising me big things."

There were a lot of truths in Noah's speech, and a pretty damned big lie. "He threatened you, didn't he?"

Noah winced, took a drag off his cigarette before admitting. "Okay, yeah, that's part of it. Nothing I can't handle."

"Until he cuts the brakes on a car he asks *you* to steal."

"Shit." He stubbed the cigarette out. "Got myself into it. I'll get myself out."

"I—"

"Want to help," he finished. "No. I've been relying on you for too long. Time to man up."

"Picking a hell of a time to realize it," I grumbled.

"I can't believe you grabbed that car for me the other night. After everything that happened, you still did that for me." He shook his head.

"You'd have done it for me."

"Yeah, I would've." He sighed. "Look, Edmund's leaving you alone—that much I know. He's freaked you'll send Havoc after him, so he's laying low, pretending he had nothing to do with the brakes being cut."

"But you know it was him—his goons," I prompted, and when he nodded, I added, "You need to get him to leave you the fuck alone too, before he decides you're as big of a liability as I am."

"I'm not connected to an MC."

"I am, though, and you're connected to me, Noah—that's not changing."

"Thanks," Noah said quietly. "I promise, I'll handle it. And I'll tell you if I'm in too deep."

"You'd fucking better."

Now, Noah turned to the matter at hand, the reason he'd come here in the first place. "Why'd you have the dream? Did Ryker do something?"

I'd much rather have kept ragging on Noah. But hell, what goes around comes around. It was my turn on the block.

I blew out a breath, feeling like I was betraying Ryker by talking about it when none of it was his fault. But Noah knew the history. "He didn't . . . It's . . ."

"Say it. Doesn't matter how stupid it sounds."

"They film porn there. And then he pushed me down for a blowjob, talked about filming it—joking—but I freaked and left and I haven't heard from him since."

For a second, Noah's mouth pressed into a grim line, but his eyes softened at the same time, like there was a war going on inside of him. "He's still keeping tabs on you."

"Good for him," I muttered.

"Do you think you might've overreacted?"

"Wait a second—now you're on Ryker's side?" I shoved his shoulder. "Maybe you should get the fuck out and go hang with him."

"Yeah, not gonna happen." Noah lit another cigarette, and I grabbed it, took a long drag.

"Linc has better stuff."

"He always did," Noah agreed. "Ryker makes you happy."

"So does Linc's shit and stealing cars and all of it's obviously bad for me."

He stared at me. "You're having that PTSD shit again, right."

It was much less of a question and more of a certainty. One I didn't want to admit to, but when he needed to be, Noah was a great interrogator. "Maybe a little."

"Maybe you should talk to someone about it."

I motioned in his direction. "What're you, a mirage?"

He rolled his eyes. "I mean, someone who can actually help."

For a long moment, I looked at the guy I'd been calling a best friend and realized that, in his own fucked-up way, he'd never really stopped. "You help, Noah."

After a couple more days just sitting around sulking, I got BT's number from Noah and called him to get myself back in the game. Because hell, as long as I was self-destructing, I might as well go all the way and have some motherfucking fun with it.

And fun it was. BT had no ties to anyone but his own racing enterprise—if I stuck with him as a free agent, I wasn't beholden to any of the MCs. But I was putting myself out there in some dangerous territory—stealing and racing in my old stomping grounds, right under McKibbins's nose.

If I'd blown things with Ryker—the best thing I might've ever had—because I couldn't get my shit together, I was going to go out with a bang. A different bang than I would've had with Ryker, but sex with anyone else held no interest for me. And at least the stealing almost matched the feeling Ryker gave me in the pit of my stomach before I came. Not quite, but close enough that I could pretend.

How long was I going to have to pretend? Forever, it looked like, since Ryker wasn't exactly banging down my door.

Had I expected that? On some level, probably. I wanted him to fix it—I'd been relying on that. But really, how could I expect him to fix something that was so deeply rooted inside of me, especially when I refused to share it?

I was the one bitching that it couldn't work out between us, but I was also the one putting up the brick wall between us as fast as I could to prove it.

For two weeks, in preparation for the next big round of races, I stole cars from North Carolina and Georgia, driving them with plates BT got from his DMV contacts. I was hoping the actual stealing would help me get back into the fun of it, and I'd found my rhythm by the end of it, if not the joy I'd expected. Since Noah and I couldn't be seen together for any number of reasons, that made it a little less thrilling than I'd hoped.

When I got to the race area, there wasn't a Havoc member in sight, but plenty of Hangmen . . . and one ATF agent pretending to be on the Hangmen's side.

Then again, he'd never actually said he was pretending.

He headed my way, a saunter that made me—and a lot of women and other men—look twice at him. An act? I couldn't be sure, but I wasn't going to blow his cover. I tossed him something between a smirk and a smile—because hell, he was the competition and as much as I was trying to forget, he also wasn't Ryker.

He rested his elbows on the hood of the 1970 Ford Mustang Boss 302 in all its C-stripe glory. "Really?" he asked, looking down at the dark-green classic.

"You're not disrespecting my car, are you?" Granted, it was a capable street performer, not a racer . . . but that's before I'd gotten my hands on it. BT had known I'd been bored and let me modify.

"Not a bit, Rush. This for Edmund?"

I rolled my eyes. "I thought we were past pretending."

Jethro shook his head and smiled. "Going rogue?"

"Completely."

"Ryker?"

I shook my head. "And before you ask me, I don't know where Noah is either."

"Threats?"

"None that I know of. But this is for pleasure, not business. I'm returning her when I'm done racing."

Jethro furrowed his brows. "You're a different one, Rush."

Out of the corner of my eye, I saw Casey saunter over in time to catch his comment. "That he is," he agreed. "Maybe he could do some business with the Hangmen. With the two of you on my side . . ."

We could make him some serious money. And I guess that's all he saw me as—a moneymaker. And maybe an easy piece of ass. Him and most everyone else. But I was the one who needed to be in control from this point forward—I'd proven I couldn't handle it any other way. "Forget it," I told him.

Jethro straightened and looked at me like I'd signed my death warrant . . . and with a good deal of respect.

Casey was studying me, the way Jethro had, and the way Ryker used to, but no way would Casey or Jethro would get it right. Or right enough. "You've got balls, Rush. I'll give you that. I see what made Ryker jump through hoops for you."

Seriously? I shot him a look that made him ask, "Sore subject?"

Ya think? "How fast does word spread?"

"Speed of light." Casey smiled.

"I'm moving on," I said firmly, meaning it for that second.

"Liar," Jethro murmured as he walked away. And that made me angry—angry enough to kick his ass in the race. Which I did, and easily, barely making use of the aftermarket mods. I took my anger out on the car, and she took it out on the road, and then I took the money and told BT I'd see him for the next round. We were doing everything in shifts and in different locations, all two days apart to make sure the police didn't catch on.

I'd driven the Mustang here from BT's place. Postrace, I'd dropped it back in the parking lot from where I'd taken it. I'd been planning on calling Noah for a ride. Instead, Jethro was waiting on the street, motioned for me to get into his car.

"Need a ride, Rush?"

I don't know why I agreed to it. But the anger had dissipated, and I was still half-floating on that warm race energy that left me momentarily pliable.

But instead of taking me straight home, he pulled into the local diner.

"Racing always makes me hungry," he explained, and what the hell—I could always eat. We didn't have to worry about being seen together at this point, and actually, Casey would just think Jethro was trying to talk me into joining the MC's racing team. So would BT, and he'd probably pay me extra for it.

I refused to think about Ryker or Havoc.

We ordered, and I played with the tableside minijukebox until the sodas came, avoiding any classic rock that reminded me of Ryker. Instead, I chose Jamie N Commons's "Jungle," and Jethro gave a nod of approval as the heavy beat shook the table between us.

It was only then I asked, "How long have you been watching me?"

Jethro grinned. "Not just you—you and Noah. And the Hangmen too, obviously. But there were jobs that started about nine months ago, before you got out of the Army. At first, I figured you were good for them, but then I started to zero in on Noah." He paused, ran a long finger along the side of the soda glass that was wet with condensation. I don't think he ever broke from watching me, but I was kind of mesmerized by the long finger. Because it'd been a long time for me without Ryker. When I finally met Jethro's eyes, he added, "But you've got a lot of guys watching you, don't you, Rush?"

I wanted to tell him to fuck off, but what came out was, "Ryker's a good guy."

"Then why isn't he here with you?"

"Because I walked away. And he let me."

Jethro stared at me. "Stupid man."

"Me, or him?"

He snorted. "Either way, it's his loss. My gain."

Because *I* was the stupid one too. "Yeah. We're not even close to being on the same side. Perfect together."

"Closer than you might think. And stranger things have happened," he commented as the waitress put down our plates of burgers and fries. He squirted ketchup on his fries and continued, "But you're not ready for anything."

No, I definitely wasn't. And it hadn't been a question anyway. So we ate in silence for a while, until he asked, "Where is Noah these days?"

"No idea," I lied.

Jethro shook his head, obviously not believing me. "He almost got you killed. Why're you hiding him?"

"That wasn't entirely his fault. Besides, wouldn't you hide your best friend?" As soon as I said that, I saw a look pass over his face. It was an expression of remorse and guilt and pain all rolled into one, a look I was intimately familiar with. "I'm sorry."

He sat back. "Yeah, well, me too. It was five years ago. You'd think I'd be over the worst of it."

"I think it gets worse, not better," I confessed. "Noah and I, we're all fucked up about Billy. Fucking nightmares."

Jethro looked concerned. "Did you talk to anyone?"

"Yeah. In the military, they say, 'You okay to go back out there?' And I say, 'Yeah.' And everyone feels a lot better." He snorted. For a second, I realized we were probably going through the same kind of thing, and that made me want to get Noah out of trouble by handing him over to Jethro. "What would you do for Noah?"

Jethro raised his brows. "Trading favors?"

"Trading information," I corrected.

"What would you want me to do for him?"

"Get him out of this mess he's involved in."

He considered, but didn't fully commit. Just said, "I've got bigger fish to fry."

"The Hangmen?"

"Actually, no. They just provide a convenient way for me to assess my target."

"And you're sharing all this with me why?"

He sighed, played with his soda glass. Finally, he admitted, "Because you served under my brother for three years."

"Captain Keller?"

"My stepbrother," he agreed. "You're a smart guy, Rush. You can make something of yourself. What do you want to do? Like really, truly, wake up every day for the rest of your life and face the prospect of doing?"

Ryker's face flashed in front of my face immediately, mainly because of the literalness of Jethro's question. But I also knew that sex wasn't enough to hold us together. Even so, was *he* enough? Would I find everything else through him?

Hadn't I already started to?

My answer to Jethro was, at least, honest. "I don't want to do anything that doesn't have an element of danger. I suck at rules and authority. And I have this problem with stealing cars. Can't help myself. Which makes me really popular with local law enforcement."

Jethro smiled. "You definitely have a future in the ATF. And yes, McKibbins has a real hard-on for you. I'll get him off your back. No strings."

"Thanks, but I've got to do it on my own."

Jethro sat back. "You do that a lot."

"My whole life. Yeah."

"Isn't it nice to get some help?"

"I thought it was," I muttered. "But it made me stupid."

"Love'll do that," he agreed. "I'm just not sure that's such a bad thing."

At this point, I wasn't either.

CHAPTER 17

OPERATOR

After Jethro dropped me home, I found a message from Greta on my phone. I'd never given her my number, met her for all of fifteen minutes, but her, "Call me back now, Rush," had me listening.

I dialed, then hung up. Five minutes later, I looked through the window to see Greta knocking at my door, holding a paper tray with two takeout coffee cups.

I opened up for her, asking, "What, are you tracking me?"

"I've been waiting a couple of blocks away," she admitted. "I was hoping you'd reach out before I had to barge in. I figured a hang-up's close enough."

Barge in, she did. I didn't know what to say to her, what the hell I was *supposed* to say, but obviously she'd planned on being the one doing all the talking, because she sat next to me on the couch and started in immediately. "You're not the first to have trouble easing into the Havoc world."

"And here I thought you were going to make me feel special."

She stared at me with that *I'm not impressed with your wiseass remarks* look people often attempted with me, but I never truly believed them. I believed her. "You're special to Ryker."

I swallowed hard, shifted on the couch, wondering how the hell I could get away from her and her impromptu therapy session. In the end, I was honest. "Fine. But what if I can't be with him?"

She sighed. "We can get you help for the PTSD."

Well, there were reasons beyond the PTSD, but hell, might as well start there. "You have biker shrinks now?"

"If I say yes, will you see one?"

"No."

"Stubborn ass." She handed me my coffee cup and picked up her own. "So you're just going to keep doing this?"

She motioned to me and the couch, and hell, it's not like I was the most productive member of society, but I wasn't sitting here moping. Much. Just in between all the stealing and racing.

"Ryker's not fighting for me," I reminded her after taking a sip. "He pulled away too." Because it was so much easier to blame him along with myself.

"So you try once, and if it doesn't go your way, that's it?" She paused. "I'll bet you spent more time researching how to steal a single car than you've spent trying to get him back."

I frowned. Stared at her. Because in all the sitting around pretending not to mope, wondering if maybe Ryker would call or break in again, I hadn't actually considered that *my* going to get *him* back was an option. It would mean spilling my goddamned guts about my past, but obviously, it wasn't reason enough to stay away. Not when I was obviously this miserable without him.

I felt like an idiot, because honestly, as Noah liked to point out, I hadn't dated. I'd always just screwed. And before Ryker, that was all I'd needed.

Now, it wasn't nearly enough. Nothing was, without him.

You walked away. Therefore, you could—and should—be the one to try to get him back. Lightbulb time.

Greta was watching me careful, like she could read everything I was thinking on my face. Was everyone in Havoc always goddamned right? Because it was super fucking annoying. Even so, I heard myself ask, somewhat pathetically, "Suppose it's too late?"

And that brought the *Gotcha!* gleam to Greta's eyes. "If you're thinking about that, you already know the answer."

I couldn't look at her—she was too triumphant. Then I had to remind myself that wanting Ryker back—and finding a way to do it—wasn't a bad thing unless I made it such. "Can you get me into Havoc? To Ryker's house?" There were a lot of steps that went after that, but first things first.

She rolled her eyes. "Of course. Are we doing this now?"

Panic rolled in. Slow down, speed racer. "No. I need a couple of days at least." Maybe more, if I chickened out further. "I'll call you."

"You'd better," she said harshly, and my face must've shown surprise, because she gentled. "I'll always pick up for you, Rush."

After she left, I stayed on the couch for a while, wondering what the hell I was supposed to do to win Ryker back, to make him forgive me. A big romantic gesture would probably work, but I was pretty challenged in that area.

I stared between the roses that were dying on the coffee table and the keys to my truck, and an idea began to form.

Maybe I wasn't so romantically challenged after all.

"Is this your attempt at romance?"

I shrugged, my face flushed, as Ryker stared at the car I'd parked in front of his house. *Judgmental much?* "Is it working?"

He stared at me like I was an alien and spoke his next words slowly. "I gave you roses."

"And I'm giving you a car." Which really, was way more practical and romantic than flowers, but I wasn't telling him that. Because he wasn't exactly full of joy and sunshine at the moment. Granted, it was close to two in the morning, but he'd been awake—or at least the lights had been on downstairs when I'd pulled up in front of his cabin. The car I'd brought him, an old-school Monte Carlo (a sexy motherfucking car that had some real street value) vibrated, because I'd put in special headers to make it loud like his Harley, so there was no way he'd missed the sound. The black paint gleamed, and while I hadn't been able to spruce up the interior much (yet), it was still a kickass car.

For a second, I'd wondered if maybe he was inside with someone else. But then he'd come storming out of the house and stopped cold when he saw me.

I turned the car off and got out.

He was still standing there on the porch, unmoving. "You're giving me a stolen car."

"The car itself isn't technically stolen," I pointed out. "I mean, the parts are from all different places. So it's not like they'd be used for anything else. They were sitting there, doing nothing. You said this was the one you drove to follow the Dead around with your friend one summer so . . ."

Ryker crossed his arms, his expression unreadable. "What the hell are you doing, Rush?"

Rush. I hated hearing that name from him. "You wouldn't answer my calls," I tried, unable to ignore how his eyes had become like daggers, pinning me and not letting me go, no matter how I squirmed. I'd been worried about just showing up here like this, so I'd tried things the easy way. A phone call to smooth things over. Because there was less rejection in a phone call.

But hell, being rejected by not being called back honestly felt pretty shitty anyway. And, in the end, I'd had no choice but to just come here cold. I had nothing to lose.

I had everything to lose.

Finally, he told me, "You were right. This can't work."

My stomach plummeted, his words like a knife to the heart. I blurted out, "Don't, Ryker. Don't say that to me. I was wrong. I was an idiot. I just . . . I don't know how to love. I don't know what it is, what it looks like."

He paused for so long that I thought for sure he wasn't going to answer. I waited for him to turn and walk back into his house, and honestly, if he had, I probably would've broken down the door to follow him in. But finally, he asked, "So what's changed?"

I'd been thinking about that over the past several days. In fact, I'd spent every waking moment, and some not so wakeful, rolling that very question around in my mind. "Nothing. And everything. See, I figured out that love looks pretty much like everything we've done. None of that other shit was as important or insurmountable as that fact." I paused to take a breath. "I'm just sorry I figured it out too late."

"Damn you." His words were a painful whisper, but somehow they vibrated like a scream in my ears. He came down from the porch like a big angry bull, charging directly at me.

I stood my ground.

I guess he'd thought I was lying, but his countenance changed in an instant when he pinned me against the Monte Carlo. "Fuck, Sean, you really didn't know."

I shook my head, feeling stupid. Suddenly, I couldn't even look at him, and I cursed myself for thinking I could—should—do this.

"Look at me." His command was rough. It immediately made me feel hot and needy, and I did as he asked.

I was fucked up from childhood. Fucked up from battle. And now I was back doing what I loved—stealing cars—and that didn't feel quite right either. I was off-balance, completely. Except things were right with Ryker. He'd become my compass. He'd seen more combat, street and otherwise, than I'd see in a lifetime. It'd showed on his face when he took care of me the night of my accident, and the night I'd freaked out on him here, but it never stopped him from being strong.

"I want to be as strong as you are," I confessed.

"Jesus—you're there without even trying," Ryker promised me, and since he'd never lied to me, I chose to believe it.

"For a long time, I thought we were just fucking, Ryk. I didn't realize . . ." That we'd been talking. That Ryker had me turned around and made me realize what I'd been missing. Longing. Wanting more sex, yes, but in between, in small doses, we'd been talking. Learning. Getting to know each other.

Ryker stroked his knuckles over my cheek. "You can learn just as much fucking someone as you can talking to them. Sometimes more. You know that better than me."

I considered that. "I'm not sure I did."

"Maybe not consciously, but that's why you used to fuck so many people. You were looking."

"So fucking's my version of the dating game?"

"Yeah, basically." There was zero irony in Ryker's words.

I tried to mentally catalogue my sexual past—and holy hell, there were a lot, most nameless, faces and bodies blending into orgasms. Some were memorable in that I could recall my orgasms, or the fact that I'd spent the night, more for the promise of morning sex than anything else. But for the most part, I'd dismissed them. No do-overs. I thought it was me being a no-commitment kind of guy—or, in my more honest moments, a complete dick.

But if I looked at it from Ryker's point of view . . . "Maybe you just fuck better," I said seriously.

Nothing threw him. "I definitely fuck better," he agreed. "Because I know who I'm fucking, and why I'm fucking him."

I wasn't just addicted to the sex we had—he'd become a part of my life. As unpredictable as his visits had been, they'd become something I depended on.

"Fuck," I muttered as the realization spread like heat through my body. "You reeled me in."

"You did the same goddamned thing to me without even trying. And it freaked me out too," he admitted.

I studied him in that moment. Really studied him. He was very tall. Built, but not in that jacked muscle-head way. From my time in the Army, I knew the difference between useless muscles and someone who used them. He was heavily tattooed, but there was space in between, like he'd thought about each of them carefully and planned his body art. Again I inspected the roses on his forearms thoroughly, tracing a single stem through the thorns, and ended with my hand on his—on his rose tattoo—before looking up into his face. He was angrily handsome, sharp and cutting, with eyes that softened when he looked at me.

He'd let me in. I'd done the same in return. I could run, again, but what was the point? He was already inside.

I'd been running from myself.

"Yeah, you were," he murmured.

"I only do this talk-out-loud thing with you."

"Good."

I suddenly wanted to bite the tattoo on the side of his neck. I wanted to lick it while he fucked me. I pictured fingers inside of me, this big rough man fucking me gently. Giving me exactly what I needed. Either he was that good—which I'd grant him hands down—or he really had taken his time studying me. Learning my body. Learning me.

I probably told him all of that, because his hand slid inside my pants, stroked my cock as my balls tightened. "Not going to last."

"Don't want you to," he countered. "Let's see if I can beat my old record."

I dropped my head back and let the pleasure roll through me. I was happy. And I didn't care what was happening around us.

The difference was, Ryker did. Always would. He had so much more than I did. A family. People to fall back on.

And you have Ryker. So didn't that mean by default, I also had Havoc? Or that he'd eventually have to make a choice between us?

I was saved from thinking about that when he stroked me faster and harder, until the only thing on my mind was crying out his name while I came.

It echoed back to me in the hills and that, in and of itself, seemed right. Really right.

"At least I learned something," Ryker told me a little while later, while I lay splayed on his couch where he'd put me after half carrying me inside. He was still dressed, but he'd slipped me out of my clothes since I'd come all over myself at his bidding.

"What's that?"

"Giving you space is never a good idea."

I couldn't necessarily disagree. But I also hadn't told him everything. "My PTSD's not a terrible case, but when it's triggered . . ."

"And being here did that. I should've thought of that before throwing you to the wolves here."

"It was a lot, all at once." But there was one very specific thing that'd thrown me right over the edge. "Listen, the porn . . ."

"Is that what's bothering you?" No judgment, just genuine surprise mixed with some concern. And then he sat up and really looked at me, scanning my expression, obviously wondering if he'd missed something.

My gut tightened, but I couldn't back away from telling him now. I'd done nothing wrong, but I still didn't like to talk about it. "How's it . . . monitored?"

"You mean, is it ever illegal? No. It's a real company, on the books. Inspected. We front money, but we don't do the majority of the work."

"Just the talent."

He frowned. "I dated a couple of them, yeah, but it's not a requirement that they fuck us. We guard during shoots. We also guard rock bands. What the fuck, Sean? Talk to me."

"I was fifteen." The words tumbled out, and his jaw tightened. "It was consensual. Stupid to tape it. Like I said, fifteen."

Ryker's voice got growly and protective. "How old was the other guy?"

"Nineteen." I could still picture him. Good-looking, and he'd seemed nice, and I'd trusted him. I have no idea why. Even then I'd known better than to trust the outside of the package. "I didn't know he'd taped it to sell it. He told me he'd erase it. And then one night, I'm out in a club with his friends and one of them congratulates me on my sex tape."

"Who was he?"

"Ryk, come on."

"Who was he?" Ryker was insistent. "And what company put the tape out?"

"I don't know," I lied. "The guy who taped me laughed when I confronted him. He handed me a hundred bucks—threw it at me, actually, told me it was my cut, and I beat the shit out of him, okay? And doing that wasn't all that satisfying, because he was just trying to make a living too."

"There's more to this."

I sighed. "I went to the production company. He said that if I wanted him to take that tape off the market, I'd have to give him something. He blackmailed me. He pushed me to my knees . . ."

I didn't have to go further. I ended up in my usual position—back against the wall with Ryker holding me. "So you don't run from me," he said.

I knew. "I know."

"Did he tape that too?" Ryker asked gently, and I shook my head. "But he didn't take the original tape down, did he?"

"No, he didn't."

"I'm sorry. I'm sorry it happened to you. I'm sorry I did something to trigger that memory."

"You didn't know. If you'd done it any other time . . ."

"But I didn't." He stared at me. "We don't do anything like that. Go, look around. Talk to anyone you want."

"I think I will. And not because I don't trust you. It's more for me. I get that people make a living doing what they need to—I'm the last one to question career choices but . . . I watched it happen to my mom. I saw her slowly lose herself trying to make a living like that."

Ryker nodded slowly. "I understand. It's hard to understand why anyone would do that consensually when *you* weren't given the choice. Now, tell me the name of the company. And the production manager."

"They might not even be in business anymore."

"I want to take care of you, Sean. *Let me.*"

His last words were so fierce. There wasn't a reason not to. I told him. He nodded. Kissed me—quick, but still toe curling. And then he let me down, lowered me from the wall. Rubbed my shoulders and as long as we were in true-confessions mode . . .

"I think Noah's involved in some really fucked-up shit, but I don't think it's his fault."

There was no *I told you so,* nothing except, "You need to stay with me until we figure this out."

I nodded. "I've got a bag with me. I left my truck at the house."

"And Noah?"

"I'm not deserting him. But he's lying low."

"He's got your number?" he asked, and I nodded. "If he calls and he's in trouble, we'll deal with it then."

I could live with that. But . . . "I've got some jobs to do. On my own. I made a deal with BT."

He sighed. Stared at the ceiling. There was no real way he could reprimand me—I knew that.

The only thing he said was, "I never wanted to change you—just keep you safe."

Later that day, Ryker said that he'd bring me over to the studio. As much as I wanted to go, suddenly, I couldn't bring myself to do it.

"Maybe another time," I said, stuffing my hands in my pockets. I'd been staring out the front window, and now he stood next to me.

"Whatever you want." He paused. "I know what those guys took from you, Sean. I really do. But by not fighting through it, you're giving them the rest."

I wanted to tell him to go fuck himself and his sudden lecture. But he was right.

"Don't let them win, Sean. Whatever else happens, just promise me that."

"Why? Because you'll miss out on blowjobs?" I couldn't help myself. And Ryker, to his credit, didn't look surprised by my wiseass answer.

Instead of touching me or forcing me to stay put, he simply stood in front of me. I'd freaked him out too much, and I'm pretty sure he was trying not to trigger me when we talked about the porn stuff. "Because you'll miss out on life. Love. Lots of shit. Your past is your past. Why the fuck are you trying to drag it across the finish line with you? Cut that shit off. You'll be a hell of a lot lighter. Freer too."

"Aren't you afraid . . ."

"What?" he probed when I paused.

"Forget it."

"No chance."

"Fine. Aren't you afraid that if I let that go . . . if I let it all go, that I won't need you as much?"

In case I wasn't sure, in case Ryker hadn't yet been convinced I was definitely in the running for the Most Fucked-up Guy Ever award, I'd just solidified my spot in the winner's circle.

But Ryker's expression softened. "No, baby. Whatever happens, you being happy is what I want. "

"What makes you happy, Ryker?"

"You."

For the first time, I could say the same of him, without reservation. And with that, I suddenly got bolder. It came out of nowhere, this next idea, but I needed to purge the bad and usher in new memories for this place.

"You don't have to take me to the studio. I think I'd be more comfortable if you auditioned me here." He stared at me, quizzically but I kept on going. "I really need a job. Figured you could get me in."

"Sean . . ."

God, the warning tone did it to me every single time. I got on my knees, sank to the floor without a worry in the fucking world. He stared down at me as I unzipped his pants, opened them to expose his gorgeous cock. His hand cradled my head lightly, stroked my hair, but it wasn't his usual touch. He didn't want to freak me out again, so I had to reassure him.

I looked up at him and said, "Make it okay. Take away the memory."

His eyes flashed, and he never looked unsure, but I felt it—the slight hesitation—and my heart skipped a beat. Could I do this? I wanted to put this behind me so badly . . . and I needed him to help me.

"Please, Ryker. Just let me." I put my mouth around his cock before he could protest. He groaned, his hand fisted in my hair, hard enough to thrill me. Mainly because it was meant to keep me in place, not push me away. My big biker was moaning my name, and I figured now was the time to enjoy that I'd pulled this off.

I put my face closer, waiting for him to grip my head harder. He did, tugged me closer, and said, "Let's see if you're cut out for this."

He took out his phone and pointed it at me. "Go."

Jesus. I closed my eyes for the briefest of seconds and then took his cock in, licking and sucking. Looked up at him to see him staring at me intensely.

"Yeah, job's yours, babe. All yours. Only yours."

And then he came, holding me in place, owning me. And I drank him, trusting him completely.

When he let me go, I didn't have time to stand before he sank to his knees in front of me. He brushed my cheek with his hand, then showed me his recent videos. The one he'd just pretended to take? Wasn't there.

"You could've just deleted it."

"Worked just the same," he said. And then I was on my back, his fingers in me, my legs spread for him. "You going to keep trying to escape?"

"Trying?"

"Are you?" he demanded, hitting my gland several times.

"Yes," I managed.

Because it was the truth, and that's what he wanted from me.

And instead of getting angry, Ryker's face opened, a smile that went all the way to his eyes. "Good," he grunted.

Like he wouldn't have it any other way.

Like he didn't *want* it any other way.

I didn't know where this was going, how to feel—hell, even what to feel. The guy sent me flowers. He'd gotten me through the end of my last deployment with his visits and the memory of them. He'd downloaded music onto my iPod (how he got my password was another one of those great mysteries)—some Grateful Dead music he always played me, plus some old-school classic rock. I had a lot of memories to keep me going through those last months.

He knew my favorite foods. He was on his way to knowing every goddamned thing about me, and even though it scared the fuck out of me every time something new was revealed, he stuck around. And pushed to learn more.

"If I stay . . . does that mean you won't try to lure me with pizza and Chinese?" I asked, stretching languidly, many orgasms later.

"Babe, this means you get me. Which means, if you want pizza or Chinese, I'll pick up the phone and get you some."

"Pizza," I managed. "Lots of it. No anchovies. Or . . ."

"You like half-plain, half-pepperoni, and you can eat a pizza and a half by yourself."

I stared at him. "You know way too much about me."

"I can eat two," he said mildly before placing the order from my favorite pizza parlor.

CHAPTER 18

I NEED A MIRACLE

Ryker left me a note—he'd be gone all day on Havoc business. If I could help it, I wasn't supposed to call him. But he wanted me to be there in his cabin when he got back later on that evening.

Things are good, Sean.

Yeah, things were definitely good.

I showered and ate some of the breakfast he'd left, even though it was sometime after three in the afternoon. I guess all that romantic shit really wore me out.

After my second cup of coffee, I put on the TV and figured I'd just stay put in Ryker's place until he got home, like he'd suggested. Because I wasn't going to walk around Havoc until I knew how pissed Sweet and some of the other guys were.

But when Noah called, all my plans were shot to shit.

"What's up?"

We tried to check in at least every other day, quick calls that let me know he was all right. Edmund's crew was protecting him from McKibbins, but I knew time was running out. He had to ditch Edmund, and fast.

"Rush, where are you?"

"I'm at Ryker's."

"So it's good."

"Yeah, it's good, man. I texted you."

"Good. Listen, I'm going to get out of town for a while . . ."

"What's wrong?"

"Rush, you're good with Ryker, you're happy. That's all that matters."

"Like you said to me before, you matter. What's going on?" I was up now, looking for my shoes. Because that's what we both did when we called each other. We prepared to go help.

"I fucked up, Rush. Bad." His voice shook. "I had to do one last job for Edmund, to fulfill the contract, he said. And the second to last car I was supposed to grab . . . fuck, it was in an accident a couple of days earlier. Totaled. There was only one other like it close by. I didn't have a choice."

"Who's car?"

"It was parked at the Hangmen's compound. Registration is Casey something or other."

Shit. I pressed the heel of my palm to my forehead and tried to remain calm. "Okay. So you took it. One more to go?"

"Right. But . . . fuck, Edmund told the Hangmen that I took his goddamned car."

"Why?"

"If you can figure that out, more power to you."

I didn't have time to parse it. But I knew what I did need to do. "Where's Casey's car?"

"In the container. Once I deliver the final car . . ."

"Wait, you can't fucking do that."

"I don't need Edmund's buyers *and* the Hangmen after me."

He was right. "Let's get the Hangmen off your back first, all right? I'll return the car."

"What?"

"I'm not going to drive there in it, but I'll go and say there was a mix-up, but we have the car."

"But we don't."

"So get it," I said through clenched teeth. "I can't unfuck this all by myself."

Noah drew in a breath. "Okay. Yeah, you're right. Thanks, man. I just . . . I can't . . ."

"I know. You don't have to say anything else. Let's get you out of this and then find something for us to do that doesn't involve shit like this."

Noah gave a shaky laugh. "We keep saying that."

"One day, we're going to mean it." I hung up and grabbed the keys to the Monte Carlo. Looked at Ryker's note one more time.

If he was around, I'd tell him. But he wasn't. And he was busy. And I'd promised him I'd stay out of trouble . . . but I wasn't the one in trouble. Someone was going to be, but it wouldn't goddamned be me.

I had shit to do.

No one stopped me when I drove off Havoc's land. I don't know what I expected—alarms or a giant net or a row of bikers with their arms crossed, staring me down.

But when none of that happened, I breathed, drove, and planned.

First stop was Edmund's. By the time I got there, it was the end of the day at the garage. I knew I'd find him in his office, on the phone, talking about absolutely nothing.

I slammed in, and he dropped the phone. He fumbled for the drawer where he kept the gun, but the drawer was always locked, which made grabbing it really inconvenient for him in situations like this.

"Get the hell out of here, Rush," he told me.

I closed the door behind me and advanced. He got up, tried to go around me, but I stopped him, slamming him facedown on the desk. I held him there by the back of his neck. "What the fuck are you pulling by turning in Noah to the Hangmen?"

"I'm not taking the blame for that piece of shit. Should know better than to involve the MC."

"What's your game, Eddie? Why fuck your own shipment over? But I guess you're not—you're fucking Noah over . . . pitting the MC against whoever your buyer is?" The pieces fell together. He didn't give anything away, but he didn't need to.

The thing was, his buyers had to be some major players for him to think he could get a foothold over the MC. Those kinds of buyers were people Noah and I didn't want to be involved with. People an MC could handle, but not us alone. "Call your dogs off Noah. I'll figure shit out with the Hangmen."

"You think you're so tough because of Havoc? You think they'll stand behind a punk like you?"

I leaned in and snarked, "I never needed Havoc to be tough, Eddie. What I do need is for you to stop using Noah to create your own war."

"He signed on for this. Fuck up can't even steal a car. He had one job."

"He can't steal shit when he's been sabotaged."

"He owes a car."

"And then he's done. Got it?"

"What're you going to do, Rush? What the hell can you do to me?"

That's when I stopped talking and showed him instead. First thing, I beat the shit out of him. I left him semistanding, though, and I made sure he knew I took his shipping invoices, plus other proof of his stealing that he left right out in the open. Overconfident asshole.

I left him bleeding and drove to Hangmen's MC.

If Havoc was tucked away from the world, the Hangmen appeared to be housed right out in the open. I drove right up to the clubhouse, only to find out it was basically a decoy meant to fool most everyone. Including me.

It was disconcerting, sitting in a private room I'd been forcefully escorted to, without being allowed to explain who I was or why I was there. By the time the door opened, I'd mentally prepped reciting my name, rank, and serial number mantra a thousand times.

Casey strolled in, looking way too pleased with himself. "Finally got bored with Havoc?"

Yeah, awkward. "That's not exactly why I'm here."

"You're here to clean up Noah's mess."

Okay, so maybe not so awkward. Or covert, given the fact that I'd walked in here alone, the doors had locked closed behind me, and I was pretty much trapped. I couldn't tell if I was getting careless or bolder. "I came here as soon as I could to try to clean up what Edmund inadvertently fucked all to hell."

Casey slammed his fists on the table in front of me. "Edmund? Edmund didn't steal my fucking car, Rush." Holy hell, I didn't want to run into Casey in a dark alley.

I tried to reason with him. "You and I both know Edmund's running some kind of game to pit you against his buyer. I don't know why. All I want to do is call off the bounty on my friend's head."

Casey's eyes narrowed a bit at the corners. "So you're here to make things right?"

"Yes. I want to make things right. I will make things right."

"So you're the rough trade?"

"What the . . ." I sat back. "Fuck no. I want to give you back the car."

Casey crossed his arms like a recalcitrant child. With a handgun. "I like the trade better."

He wasn't exactly giving me an option. More telling me what was going to happen.

I tried to ignore that piece of it and lure him back onto the subject of his car. "So if I return your car, can you forget Noah's involvement?"

"Forget? Do you have any idea what kind of shit he's involved in? We're the least of his problems."

"Good. So we've got a deal?"

"Think about what I said, Rush. *That's* my deal."

From my perspective, *Think about it* seemed to mean *Come back and let me fuck you or we'll kill Noah.*

To be fair, I'd had worse propositions. Either way, Noah had to get the car back to me so I could get it back to Casey, because maybe the guy would feel differently or get sentimental when he saw his car. "I'll think about it," I told Casey.

Casey stared down at me. "Ryker know you're here?"

"Yeah, right," I muttered. "That would've gone over really well."

Casey jerked his head toward the window behind me. I froze for a second, unable to turn around. He lifted a brow. Finally, I stood and glanced outside to see several Harleys. One of them was Ryker's. With Ryker on it.

I turned back to Casey. Honestly, I didn't know which one of them I was in more trouble with at the moment.

Casey merely shrugged, a self-satisfied smile on his face. "Like I said, consider it. Maybe after this, you won't have any place else to go." Then he told the guy guarding the door, "Let Rush out the front gate."

Right into Ryker's arms. "I could just slip out the back," I suggested.

"I don't think so," was all Casey said before pointing me in Ryker's direction.

I walked out, not sure if I was supposed to go to Ryker or to the Monte Carlo. And I was honestly trying to wait for direction and not piss him off in front of his MC, out of respect, not because I wanted to be ordered around.

See, I could learn things.

Ryker made the decision easy by motioning to the car. I got in and drove back to Havoc, while Ryker and the other bikes formed a semicircle around me. Protective . . . and not letting me out of their sight.

It gave new meaning to the word cage.

CHAPTER 19

THE RACE IS ON

"You," was all Ryker could say to me when I got out of the car in front of his cabin. I'd been hoping that maybe seeing the Monte Carlo would remind him of the gesture and then he'd soften.

That seemed to be a total pipe dream.

Besides Ryker, the rest of the bikes had also followed me. And blocked the car in, like I was thinking about gunning it and running or something.

Again.

There was Ryker. And Sweet. And the guy I'd fought—the biggest one, at least, who Ryker turned to now and said, "What the fuck does, 'Don't let him out of your sight.' mean to you, Tug?"

His answer? "I wasn't about to stop him from beating the shit out of Eddie."

Okay, that was good. I'd expected Tug to throw me under the bus and run me over.

Apparently, that was Sweet's job, because he demanded, "And how does that help us? It got Eddie more pissed at Rush and Noah. And then, Rush . . . you went to Hangmen's and what did you do once you strolled in?"

I swallowed and wondered if they'd been there the entire time. "I asked to see Casey. He told me I could come see him anytime."

Ryker and Sweet just stared at me. I'd pushed my luck, I knew, but I swore I saw the gleam in Ryker's eye . . . like the punishment would fit the crime.

I pulled the manifests I'd taken from Edmund's office out of my pocket and handed them to Sweet. "I was going to give them to Casey when I dropped his car back."

"Where is his car?" Ryker asked slowly, his voice a dark, dangerous rumble.

I turned to him. "Noah's got to get it back."

Sweet raised a brow. "Get it back?"

This was like a tennis match. "It's already in a container. Noah's supposed to deliver the final car tonight, then the shipment goes." I paused. "Noah's first choice wasn't Casey's car. But the one he was supposed to lift was totaled in an accident. And then he was desperate."

"And you figured going out on your own was a good idea?" Ryker asked.

"To be fair, he kind of covered everything," said my new biker BFFL, Tug. Ryker and Sweet stared at BFFL-Tug. BFFL-Tug looked at me, and we both shrugged.

"Think we can use this to get rid of Edmund?" I asked all of them.

"There's no 'we' in this," Ryker told me.

I nodded seriously. "Oh, so you want me to do it?"

BFFL-Tug smiled, Sweet looked like he wanted to strangle me, and Ryker basically dragged me the hell away from them and into his cabin.

He let me go for a second to call out, "I'll handle it, Sweet," before closing the door and advancing on me again. I didn't have many places to go, except against the big oak table. So I stayed there, half sitting, trying to pretend I wasn't freaked out over everything I'd done.

It was one thing to do what I'd done. Another to realize I'd done it. Before Ryker could ask me, I told him my theory about Edmund, that he was trying to actively start a war between the MC and his own buyers, in hopes of wiping out the competition at the docks. And he was using Noah, hoping to reinvolve me, and by extension, Havoc and Hangmen.

"That's exactly Eddie's style," he said. "Always has been, from his New York days."

I was about to ask how he knew that, but hell, from this point on I'd just assume that Ryker knew goddamned everything.

"What were you thinking, Sean, walking right up to the Hangmen and handing yourself over to them?"

"I didn't exactly hand myself to them. I told Casey I'd get his car back. And Casey did let me go out to you," I pointed out. *Even when I wanted to slip out the back instead.*

Ryker was staring at me again. Sometimes it hit me randomly how big he really was. Brick wall big. "Casey expects you back."

I couldn't deny that. "I didn't actually agree to his terms."

"Don't even think about it," Ryker growled. "I fucking know what kind of terms Casey expects from you, that motherfucker, and it's not happening, because I don't share what's mine."

I stood then, my hand up. "Hold on there. *Yours*? You serious with that shit?"

The growl that followed informed me that Ryker was very serious. "It's not like I haven't used that term with you before."

True, but . . . "I thought maybe that was just a . . . sex thing."

Ryker growled again.

"No, I mean, look, it's definitely hot in that context, but you mean it, like, for real. That's like beyond commitment. Married people don't go around talking about owning each other."

"But I am." He walked toward me, and I held my hand up. Then I backed myself against the wall, assuming the position and motioned for him to come forward. He stared at me for a long moment, dumbfounded maybe, or thinking of ways to make me pay. And then he did come forward, put his hands on either side of me and promised, "If Casey touches you, I'll fucking kill him. Understood?"

I nodded. Vigorously. I wasn't starting a Havoc-Hangmen war like I was some kind of man version of Helen of Troy. "Listen, you know that Casey's not battling for my heart, Ryker. All right? I'd never pretend he was—not even for Noah. And he'd never ask me to."

"Right. Noah's such a fan of mine."

"He's the one who told me I'd overreacted, and that I needed to come back here and make it right," I explained.

Ryker sighed.

"He's not malicious, Ryk. He just can't control himself. I understand that better than anyone. I can't judge him."

"Fine. Don't judge him. But I'm judging that motherfucking Casey, because he knows better than to entertain any thoughts of you making a deal with him. He knows better than to ask someone who's mine to even think about that."

"I'm not the goddamned crackerjack prize for you and Casey to fight over."

"You're a prize, all right. My prize."

"I didn't think fucking you meant that I was owned by Havoc."

"By me," he emphasized.

"Whatever, *Ryker*. The real world doesn't work like that."

"My world does, *Sean*."

And I was in his world, according to him. And I was hard from the second he used the words *owned* and *mine*, so yeah . . . "This is so fucking crazy."

"Yes, it is."

We were talking about two different things, though. But I guessed any way I looked at it, this was insane.

Owned by Ryker. Like I was his . . . something, no, some*one* special to him. And hell, I really liked that feeling. "I'm not exactly the damsel-in-distress type, in case you didn't notice."

"I notice everything about you, Sean."

There was such a promise, a sweetness to that, despite the fact that it was growled.

I sighed. At least I'd gotten Noah off the hook for the moment. "I have to make a call about recovering the car."

"Sean . . ."

"That's what I promised Casey. All I promised in return for them not killing or otherwise maiming Noah. And dammit, Ryker, I'm only as good as my word."

He considered that and nodded. "Make the call."

He handed me his phone.

"I have a phone."

"I insist."

Pick your battles, I told myself. I dialed Noah's number, and he answered on the first ring, just as Ryker leaned in and hit the speaker button. "Noah, it's Rush. Where are you?"

"Getting ready to grab the car. Waiting for it to get dark," Noah said. "You with Ryker?"

"Yeah, he's here." I avoided looking at Ryker, asking casually, "And you can do this?"

"Yes, Rush," he assured me with all the sarcasm he could muster.

"Can you do it without getting in trouble or hurt?"

There was a long pause. "Oh. Well, when you put it like that, probably not. Is that part of the deal?" Noah asked, and Ryker threw his hands up in the air. "Rush, I'll be fine. Where am I meeting you?"

I glanced at Ryker, who told Noah, "There's an abandoned garage three miles out from the Hangmen's clubhouse. Pull in there. We'll be waiting."

"See you when I see you," Noah said, then hung up.

Ryker looked like he wanted to strangle Noah through the phone. "You two are fucking impossible. I'll take care of it."

"Do you even know how to steal a car?"

Ryker narrowed his eyes. "I was doing that before you were born, son."

"You were, like, eleven when I was born." I paused. "I see your point."

Eleven-year-old Ryker. His eyes told me he'd been born an old soul. No one who tried to protect people as much as he did hadn't had a ton of bad shit happen to him. Which is why I gave him the kind of slack he gave to me.

But I never talked about anyone being *mine*. I felt like he was going to piss in a circle around me.

"Not a bad idea if it'd keep you in line," Ryker called over his shoulder as he walked out of the cabin to his truck.

I cursed under my breath and followed him out.

WHEN PUSH COMES TO SHOVE

We drove to the garage, with several Havoc members following us, including Tug and Sweet. I fiddled with the radio as Ryker drove his truck, his bike in the back.

Finally, he switched off the radio and I was left with dead silence. Which I didn't like. "Look, I know you said Havoc doesn't deal with cars."

"Getting Eddie off our docks is beneficial for everyone," was all Ryker said.

My gut was already tight, because I didn't want Ryker to get hurt because of me. This shit was getting real, and having the Havoc presence let me know that this wasn't being taken lightly. Nowhere near lightly. Ryker was armed. They all were.

"I won't get hurt," he said.

Shit. That talking-out-loud thing. Again.

Ryker put a hand on my thigh. "Seriously, Sean. I'll protect you. This will be fine. This is what I do."

"You're not pissed that I'm helping Noah, are you?"

Ryker sighed. "I'm pissed you didn't reach out for help before storming off on your own. But the way I see it, you and Noah and Billy took care of each other. In his own way, Noah's trying to keep you out of trouble now. If he wasn't a good guy, you wouldn't be friends with him. I told you I thought you were being naive about him, but I was wrong. You were being a friend."

"Thanks," I managed. I'd thought maybe the only way I'd ever get Ryker to really understand—to back off and to maybe even like Noah a little—would've been by telling him a story that really wasn't mine to tell. But he'd gotten there all on his own. And still, I felt like Ryker needed to know about it. "You know I met Noah first in juvie? We were fifteen. I was doing six months."

"For?"

"Vandalism for Noah. On my end, fighting."

He glanced at me for a second, then back at the road, and I saw his hands tighten on the wheel. "Because of that asshole who taped you?"

"Yeah," I admitted, and Ryker ran a hand along my hair, stopped to rub the back of my neck while we waited at a stoplight. I was conscious of the MC members all around us. Obviously, so was Ryker. "Noah was doing three months. He came in scared as shit and you know, place like that, you come in smelling like fear and you're dead."

I hated thinking about this. "The second night, a group of older guys cornered him in the showers . . ."

Ryker's hand stayed on the back of my neck.

I sucked in a breath and forced the rest out. "I got there too late to stop all of it, but . . ." I didn't have to close my eyes to picture Noah, naked, bloody, and still defiant. He'd pretend none of it affected him until he actually believed it. "I kicked their asses. Told them I'd kill them if they touched him again. Noah went to the infirmary for two weeks, and I went into the lockdown ward where the violent guys were held."

"Did anyone hurt you?" Ryker's voice was tight.

"Actually, news of me beating up three of the biggest guys there spread pretty fast. The guys I met actually taught me more about fighting dirty than I'd ever wanted to know. I mean, my mom and dad were both violent. In a way, it skipped me. I didn't have that quick-to-rise anger, that inextinguishable fury. I was smart. Strong. I could fight, and I could defend myself. But none of that fed my soul."

I took a breath that sounded shaky to my own ears. "When I first heard my dad talk about why he robbed banks, I didn't get it. Not until Al put me behind the wheel of a classic Mustang and told me the police would be there in five minutes. I pulled the wires like we'd practiced—rote by now—and something in me sparked to life with that engine. I got it then. And I also knew there was no turning back."

I shook my head and continued, "I understand this world, Ryker. Your world. I might not be used to it all the time, but I understand the violence."

In response, Ryker simply reached over and grabbed my hand. For the rest of the ride, I looked down at the rose on the back of it while his fingers remained threaded tightly in mine.

Ten minutes later, we pulled into the deserted garage, and we both spotted the baby-blue '76 Chevy Impala convertible drive in from the opposite end of the lot, looking really worse for wear.

I opened the door as Ryker managed, "What the fuck?"

Noah climbed out and the door almost fell off. He cursed, propped it up a little with his foot and then slammed it closed. There was smoke wafting up from the hood.

I slid out of the truck and went over to him. "Please tell me that's what it looked like when you took it from Casey."

Noah shook his head. "I ran into some trouble."

"Return it to Casey," Ryker said from behind us. He was one hundred percent serious. "You never promised mint condition."

I stared at him like he had three heads. "That was heavily implied."

"Fuck implications. Get in the car and return it. I'll follow," Ryker said. "Better yet, I'll drive it, and Noah, you take my truck."

Noah nodded, his eyes wide that Ryker would actual let him do something. And then everything started going to shit too fast for me to really get it straight.

Sweet was calling, "Noah was followed," and I heard BFFL-Tug say something about Albanians. I heard the cars a few seconds later.

"Sean, you and Noah go to Casey. Now," Ryker told me, his eyes on the road behind the garage instead of on me.

"What are you going to do?" I asked.

"Whatever I need to," he promised, and then he handed me a Sig. A good all-around piece. "Go. Drive the shit out of her."

I got into the driver's side of the convertible, and Noah slid in next to me. I put the gun between us on the bench seat, and Noah put his hand on it so it'd stay put. We took off the way Ryker and I had come in. Noah, looking behind us, reported that the guys who'd been after him had pulled in.

Havoc was the only thing standing between us and them, preventing them from crossing through the lot to follow us.

I still floored the car, rubbing the dash, apologizing as it throttled and wheezed and clunked its way through the asphalt streets.

"Two blocks to go," I said finally. We'd both been white-knuckling it, and I let myself relax for a millisecond. Long enough for a car to pull across the road from out of nowhere.

"Back up, Rush," Noah said, turning his head. I went to do exactly that and nearly hit a car behind us. On either side of us were houses, all with driveways leading into a garage and no egress to the other street behind them. I seriously thought about crashing through an empty garage and coming out the other side, especially when I saw the men with machine guns.

"They want me, Rush," Noah said quietly.

"They're not getting you." I went to grab the gun, was prepared to shoot whoever came close.

But the gun wasn't there. Noah was holding it. Aimed at me. "Get out, Rush," he said quietly.

"No."

"Rush, don't do this. They're coming. They'll let you go. Just get to the Hangmen clubhouse."

"I won't leave you behind. Fuck you for asking. And get that thing out of my face. What're you going to do, shoot me?"

"He might not, but I will." One of the men from the car was leaning in the window next to me now. I stared up at him. "Get out of the car, Rush. Noah, stay right where you are."

Noah nodded. I knew this other guy wouldn't hesitate to shoot me, so I did open the door. Hard enough to knock him down. I got back in and tried to plow the car into the one ahead of us. I succeeded in pushing it out of the way, and hitting my head on the windshield at the same time. I drove further, until Noah forcibly took my hands from the wheel, put his foot over mine on the brake.

That was the last thing I remembered.

I woke up, cotton-mouthed, and tied to a bed frame. The bed wasn't Ryker's, so not a good sign right off the bat.

I tried to move and was rewarded with a shooting pain along my temple. "Shit."

"You took a good hit to the head." It was Casey, brushing the hair from my forehead. Gently. Placing an ice pack there.

"Why'm tied?"

"You were thrashing." Casey loosened the bindings, and I groaned again at how sore I was. "I didn't want to give you anything until I knew what you were allergic to."

"Who cares," I groaned. "Give me whatever the fuck you've got." Casey shook his head, handed me some pills and a drink of water. Just lifting my head to take the sip nearly fucking blinded me with pain. I lay back and let him put the ice on my head again. "Those better be magic pills."

"Do you remember anything?"

"Noah . . . shit." I tried to sit up but thankfully, Casey stopped me. "Where is he?"

"Eddie has him."

"What do you mean, *has him*?" I was getting fuzzy from the magic pills.

"You were surrounded. He pretty much threw you out of the car, from what I could gather, and Eddie didn't bother to stop and pick you up. Maybe Noah convinced him that you were dead. He fucked up."

"But I fixed it." I'd tried, anyway, but all Casey had was me, and no car in sight.

"You fixed things for Noah with *me*, and that's only because Eddie forced Noah into his own car. You didn't fix anything between Noah and Eddie."

Shit. "Where's Ryker?"

"I'll call him," Casey assured me. And I didn't entirely trust that.

"Tell him about Noah."

Before I could do or say anything else, I passed out. When I came to, both Ryker and Casey were staring down at me, and I guess I'd been wrong about not trusting Casey.

"Sean, are you all right?" Ryker was asking.

"M'all right. Just been a rough coupla days. Weeks. Years," I managed.

There were both still staring at me. "You guys ever . . . you know, together?"

I was making obscene hand gestures without realizing it.

Finally, Casey turned to Ryker. "He's cute. And deadly. It's a good combo."

"He's also mine."

Ryker was getting growly. I changed the subject. "Hey, did you really get the car back?"

Ryker snorted. Casey glared and pointed out the window. From the bed, I could see the car, worse than I'd remembered it. "Right. I had to ram the Albanians." Casey winced. "I'll make it up to you. Noah can fix it."

Casey did his angry crossing arms thing again. "The same Noah who fucked it up in the first place?"

"Yep. Same one. He's better at that than me," I explained. "He's got a lot of patience."

"Well, I'd have to find him first, yes?" Casey asked.

"Right. I'll get on that."

"Sean, it's taken care of," Ryker told me. "Last I heard, Sweet and Tug had Noah."

"If they bring Noah here to fix your car, do you swear you won't hurt him?" I asked, and Casey rolled his eyes, but he nodded. "Oh, and he's not gay. Or bi."

Casey sighed. "Luckily, that's not a requirement."

EASY ANSWERS

Several hours later, I lay back on Ryker's bed, staring at the wooden-beamed ceiling as the fan spun lazily overhead. I'd have to face the music on this one, so I was forcing myself to stay put, even though the pain pills were working and adrenaline from the day's events still raced through me. It was like I was still in the car, my body buzzing from the electricity as if the engine'd brought me to goddamned life.

I was hot. My cock was hard, and I needed to be fucked. Hard. Right now.

Ryker obviously felt the same, judging by the fact that he was stripping as he walked into the room, the familiar heat in his dark eyes. He might be pissed, but whatever was happening between us overrode that.

"You sure you're okay, babe?" he asked me suddenly.

I was afraid he was pulling back, for all sorts of reasons. "Don't you fucking feel sorry for me," I growled.

Ryker's eyes flashed. Humor and understanding the foremost emotions. "I feel a lot of things, Sean, but sorry isn't a single goddamned one of them."

"Okay."

"One more thing."

"Yeah?"

Ryker pushed me back on the bed, held my wrists immobile over my head. "You don't get to tell me what to do."

"But you get to tell me?"

"Yeah." Ryker's eyes flashed again, his cock diamond hard against mine. "Problem with that?"

"Fuck no," I breathed, because at that moment, I couldn't think of a single reason to argue, not when I'd be getting exactly what I wanted. What we both wanted, which was more of each other.

"Don't move your hands then."

But the second he took his hands off my wrists, I did move my arms, causing him to grip them again. "You like to be held down, Sean? You need that?"

"Yes," I managed. "Please, Ryk . . ."

He let me go for a second so he could drag his shirt off. I managed to do the same before his body covered mine, pinning me, stretching my arms up over my head again. His mouth took mine, his tongue stroking mine as he held my wrists in place with one hand . . . and took off his belt with the other.

When he pulled his mouth away, I looked at the belt, and my face flushed. He grinned, that *I've just learned something about you* grin, and he said, "Now that I know, I'll be happy to use this to do more than hold you in place. Your ass will stripe well from this."

Jesus. I clenched my ass cheeks together at the thought and my cock dripped pre-cum.

"Yeah, definitely." He smiled. Wickedly. "But tonight, you're getting a different kind of punishment."

He wrapped the belt around my wrists. There'd be marks there tomorrow, and the next day, and I liked the thought of that, of being marked by Ryker. Marked as his. And then he opened me with his fingers, made me watch as he did it, one finger, then two, lubed. Gentle.

Too gentle.

"You're so fucking pissed at me."

"Yeah," Ryker agreed as he fingered me, not hard and fast like I wanted, but torturously slowly.

Showing me why he was pissed. Showing me he cared. And that was way more effective than yelling at me.

"Stop, Ryk," I begged, but he wouldn't, not now. He just kept up the slow grind, his gaze so intense that I found myself unable to look away. Which was the only way I could think of to apologize. It didn't matter what I begged for, didn't matter what words came out of my mouth. Keeping my eyes locked to his said more than I ever could.

He didn't touch my dick. I had no friction, nothing to relive the ache.

He just concentrated on me. Murmured "Mine" a couple of times.

"Do you say the 'mine' thing because you know it turns me on . . . or because you mean it?"

He continued sliding his fingers in and out of me. "I say it because it's true. That's why it turns you the fuck on."

And oh, I hadn't considered that. But I liked it, more than I thought possible.

"Don't you get it, Sean? I get 'you' better than you get yourself. I understand your impulses. Your needs. Your PTSD shit, as you call it."

"You get it . . . but why do you want to deal with it?"

"Because," he said as he entered me with his cock, finally. "As much as I love this MC, and what I do for it—you, Sean, *you* make me feel alive. You make me want to be better, so I can protect you."

"So you can stop me."

"To protect you so you can do what you need to do."

He never took his eyes from mine as he fucked me, pounding me with long, hard strokes, pushing one of my legs onto his shoulder so he could take me more deeply. Forcing the surrender from my body. His eyes were dark, with striations of brown and black, almost blue-black. Ever changing, like a mood ring. A predator's eyes, guarding me, wary and fierce. Piercing, and there was no escape for me under his gaze.

Ryker threatened my heart, and I welcomed that shit. Every single time. "Yeah, that's it . . . Christ, don't stop, Ryker. Don't you fucking dare . . ."

My orgasm caught me off guard, slammed me with the force of a freight train traveling down a mountain without brakes.

I trusted Ryker to get me to the bottom safely.

"I really can't leave you alone for a second," he growled after he'd come—and I'd come twice.

"No," I agreed. Not if we could do this like all the fucking time.

"We might have to take some time out for food and sleep."

"Do you have a direct link into my brain?"

"You really don't realize you say whatever the fuck comes to your mind?"

"No."

"You've been doing it since that first night. You seemed like you were telling me. Took me a bit before I realized you thought you were saying it to yourself." He smiled. "Like you can't control anything around me."

"Obviously." I curled against him, my cheek against his shoulder, tracing the tattoos on his forearm with my fingertips. "Did you get these done here?"

"Some of them. Some were done at other MC's shops."

"Who does them here?"

"Gavin. Why? You've got an urge for ink?"

Your ink all over me, I thought, and thank God I hadn't been drinking or else that would've come out of my mouth and I'd never live it down.

"Say it," he growled, held up the belt. "If you say it, I'll use this."

"Your ink all over me," I agreed easily, no hesitation, and then closed my eyes and cursed internally. Because he played dirty.

I heard a soft chuckle and said, "You know what I mean."

"Oh yeah."

"I didn't mean it like that."

He shifted so I was forced to look at him. "Tell me how you meant it then."

"You look entirely too fucking pleased with yourself."

"Said from someone who wasn't sure if they wanted to ride on the back of my bike a few weeks ago."

But I did it.

"But you did it."

Fuck. Me. "Stop, Ryk. You're turning me into a . . ."

"Romantic?"

I huffed and put my forehead against his chest.

"You rode my bike," he reminded me.

"I rode a lot more than that," I griped.

He swatted my ass with the belt, and I stiffened and groaned, but the good type of groan. "You were right, you know. About what it means to get on the back of my bike."

"So what now?"

He cupped my ass and rubbed. Jerked me closer possessively. "You don't run off and do shit without me."

I glanced up at him. "Did you want to?"

"Want to what?"

"Want to own me? Or was it that you had to get me out of there?"

"I could've easily taken my truck to come get you."

"Point taken," I muttered, feeling my face flush. "Ryk, you're killing me."

"Good, Sean," he said. "Because you've been killing me since the goddamned day I laid eyes on you, when you sauntered by me, telling me to catch you if I dared."

And he'd dared all right. It'd been like poking a hungry lion with a stick... except I really didn't mind being mauled.

But owned? That was different. And I couldn't say, at the moment, that I minded it all that much.

CHAPTER 22

SIMPLE TWIST OF FATE

Noah thought I was fucking nuts (his words) when I told him about fixing Casey's car. To his credit, after much convincing, and several days' rest at Havoc, because Edmund's goons had beaten him up, he went to the Hangmen's clubhouse with me, grumbling the entire way there about how he hoped I knew he was going to kick someone's ass if they started with him.

When we got there, the first person Noah zeroed in on was a tall blonde woman. She was cute pretty, with freckles across the bridge of her nose and a killer body.

And she was fixing a car. Which for Noah was like porn with a side of porn. He went over to talk to her while I went to Casey, who was sitting with a group of guys, all looking at Noah like they wanted to rebeat him for talking to an MC woman without anyone's permission.

Noah and I had always lived by the *easier to ask forgiveness than permission* motto anyway. It was too late to change either of us.

Casey had stood to greet me, all while looking over my shoulder, his face darkening. I turned to see Noah and the blonde woman discussing . . . something. And they were both laughing. Casey marched over there and I followed, really hoping that the chick wasn't like, Casey's woman. Because Ryker'd told me Casey was bi, like me.

"Hey, Noah, this is Casey," I managed, just as Jethro popped around the corner.

Noah barely glanced up at Casey. "Dude, sorry about your car. It wasn't in the greatest condition anyway. Did you ever do any maintenance on her?"

Casey's brows rose and Jethro snorted. I was killing two birds with one stone by delivering Noah to both of them at the same time . . . and keeping Noah inside the MC was better than keeping him out.

But Casey ignored Noah and put a hand on my shoulder instead. "You ever get bored at Havoc . . ."

"He won't."

I turned to see Ryker. "You really are following me everywhere."

"Because you really do need a keeper. Speaking of . . ." He turned to Casey. "Still pretty hot out there. Can you keep Noah here for a couple of days? Or else I'll pick him up and drop him off."

"Hope he's got a bag packed, because he's not going anywhere until the car looks as perfect as if did before he fucked with it."

"No offense, but I'd never describe that car as perfect," Noah muttered. If he hadn't been running his hands over the hood at the time, that look in his eyes I knew all too well, Casey probably would've decked him.

Instead, Casey looked at me. "He's lethal too?"

"Pretty much," I agreed.

Casey stared at Ryker. "This is why we don't let outsiders in."

"Too late." Ryker put a hand on the back of my neck and steered me out to his truck.

"Want to put your bike in?" I asked. "We can go have lunch."

Ryker studied me for a long second. "Yeah, I'd like that."

Lunch led to a couple of drinks at Bertha's—for Ryker, not me. Because those damned drugs from the other day had fucked me up enough. He played pool while I looked around and tried to remember all the little details of the first night I'd met him.

His phone rang. He listened for a few seconds then said, "I've got plans tonight," before he hung up. Then he motioned for me to follow him, and we stopped in the long hallway that connected the two rooms of the bar. He pulled me against the wall and said, "Here. This is where we first talked."

"This, I remember."

We stood side by side, backs against the wall. This time, Ryker was drunk, and I was in control. As much as in control as I could be around him.

"I'd like to put you on that pool table," he started. "Strip you. Hold your hands behind your back. Fuck you, holding you helpless like that. Helpless, taking whatever I give you."

I bit back a whimper.

"When I get you home, that's what we're doing. Kitchen table. Bed. Maybe the porch."

I shuddered. "You said you had plans."

"I do. I plan to spend at least several hours between your legs tonight."

Jesus. I flushed, and he grinned. Yanked me to him. "Love making you blush, baby."

His smile was lazy. Heavily lidded. If he could bend me over the bar (if I asked), he would. But instead, he backed me against the wall, put his arms up, blocking me in (like he needed to), and kissed me. Like, kissed me so well, there was applause at one point.

A woman walked by, trailed her fingers across Ryker's arm and said, "I'm definitely jealous. I know you're sometimes looking for a third . . ." and dropped a card in my pocket.

I glanced up at him. "Seems like she might know something about you that I don't."

Ryker grinned sheepishly. "I haven't done that in eight months, Sean."

"But before that? Threesomes? Was she an example of how you and Casey shared?"

"You little shit. How did you—" He seemed to realize that I'd simply guessed. And then he raised his brows. "Interested?"

"I just like hearing about it. Turns me on."

"Sometimes women. Sometimes guys," he said, running a finger along the side of my neck. "Always tied down."

"So you and Casey never . . ."

"Nah. Not like that. More about the person in the middle than us."

"And Sweet was okay with that?"

"Despite all the false shit out there, most MCs couldn't survive without cooperation between them. Casey brought this Hangmen's chapter up here from Florida. Settled in and everyone waited for us to kick their ass."

"Seriously, will Noah be okay there?"

"Can he restore that car?"

"Yes."

"Then he'll be fine."

CHAPTER 23

FIRE ON THE MOUNTAIN

I woke from a deep sleep to the sound of an alarm. Before I could jolt out of bed, Ryker's hand was on my shoulder, and he was turning off the high-pitched shriek coming from his phone.

"It's okay, Sean. Just something I have to take care of now."

"Is everything all right?"

"No. But it will be."

"Can I help?"

"Yeah, by staying here. By being here when I get back." He touched the side of my face, and I nodded and watched him pull his vest on, grab a knife and his keys. When he left the room, I got out of bed and followed him out the door. From the porch, I watched him take off on his Harley.

He wasn't alone. I watched more motorcycles following him, flying down the hill, a single-file trail of destruction ready to take on the world. With Ryker at the helm.

"He'll be okay."

I hadn't heard Sweet come up onto the porch, because I'd been so enthralled watching them. "I feel like I should follow."

"No, you shouldn't. If you've never done it, you'll scare the kid."

"Scare the kid?" I turned to Sweet. "They're picking up a kid?"

"A twelve-year-old boy."

"And what? The bikers from hell aren't going to give him nightmares?"

"He's met Ryker and the others before. That's how he knew to call them if things got bad."

I didn't know what his definition of bad was, but I could only imagine. "I don't understand what's going on, Sweet."

And honestly, I didn't expect him to tell me. Not after all the shit I'd put Havoc though. But he said, "We help kids—sometimes kids and their parents, mom or dad—who need us. Some of them have been abused. Some of them are witnesses to unspeakable things, and we protect them until they testify. Or we relocate them."

I stared at him, trying to process what he was saying. It's not that I thought Havoc was the worst place ever, with the porn and the bodyguarding and whatever else they wouldn't admit to. They were a biker club, not angels. But I never expected them to be involved in something like that. "You guys could get into real trouble for that."

"For some of it, definitely. Then again, sometimes federal marshals ask us to hide the kids here. Who'd want to come in here and deal with us to get to their witness, right?"

"What's going on with the kid Ryker went to get?"

Sweet looked angry. "There's some bad shit going on. He's supposed to testify against men his father knows. At first, his father was supposed to be cooperating, but Ryker never believed that. Told the kid to call him at the first sign of trouble."

"What kind of trouble?"

Sweet looked at me. "His father tried to beat him to death to stop him from testifying. He ran when the neighbors heard the screams and called the cops. He called Ryker first, so I'm hoping he'll get there before the police do."

"The police won't help?"

"The police aren't US Marshals. This kid's already supposed to be hidden."

God, I couldn't believe this. "So Ryker will get him and bring him here?"

"Depends on how badly he's hurt. If he doesn't need surgery, my sister will come here and help him out."

"Your sister's a doctor?"

"Works the ER down in Montgomery County. I try to keep her out of most things, but for a kid, there's no stopping her." His phone beeped and he stared down at it, muttered, "Good, good," then turned to me and said, "They're bringing him here. Gotta go call my sister."

He jumped down off the porch and disappeared into the night. I waited out in the semidarkness, curled on a chair, listening for the sounds of the Harleys to come dancing up the hills again.

From my vantage point, I could see the main clubhouse had a few lights still on. From what Ryker had told me, there were men in the trees, guarding Havoc too. Maybe one day, I'd be one of them.

But being in the club (or not) didn't seem to be a deal breaker for Ryker.

Goddammit, I was freaking myself the fuck out. We'd come so far. I'd given him more trust than I'd ever given anyone. Even Noah.

Noah. Jesus. I stood and paced the generous porch, my bare feet padding against the smooth wood. Ryker said he'd made it by hand, and I could picture it.

I wasn't sure how much time had passed, how long I alternately sat and stared into the darkness, then got up and paced, went inside to grab something to drink. Came out again, prayed for a little boy and for the men who were helping him.

I was just about to go inside and maybe try to sleep when he spoke.

"I came into Havoc when I was twelve, and I never left." Ryker's voice—quiet and serious but still riveting—and my hand stilled on the doorknob. I hadn't heard him come back. I let go of the doorknob and turned around, went to stand next to him. We both held on to the railing of the porch and looked out into the night as I asked, "Were your parents bikers?"

"My mom was a teenager when she had me. And she was a drug addict—she got clean when she was pregnant but went right back to it after I was born. I don't think she knew who my dad was. I never cared much to try to find out."

"Were you taken away from her?"

"Child protective services probably tried, but she moved around a lot. Until we moved around here, and Havoc intervened."

I got it then, the pieces clicking together faster than I could get the words out. "Havoc rescued you through their Underground Railroad–type of system."

The silence told me I was right. A big burden for a little kid, but the guy'd always been an old soul. I knew that from the second he'd stepped into my bathroom to rescue me. I should've noticed he'd been rescuing me all along.

Havoc really was his family, and I'd threatened everything about this place and the people who'd kept him safe. How the hell could he even look at me after that? I could barely stand it myself.

His hands came down heavily on my shoulders, but I still couldn't look at him.

"This is so fucked up, Ryk."

"Yeah, it is." He moved a hand down to slide it around my chest, tugging me against him. "Come back inside."

"How the hell can you still want me here?"

His nose nuzzled my cheek. "You've done nothing wrong, babe. You've been being you. All right? This shit takes time to figure out, and you're figuring it out. And you're loyal."

"You know I am."

"When this started, I didn't think any of it would go this far. But I'm not sorry at all."

"Me neither." I paused. "Sweet told me about the boy."

"Charles."

"Is he okay?"

"Physically, he will be." Ryker put an arm around my shoulders and pulled at me. We went inside, where he put on some coffee, then joined me on the couch.

"I was the first," he admitted. "I'm the start of the whole program. When Sweet's father found me, he didn't know what to do with me. But he knew enough not to leave me where I was. So he put me on the back of his bike, and he drove me here. And later, when my mom sent her boyfriend here with his crew to get me, Havoc stood around me and told them to try to get me. And they did try."

"I'm guessing it didn't go well for them."

"Not at all." He paused. "Sweet's mom took me in. They lived in the cabin right over there. That was the first one built on the compound. The only one for a while, but then, over time, the MC decided it was safer for members to have a place here. If they wanted it."

"So the whole MC lives here?"

"Not all of them want that kind of closeness. But a group of them live down the road, along a regular street. Still well hidden, though." Ryker smiled. "It was a good place to grow up."

"I can imagine." What I couldn't do was shake the image of a scared little boy, like I'd once been, from my mind. "What'll happen to Charles?"

"He'll be all right."

"You'll keep him here?"

"Maybe. Maybe Sweet's sister knows about a good family who wouldn't mind raising a hellion. No one's giving us foster kids. But over half of us were. The guys who started this club were four foster brothers with the same foster care mom. Tough SOBs who went to war, came back fucked up, and made a place for guys like them and the people who loved them. One of them was openly gay, so that has a lot to do with the nonjudgment around here. They don't care who you fuck as long as you don't fuck over the MC."

I wanted to ask him more about the men who'd started Havoc. And why here. Because anyone who lived close to the hills where the MC was situated knew the legend. Part of it helped to elevate Havoc's status from dangerous to almost supernaturally dangerous.

I wasn't sure if it was a story parents told to keep their kids out of the woods and away from Havoc, or if Havoc'd started the story themselves, but either way, it was a pretty cool one.

I told Ryker that now, and he nodded and told me, "The way I always heard it was that the four horsemen of the apocalypse rode through the hills where Havoc's compound now sits. Then it became an Indian burial ground, sacred land. Everyone was really superstitious about it, too scared to touch it, because whether or not they believed the first part, the burial ground was indisputable. And so it stayed empty for a long time, until the mayor of Shades sold it to a developer in the sixties. The land was supposed to be stripped and cleared to make room for malls and apartments and houses, a continuation of the rest of Shades Run." He sounded serious, like he believed it, and I always had too, but I'd never heard it laid out quite like this.

"They got the equipment up here. Every time they tried to use it, something broke. One night, all the construction trailers caught on fire." I looked around to where he'd been pointing, showing me where the trailers had been. "Everything burned, except the trees and the grass. People who saw it said it looked like just the equipment had been targeted, but there wasn't any sign of vandalism or accelerant that would prove someone did it on purpose. The developer got spooked and decided to start small. He was going to build a couple of houses side by side, and he was going to live in one of them to show people not to be scared of an old legend. But those houses never got built. Anything anyone brought to the land went bad or broke or never made it to the site. So the developer tried to sell it for years. Until the guys who founded Havoc came in and changed everything."

"Looks like it," I murmured.

"My house is one of the earliest ones built. It belonged to Peter, who was one of the four original members." He looked understandably proud of that. "Besides Peter, there was William, Finn and Darren. They came back from Vietnam, and they'd lost their jobs because they'd been gone for so long. They were broke, and the land was on sale cheap. And they knew why—it wasn't like the guy who sold it to them duped them. But they figured, after what they'd seen during war, what the hell could be scarier than that? What could be scarier than the way they were—the way they felt?"

Was that why I felt so comfortable arriving in Havoc's territory? But hearing Ryker explain it, the whole thing made sense. "So they moved in here?"

"In tents," he said. "There was nothing here and since they'd heard that even the simplest structures fell or burned down or rotted, they started slow. They didn't have much anyway. And, the way Sweet tells it—the way his grandfather told him—Finnean said that after about three weeks of sleeping in the tents and riding around the land, figuring out what they were going to do with the rest of their lives, they woke up to find crocuses blooming. It was February, still really cold, but the flowers had popped up all around them in the middle of the night. The first thing that had grown here in a hundred years or more."

As he spoke, my gaze caught on the mess of crocuses, highlighted by the now-rising sun, in the field beyond Ryker's house. Which didn't make sense, since it wasn't their season.

"They're always here," Ryker said. "Doesn't matter the season—they come up, die and more follow them. It's never ending."

A shiver went through me, although it wasn't a spooky, creepy feeling. I tried to imagine the guys, back from war, living in tents.

Probably having nightmares, knowing they weren't ready for society. That they might not ever be ready. "I feel like that," I told Ryker.

"Yeah, baby, I know."

"So from those tents . . . all of this?" I motioned to the compound, which was really endless. It was built cleverly, so many of the structures seemed to blend into the woods.

"All from those four men. And their significant others," he was quick to add. "William was the one who suggested the name Havoc—he wanted to play off the legend and to keep people the hell away. And for a while, anyone who wasn't part of this group who tried to come here? Their car would stall on the hill."

"Does that still happen?" I asked. "Because I didn't have any trouble."

He glanced at me but didn't answer. Just said, "William and his partner, Mark, were the first couple here. Guess that's why no one blinks an eye around here if you're gay or bi or straight. Doesn't matter. Loyalty does."

Ryker was more than loyal, his protectiveness scary, but mainly because I'd never had anything like it. Shit was always up to me. I protected Noah, and Billy. At least I'd tried.

"And who protects you?" Ryker asked when I'd admitted that.

"Before you?" I shrugged because I didn't want to answer. Because I couldn't. Because there'd never been anyone.

"Your parents?" I shook my head, and he said, "Sorry, babe."

"We can't all have a Havoc to take care of us," I told him, although I felt like, as much as Ryker owned me, I owned him as well. But I couldn't put that into words.

His hand rubbed the back of my neck before he slid a finger under my chin. "Havoc's not the only thing that takes care of me. You do too. But you know that already, Sean. Don't you?"

I stared at him. "I guess I do."

CHAPTER 24

SAGE AND SPIRIT

Ryker's phone woke me up again later that same night. He'd grabbed it on the first ring. "I spotted them ten minutes ago on the monitor, old man. I'm on it."

He referred to Sweet as old man at times, which always made me laugh, although not to Sweet's face. Mainly because Sweet had warmed up to me a bit more, even going so far as to let me drive him in the Aston Martin the other day.

Ryker was dressing. "Trouble's coming. More trouble."

I got dressed too. "Then so am I."

"Sean, no. You need to stay put. I can't worry about you and fight."

I thought about it for a second, and I agreed. To his face. In seconds, he was out of the house and on his bike, reiterating over his shoulder for me to stay put.

But I just couldn't. Something was really fucking wrong, and every instinct told me this time, whatever was happening had nothing to do with me. And I wouldn't let Ryker face any kind of danger without at least trying to back him and Havoc up.

I grabbed a Sig from the drawer—he'd shown me where he kept his weapons, just in case—and I followed the trail of bikes down the hill. They were silent as ninjas, and they weren't speeding, so I was able to keep up somewhat. I'd learned that most Havoc guys had two bikes—loud ones and quiet ones, and now I understood that need. My feet took the terrain instinctively.

Once I got almost to the bottom of the first hill, the one behind Ryker's place, I saw a couple of cars. And although there were men getting out of the cars and off their bikes . . . it looked like there were others inside of them, trying to start them.

The cars had stalled on the hills. Like the hills wouldn't let anyone up who didn't belong.

"Jesus Christ, Rush," I muttered, because I was spooking the fuck out of myself.

At the bottom of the hill, there was an open circle of land, spotlit by the bikes. In the center was Ryker, taking on at least three men. Sweet was fighting too, along with a lot of the guys I recognized from hanging out here. I saw brass knuckles and knives. Figured they had guns, but for now, it appeared to be a brawl. I was still half-stunned by violence from the Army, and what was happening was violent enough to make my PTSD stand up and take notice. I stayed behind the tree line, partially because Ryker told me to stay out of it, but also because I didn't know this enemy, how they fought, why they were attacking Havoc . . . what the hell was going on. I needed to recon.

"Should've made Ryker tell me how he fights," I muttered to myself as I held my weapon down by my side. I got closer and made out the cut on one guy's jacket. Heathens. An MC from North Carolina. I didn't know much about them except that their rep wasn't good. They were into meth and God knew what else.

I stood at the ready. But Havoc was a well-oiled machine, working together to take down the Heathens, and I waited for an opportunity to help, to prove I was needed for more than just patching him up afterward. Ryker's lip was bleeding, but he was too busy slamming men to the ground to notice or care. He looked fierce as he defended his club, his family.

The wind picked up. I was about to say fuck it and go in anyway when something told me to stop. I swore to fucking Christ I heard what sounded like a galloping horse. I turned around and felt a rush of air slide by me.

I glanced back to the fight and knew Ryker didn't need me. Not there. But somewhere.

Maybe it was Billy. Or Finn. Or those horsemen. But whatever or whoever it was, I was heading back in the darkness toward the main house. The wind picked up again, and the hairs at the back of my neck stood on end. I ran faster, trying to figure out what the hell was going on.

I made a quick circle around the houses. All quiet. Woman and children went into lockdown when there was any threat on the compound They wanted to deal with it themselves, rather than risk police poking around their land.

Horses again. I hadn't had anything more than a beer. But I followed the sounds until they faded away, and I found myself in front of Greta's. The doors were closed, but I caught a hint of movement through a hastily closed shade.

Greta. A gun, pointed at her. A young boy. Dammit. I wanted to burst in there, but suddenly, there was another young boy next to me. He must've snuck out another front window. I caught him so he wouldn't land heavily on the porch and attract attention.

The man was agitated. I didn't have time for complicated. I picked up a loose brick and handed it to the kid. Pointed to the window. Whispered for him to wait ten seconds, throw, and get out of the way. Duck.

He agreed. I hightailed it to the back and kicked the door in as the window broke. Shot the guy in the shoulder. Greta grabbed his gun and held it on him, and I went over and tied his good arm to the nearest chair while he cursed me.

Some other Havoc guys came in, and they took the gun from Greta. That's when she hugged me tight. I pretended I hated it, but I didn't.

Ryker limped in at that moment. He'd given several beatings but he'd taken one as well. His cheek was swollen, his lip bloody, and he was giving orders. "The boy's got to get out of here before the police catch wind of this."

Greta grabbed for her cell phone. "I'll call the marshal and get him here."

I stared at Ryker. "Do the police cars come up the hill?"

He shook his head. "They know better—they get out and walk."

I didn't let him say anything else before I was out the door and down the hill.

CHAPTER 25

I FOUGHT THE LAW

Getting arrested isn't all that hard. I had a lot of options, but in the end, I figured that stealing a police black-and-white was the best bet to get all hands on deck. I hoped it'd give Ryker enough time to get Charles out of Havoc and giving the police a merry trip through town seemed the best way to do so.

Letting myself get caught? That part would suck, mainly because I'd have to make it look realistic. But watching the cops get out of their three cars and leave them to walk up the hill gave me a second of pleasure, because that was my in. I let myself inside one of the cars, started it easily, hit the alarms and watched them come running. They got into the remaining cars and followed me, and I made sure to keep them on the road for a good fifteen minutes.

Shades didn't have a giant police force, so I figured I'd kept enough of them busy. Finally, I pulled over and waited.

Over a megaphone, I heard, "Get out of the car with your hands up."

McKibbins's voice. Of course. But I followed his directions, and then he shined a flashlight directly, deliberately, into my eyes. "Sean Rush. What a fucking surprise. Kneel."

I did, with my hands locked behind my head. McKibbins approached me, pushed me down, holding my arms so I didn't crash facefirst into the pavement.

"What the hell were you thinking, Rush?" he muttered as he searched me, probably pissed when he found nothing. When he pulled me off the ground to a standing position, he stared at me. "Sloppy? Or desperate? Either way, hanging out with an MC will do that to you."

I didn't say anything, not even when he jerked my arms roughly before shoving me into the back of the police car. I stared at the partition, the back of McKibbins's head as he talked to his partner about how the American military really needed to take in a better grade of soldiers.

I rolled my eyes and bit my tongue for the short ride to the stationhouse. Once there, I was taken into a room, shoved into a chair, handcuffed to the table, and left for several hours.

They'd forgotten my legs. Always the first mistake. Hook, a mercenary type I'd met along the way in Iraq, had told me *You can kill anyone with your legs if you know how.*

He'd proceeded to show me how. And even though I'd never pull that here, just knowing I had options made me sit more easily.

Still, I fucking hated this place. It was better than the jail, where I'd made a visit to my father right after the judge's ruling, before I went to Basic.

He was only housed half an hour from where I lived. He'd been there for ten years, but I'd only been to see him a handful of times.

He'd been seventeen when I was born. When I saw him, he'd been thirty-four, and he'd actually looked like he was living the life in prison rather than suffering. Beyond the sickly pale of his skin, he'd looked clean and relaxed. He'd even shaken hands with the prison guards.

They'd sat him down across from me and chained his hands the same way they'd done with me today.

Like father, like son.

He'd known why I was there—the prison grapevine was better than TMZ. We'd both looked between the chains on his hand and then back at the invisible ones on mine, the sentence that was to be served in the Army instead of in prison. And then we'd looked back at each other.

"You going to leave me alone with him?" he drawled finally.

The guard pointed to him. "No funny business, Kevin."

"And turn off that goddamned two-way shit. I find out you're listening in, I'm calling my lawyer."

"Yeah, you do that," the guard muttered, then closed the door behind him.

"You know they won't turn it off. Assholes." He spat toward the two-way mirror before looking back to me. "They said you wanted to see me."

"They were wrong."

"What'd you do?"

"Stole a few cars."

He snorted in disgust. "And you got caught? Rush, I taught you better than that."

Actually, he hadn't, but now wasn't the time to argue about how I was raised. "I'm going into the Army."

"I heard." He rolled his eyes. "You really fucked up."

I fucked up? I didn't lash out, though—remained calm and finally asked him what I'd always wanted to. "Why'd you do it?"

"Do what?"

"All of it. The stealing. The killing."

"Alleged," he called toward the mirror before he turned back to me. "Come on, Rush—you know the answer as well as I do. I liked it."

"And if they let you out?"

"I'd do it again the first chance I got." He smirked a little. "So would you."

I hated that he was right. "Maybe."

"According to that asshole cop, you're going to end up in the cell next to me. I told him no way." My father leaned in like he was about to tell me a secret. "You know why I told him that? Because you're too damned smart to let yourself be caged. You might be caught, but you'll always have your freedom."

The Army wouldn't be freedom, but it was a hell of a lot better than jail. I couldn't ever remember my father complimenting me. I didn't know if I was supposed to be proud or say thanks.

"You're smart because you're alone," he continued. "Worst thing I could've done was get myself tied down with a woman and a kid. Totally fucked me over."

"Wasn't all that great for me either, Dad," I said wryly.

He pointed his finger at me. "Remember that, then. Don't fuck it up by attaching yourself to someone because they make you feel good between the sheets for a few minutes. Always plenty of women around for fucking. Wear a condom. Don't get distracted, and I'll never see you here. Because let's be honest, Rush—as much as someone could fuck you up? Because of what you do, you'll fuck anyone up who crosses your path. You're better off alone. Guys like us always are."

The guard opened the door. "Time's up."

"Great father-son bonding time," I muttered as the guard walked him out of the room.

I blinked and it was just me again, alone in the interrogation room. Alone being the key word.

McKibbins came in about ten minutes later, when I was still turning around my father's old proclamations in my head. As I sat here, stupid enough to have let myself get caught on purpose. For Ryker.

No compliments from the old man on this one, I'd bet.

I looked up at McKibbins warily, especially when he dragged the chair around the table to sit next to me.

"Mirror's off," he said, before I could tell him to do that.

"Okay." What did he want? My undying thanks for giving me my rights? Although not all of them, because where was my phone call? I tamped down the wiseass as much as I could, but who knew how long that shit would hold?

"You're lucky I was the one to catch you tonight," he told me.

I shifted, but it was impossible to get comfortable with my wrists twisted. "Right, you're my guardian angel."

Yeah, didn't hold long at all. But hell, McKibbins would think I had a head injury if I was normal to him.

McKibbins frowned. "Rush, you need to get the fuck out of this life before you end up like your old man."

"Or Billy?"

He stared at me, and his voice softened. "Or buried, like Billy."

"You think I deserve that."

"I think neither one of you would've gone to Iraq if you hadn't started stealing."

I wasn't getting into that, because we'd never, ever see eye to eye. "So mentioning my father's supposed to scare me straight?"

"For Billy, Rush. For Billy." He spoke through clenched teeth and my gut twisted. Billy would hate him for doing this to me, for using his name like this.

"Billy never judged me, or anyone. Even you," I said quietly, and that was the God's honest truth.

McKibbins's expression tightened, but he ignored my words. "You've been running with Havoc MC."

"I wouldn't say that, no." Because that was also the truth.

"You've been spotted with Ryker."

I shrugged. "I don't even know his last name." Another truth.

"You are spending time with him, fixing his bike."

"We're fucking. Is that against the law now?" I asked.

"Depends on what you're doing." I swore I saw the hint of a smile on his face, like he was making a joke, but then he sobered. "Rush, what do you know about Havoc's activities?"

"I know they ride motorcycles," I said innocently.

"Fucking can't help yourself," he muttered. "Rush, Havoc runs a car theft ring—they steal and export expensive luxury cars out of the country."

I tried not to react. "I have no idea what you're talking about."

"Right. I'm actually going to believe you on that. I've got no proof, other than what I've suspected for years. But we've never been able to make a connection, not the way we've been able to connect Edmund to things. But when Havoc brought you in . . ."

"I'm not *in* Havoc."

"Coincidence that they started hanging out with a car thief?" he asked. I'd been thinking the same thing.

"They're not hanging out with me. Ryker is."

He stared at me like I was the most naive person on earth. "Hanging around Ryker is hanging around with Havoc. You want to know what I think? Either they're looking to hire you or to kill you."

"Kill me?"

"They're not Boy Scouts, Rush. And they don't appreciate competition."

A chill ran through me. "I don't pose a threat. I'm out."

"Bullshit."

Yeah, it was. And Ryker knew I was still stealing and racing. "If an MC I'd known about my whole life was into stealing cars, wouldn't *I* know about it?"

"Obviously not."

Now the question was, did Noah know about Havoc and the ring? Because reason stood to follow that Edmund did, hence his freak out when he discovered I was involved with Ryker. And that would be a really good reason to try to kill me . . . but a really good reason to leave me the hell alone too.

Either way, they'd gotten Havoc suspicious. But no one said you needed to be a brain trust to manage thieves. You just had to dangle the right carrots, and we'd come running. "Why are you sharing all of this with me?"

"Thought you might be interested in helping."

"Why'd you think that?"

"Rush, I've been goddamned pleasant as hell, trying to get this through your thick skull. You're a thief, but you're nothing like these MC guys. You have no idea the kind of shit they do. And trust me when I say, if you don't get me information, you're going down the way you should've a long time ago."

"What, I'm supposed to waltz in and ask them?"

"You could. Maybe when you and Ryker are having a quiet moment. Although you'll need to be wearing this, so that probably won't work well." He pulled a wire out of his pocket. He held up the thickest part. "This is the microphone. Position it out like this. Don't put tape over the microphone."

"I'm not wearing that. Are you fucking kidding me?"

"I need information I can take to the DA. They're not going to take the word of a car thief." He paused, stared at the chains on my wrists. "Do this, and I'll wipe this latest incident off your record."

Anger coursed through me.

Of course it was true—my gut had told me weeks ago that Ryker was lying. I'd grown up with the MC around me. I'd heard a million rumors, but never this one. Was I the only one who didn't know Havoc was into stealing cars?

How had they kept it so quiet?

Because they use disposable guys, like you. Like Ryker accused Edmund of doing.

Dammit. I took the wire from him and nodded. He clapped me on the shoulder and left. I didn't even bother to ask him how long he planned on keeping me here like this, because I wanted him gone.

I wasn't going to spy on Havoc or Ryker, but I was going to find out what was happening, if it killed me. Which it might.

In my world, snitches were the worst. I'd gone to juvie because of porn guy turning me in for beating him up, mainly to keep me from hunting him down and killing him. And my whole life depended on people keeping confidences, from childhood through the Army. I could understand Ryker's need as well, but he sure as fuck didn't need to use me.

A brief knock on the door, followed by sounds of men arguing—and I swear there was a chair or something heavy thrown against the two-way mirror because I heard some kind of crack. It all had me craning my neck to see what was going on. I half expected Ryker to barge in, but it was actually Jethro who came banging inside.

He looked pissed. He was out of breath, and fuck, I hope all of that wasn't directed my way.

I tensed when he slammed the door behind him and came over to me. He leaned down and looked at me, and his eyes were angry when he murmured, "The ATF didn't bail you out—the guy who races for the Hangmen did, got that?"

I nodded. Because angry or not, this was a good thing. I think.

Jethro motioned to the mirror and then another cop came into the room.

"Meet you outside after you get your stuff," Jethro told me, and I guessed Ryker wasn't out there at all.

The cop unlocked the cuffs, and I flexed my wrists, rubbed my hands together to get the blood flowing. He motioned for me to follow him, and I did, stuffing the wire into my pocket. I collected my wallet and keys from the desk clerk, and then I was free and in Jethro's car, the same one he'd raced against me that first night we'd met.

He gunned it away from the police station, and once we got onto the highway, I turned to him. "If you go to the bank, I'll pay you back."

"Why? You're jumping bail?"

"No."

"Relax. I just said that so McKibbins would think it. The chief knows who I am. There's no real bail involved here. This will just go away, for all intents and purposes."

I frowned. "But I didn't give you Noah."

"Noah turned himself in to me today," he explained.

"And if he hadn't?"

Jethro shook his finger at me. "Think about this before you make fun of someone's vintage T-shirts again."

"You'll help him?"

"Of course I will. No one knows he came to me but me. He's not snitching on anyone. I'm just extricating him from his situation with that asshole, Edmund. Once Edmund's out of the way, my job's easier." He glanced over at me. "Really, Rush, your friend's okay. He did this as much for you as for him, you know."

I nodded. But I was all goddamned hollowed out inside. "Is it true about Havoc and the car theft ring?" He didn't say anything. "You knew."

Jethro glanced at me. "So did you."

That was fair.

"You going to see Ryker?" he asked after a few minutes.

"Yes."

"I'm not going anywhere near Havoc with you. I'll drop you at your place to get your own ride there."

Once he did, I sat in my truck and brooded for a while before I started driving. I guess I couldn't be trusted or accepted. That hurt enough. But the worst part of the betrayal? I understood it. I could fuck up Havoc and everything they'd built because of my reputation. My compulsion to steal. The way I understood it, my rep would bring unwanted scrutiny to Havoc. And I'm pretty sure I understood the reason why they kept the car thefts so far under wraps. That had to fund whatever they were doing to help the kids.

So I'd make it easy on Ryker. Easy and believable. Because that kid's face flashed in front of my face. That kid could be me, or Ryker, or Billy, or Noah, but I'd be damned if he wouldn't have a chance at normal. A chance for a family.

CHAPTER 26

SHELTER FROM THE STORM

Ryker knew I was coming. The front gate had to call ahead to Ryker to get the okay for me to come in. But my truck, unlike most vehicles around here, was really goddamned quiet. And plenty fast. I pulled along the side of the house and walked up to the porch. The screen was closed, but the main door was open, and I heard them talking.

"He's a time bomb, Ryk." Sweet's voice. I stilled and listened, because I needed to know this shit.

"I know."

"And what the hell does that mean for Havoc? He's not going to stop taking chances."

Ryker didn't say anything. Didn't defend me. Because really, everything Sweet said was true. It wasn't like he was saying I was an asshole. He was just outlining . . . me.

And me and Havoc? Not a great fit.

I went back and stamped noisily up the porch, calling for Ryker. He and Sweet came out immediately.

"Sean, are you all right? Jesus . . ." Ryker grabbed for me, inspecting me.

"I'm fine. McKibbins didn't try anything. Nothing physical, anyway," I said. Ryker led me inside, sat me down, and handed me a soda and a roll. It was almost five in the morning.

Sweet followed us in, sat at the table across from us. And I'd have to play this really well.

I dug into my pocket and threw the wire on the table.

"What the fuck, Sean?" Ryker demanded when he saw it.

"It's not active," I said. "I took the battery out already. And how do you know what it is?"

He didn't answer that, merely dug into his pocket and pulled out a similar wire. "McKibbins's partner came to see me."

"So what, he's pitting us against each other?"

"Said he'll leave Havoc alone—you're McKibbins real target. Have been for years."

Jesus. There was a hell of a lot of truth in that. I ran my fingers through my hair and said, "He said you guys were into illegal shit."

"Did he mention Charles, or anything about witnesses?" Sweet asked and I couldn't leave him hanging about that.

"No, not a word. He seemed to have something specific in mind, but he wouldn't say it. Is there something about the porn that he might be confused about?" I asked.

Ryker shook his head. "That's all buttoned-up."

"Rush, can you give us a few minutes?" Sweet asked.

"I'll wait outside." On Ryker's porch, I put my hands on the rails and stared out at the darkened field of crocuses.

A few seconds later, a bike's tailpipe backfired or maybe someone was practicing with their rifle. Everything echoed in these hills, and it didn't matter. I winced, because I knew—I knew—it wasn't Iraq or insurgents but I couldn't stop my goddamned mind from going there. I gripped the porch rails, knowing that if I couldn't go inside, it would get worse.

But with Ryker and Sweet inside, it was better to have the fucking meltdown out here. With any luck, it'd pass before they came out. Or maybe I could keep it away by the sheer force of will.

"Sean . . . hey, Sean, it's me. It's okay." Ryker's voice, and he was doing a pretty damned good impression of Noah's mental patient voice. The fact that I could think that told me this episode wasn't all that bad. But still, I was gripping the porch railing so hard I was sure either it or my hands would break. They ached from the pressure.

Ryker was close. I don't know where Sweet was. But Ryker's hands were on top of mine, rubbing, urging me to unclench them, and I did. Not before saying, "It's my fault Billy's dead."

"I don't believe that, Sean."

"McKibbins does."

"He's grieving. Looking for someone to blame."

"Well, he found that person pretty easily, because I am." I jerked away from him and turned around fast on him.

He circled me carefully, like I was some feral animal. Which I was.

I was also broken. Maybe I'd always been and could just admit it now.

"Sean, come on. Come sleep."

"No. No more rescuing me." I'd come here to tell Ryker I was leaving. He should be kicking me out of Havoc now, but he wasn't.

"Okay, no more rescuing," he agreed. "As long as you come inside."

"You're just saying that. You won't stop," I told him, fisting my hands to get rid of some of the agitation. "Don't you get it? *Noah's* bulletproof—he's the one guy I don't fuck up and kill. You—"

"Sean, please. Let's not—"

"Do this now?" I finished for him. I knew he was right and that bothered me the most. "You don't control me, as much as you want to."

"It's not about me wanting to, babe. It's about you wanting me to."

"Fuck that. I'm not walking around on a leash four paces behind you."

"I never asked that," Ryker said through gritted teeth. "I don't want that. I want you."

I was cold. Freezing. Didn't want to be here when I came down from this part. I wanted icy rage, not icy fear gripping me in frozen fingers.

He was still saying my name, but it sounded far away. I was probably running by that point. My body was full of adrenaline and terror that nothing—no one—could've stopped me. I was bathed in sweat. Shaking. Anger and pain, and I'm not sure if he found me or if I found him. I was numb by that point. Didn't apologize, and he didn't ask for one. All I knew was that I was in the tub, curled up, and he was using a washcloth to sponge water over my back and shoulders, until I sat back—submerged.

When the water threatened to chill, he ran more. I stayed in until I pruned and then I got up and dried and dressed. And then I told him, "This can't work," my voice sounding dull and distant.

He never answered me, and I fell asleep in his arms.

CHAPTER 27

AIN'T IT CRAZY

I went into Greta's place with Ryker. She hugged me again and a couple of guys patted me on the back. Even the guys I recognized as the ones I'd fought with earlier in the week nodded in my direction.

"Hey, Rush, you gonna help me fix a car today? A sweet '67 Chevy. I can't get her to turn over," BFFL-Tug said.

"Yeah, sure, I'll help." After he left, and the food came, I picked at it, and Ryker watched me, the concern in his eyes too much to take. Finally, I stood and walked outside, and he followed.

"What's up, Sean? The wiretap shit still bothering you?"

"Little bit, yeah." I stuck my hands in my pockets. "Is it all right to help Tug and those guys with the car?"

"Yeah, of course. More than all right."

"I wasn't sure how Sweet felt about me helping out with that stuff."

"He's grateful someone knows what they're doing with the cars."

"Really?" I crossed my arms. "Because I'd think a place that specializes in stealing high-end cars and shipping them overseas would know exactly what they're doing."

He stared at me. I waited for the denial, but none came this time.

"So these guys, they pretended to know nothing about cars just to test me?" I asked.

"Sean—"

"It's a yes or no?"

"Yes."

"Awesome."

"I can't trust everyone I fuck with this information."

I froze. "Wow. I'm sure it's a pretty long list."

"Before you, it was. I'm sure yours was too, before me."

"How do I know you're not lying about that too?"

"It's not like you introduced yourself as a car thief."

"That's different."

"How?"

"Because I didn't deny it when you found out."

"It's complicated."

"I'm learning that it always is with you, Ryk." I'd seen no signs of it at Havoc. Cars, not bikes, but they'd asked me to show them things. And like an idiot, I had. Was that the way they kept everyone unsuspecting?

What kind of idiot was I? "You set up all that shit about fixing Sweet's car to throw me off track. Was Havoc going to compete for the same jobs as Edmund?"

"Eddie's a fucking lowlife. He needs to pack up and leave town."

"Taking my job with him."

"His jobs were killing you," he reminded me.

"You're trying to distract me. The point is, you didn't want me to know about Havoc."

He nodded slowly, then said firmly, "I didn't see you selling out Noah—you called him your best friend. Even after he almost got you killed and ditched you, you gave him a second chance. Funny, Sean, I've never had to give my MC a second chance because they've always had my back. Even if I did something stupid, they'd bail me out, give me hell for it for my own good. So tell me, Sean, I'm supposed to ditch my MC's trust for a guy who won't even listen to me about personal safety?"

"A guy, huh?" Jesus, that stung. I went after him, mainly blind rage. Ryker was strong, but I gave as good as I got before we were pulled apart. Someone held my arms behind my back and that's when I really started to lose it.

Someone was holding Ryker back too and the weird thing was, he was yelling at them, "Let Sean go. Let go of him . . ."

He sounded more angry than worried that they were holding me, unconcerned that he was restrained.

When whoever held me finally listened, I was too numb to do much more than walk away.

Kid can fucking fight.

Heard he's good with a knife too.

I stood on his porch, not sure why I was waiting for a guy who was pretty pissed at me, if the way my jaw and ribs ached were any indication.

He wasn't far behind—wasn't surprised to see me. Barked, "Stay," then came back with ice for both of us. "Guess you know how to defend yourself."

"Did you really doubt me?"

"It's a hundred times more difficult than you can imagine in this world. You see it from the outside. You need to think of it like the Army. You want in, there are rules. You marry into it? There are still motherfucking rules. And don't tell me you never saw a spouse fuck up an Army guy's career with her *I won't follow rules* crap."

When he put it that way, it made sense. But Ryker found me. I didn't know what I was in for when I let him into my bed. The farther I'd got pulled in, the more I'd resisted everything. Mainly because that's just who I was.

And the worst part? Ryker knew that. Because he seemed to know every goddamned thing about me. And I was still fascinated by that. "I didn't sign up as spouse."

"You came here. To my MC. My house. You represent me," he said through clenched teeth.

"I was a job," I countered, with clenched teeth of my own.

He sighed. Closed his eyes, balanced the ice where I'd landed a great right hook. My hand would ache for days, but that was all right. No one at this motherfucking compound was going to take advantage of me.

Finally, he said, "You started out as a job."

"When did it end? After the first night you fucked me?"

"No."

"Second? Third? Fourth? Twentieth?"

If Ryker clenched his jaw any harder when he ground out, "No," I was pretty sure it'd break.

But I didn't let that stop me. "Last week?"

"I'm still on it."

"So this protection bullshit—it's for Havoc, not me."

"It's both," Ryker said. "Because Havoc is my family, and I protect what's mine."

"Right." My throat tightened bitterly. Because I didn't have a family beyond Noah and Billy, and Billy was gone and Noah was . . . *Fuck*. "Okay."

Because what was the point of arguing or trying to make this something it wasn't. Sweet already told me that Ryker never committed, that he rarely spent long with any one person, and when he was done, he never went back. And sure, I could argue that he'd been with me for a while, but since it'd started out as protecting Havoc and that hadn't changed, I figured it pretty much canceled any hope out. "How the fuck was this ever going to work between us?"

"This is coming from Mr. No Commitment?"

I pointed to him. "Fuck you, Ryker. Because you changed that. You let me change it, and what, you knew you couldn't tell me things?"

"Lot of people who marry into the MC don't know things."

I threw my hands into the air. My brain was spinning as I tried to process all of this. He'd reeled me in, for what? To keep me dangling whenever he wanted me? To keep me in line?

"Right, because that's happening," Ryker muttered.

"Dammit." I took a deep breath and stuck my hands in my pockets, stared at the floor.

. . . let's be honest, Rush—as much as someone could fuck you up? Because of what you do, you'll fuck anyone up who crosses your path. You're always going to be alone. You're better off like that . . . guys like us always are.

My father's words played over and over in my mind as I went inside and stuffed my clothes in my bag. At some point, Ryker came inside, and he was watching me. "I'm going home. I'm quitting my freelancing with BT. I've got money saved. I don't want to hear from Havoc or the Hangmen or Noah. Or you."

I waited for an argument, and I got none. He let me go. Even if he'd come after me, I wouldn't have gone back with him. This wasn't one of those showboat moments, and at least Ryker knew me well enough to know that.

I got home, threw my bag down, and sat on my couch. The rest of the day was passed watching mindless TV. I didn't want to have to think or deal. The truth was, I did have good savings. My rent wasn't much, and I owned my car outright. But I couldn't sit around all day because I'd go crazy. Eventually.

But for a little while, until I got my shit together, I could. For a week, I ordered takeout and I read and I watched mindless TV. And I thought a lot about what I wanted to do next, all while ignoring Noah's calls.

Ryker didn't call, text, or come over.

I deleted the Grateful Dead tracks from my iPod shuffles because if I didn't, I'd lose my resolve.

I'd have to start over, and leave Havoc behind, along with Ryker, Noah, and Officer McKibbins, and my memories of this place. And maybe that was a good thing. A fresh start.

Like the Army was supposed to be.

Well, it had changed me. So had Ryker. And I tried hard not to miss him, but I did. Every time I crawled into bed, I thought about him. My body tensed, cock hardened. I told myself it was the bed. So I'd go to the couch. But then I'd sit and wonder, how *did* he get in here in the first place, because he never did tell me.

Guess it was going to be one of those great mysteries.

I did sleep though, with the aid of Scotch. And being without him wasn't getting easier. He was too close, too easily accessible. I had to put as much space between us as I could.

CHAPTER 28

PAIN IN MY HEART

"Heard about Noah," Linc told me from where he was splayed across my couch.

"Heard from him?" I asked. He glanced at me, and I sighed. "Forget it. I don't want you to have to lie."

"He feels like shit about everything."

"He should. Fucking asshole almost killed me," I shot back. "You sure he's all right?"

It was Linc's turn to sigh. "He will be, now that he knows you don't hate him forever."

"I'm worried about him." I didn't mention the Jethro stuff—I didn't know what Noah had said to Linc, and hell, I knew Noah was in good hands. Finally.

Took the fucker long enough.

Linc nodded. "That's cool. But you can't fix him, you know."

"Thanks, Dr. Linc."

"Fuck off, Rush."

When he'd come in, he'd thrown a large envelope on the coffee table before heading to the kitchen to grab a beer. I hadn't touched it. Now, he motioned to it, asking, "You're really going off the grid?"

I was. Moving to Florida was the first step. There was a pretty good need down there for mechanics on high-end cars and boats. I'd reached out to Linc to grab me new IDs and credit cards and shit, so I could open a bank account. I didn't want anyone to know what I'd done in my former life. I'd planned on no stealing, no racing.

I'd paid ahead a month for my place here, in case it didn't work out. I was leaving tonight. "I've got to start over. I'm already packed."

"Yeah, I saw that. Listen, I was thinking of sticking around Shades for a while. My brother's on my case, and I need some time away. Is it cool if I stay here?" he asked.

"Place is paid up for the month. Don't fuck it up—I want my security deposit back." I handed him the extra set of keys, all while thinking, *Worst idea ever.*

But hell, old habits died hard. And Linc had dropped everything to get me what I needed.

Linc smiled. "Cool. Thanks. I'm going to go look around for a bit—I'll be back before you leave." He gave a wave and closed the door behind him.

When the bell rang five minutes later, I called out, "You have the goddamned keys, Linc." But when I opened the door, it was Greta standing there.

"I'm not going back," was the first thing I said to her.

"Good for you. I'm not here to bring you back."

Oh, snap. "Fine."

She narrowed her eyes. "Think you're too old for a lecture?"

"I supposed the correct answer's no."

"Wiseass. You're all that way when you're hurt or scared." She brushed past me. By the time I'd closed the door, she was in the living room, cleaning, gathering up the take-out containers and beer and soda empties. I was going to argue, but really, why? So I sat and waited.

She ended up in the kitchen. After a few minutes, I smelled fresh coffee brewing.

She stuck her head out of the doorway. "I'm not bringing it to you."

I went in and joined her at the table. After we took a few sips, she said, "Your parents?"

"Not around," was all I offered. She raised a brow, and I sighed. "My mom split and Dad's in jail."

"For how long?"

"He's still there." She stared at me until I admitted, "Life sentence."

"For?"

Jesus. "He shot and killed two security guards while he was robbing a bank."

She studied me, turning the mug around in her palms. "You pulled yourself up and out and escaped. Why?"

"I didn't want to live in the shitty places I grew up in. I saw a lot of losers."

"So you learned how to be a better criminal, and, somehow, a better person."

"I guess. I've never hurt anyone. Cars I steal are insured to the max. And rarely driven. Hell, they're like chess pieces to most collectors."

She considered that. "So what now?"

"I'll let you know when I figure it out." Because the last person I was telling where I was going was her.

"Like I said, hiding the hurt."

"Obviously not successfully," I muttered. "I like fixing cars. I like stealing them too. Doing either of those around here now without protection is suicide."

"You've attracted attention. But that's not new. Boys were talking about recruiting you long before this."

I glanced up at her. "I'm glad I get St. Ryker's approval."

She snorted. "That boy's the farthest thing from an angel. Gave Havoc a run for their money and then some. Because of him, the police raided our compound—the first and only time—when he was seventeen. So he gets you, Sean. Ryker's had his eyes on you since you were just past jailbait. But then you went into the Army and came back more of a man. And scarred, in here." She pointed to her heart. "Just like Ryker."

"He lied to me."

"So?"

I stared at her, trying to think of something. Finally, I did. "He doesn't trust me."

"Honey, he doesn't trust the world. He's all about protecting Havoc, but this had just as much to do about protecting you as it did the MC."

"What, you're his matchmaker?"

She wagged a finger at me. "Be a shame if your smart mouth stood in the way of being happy. Stupid too, and I know you're not."

"I don't want to talk about this."

"I don't care."

"Look, I don't owe you shit. You're not my mother, and Havoc's not my fami—" I stood and walked away before I could finish the word. In my head, I cursed.

I heard her get up. I was figuring she'd be out the door. But then her hand was on my shoulder, and she said, "That's what I thought."

"Right. So now you know. Thanks for stopping by."

She shook her head a little. "Forest for the trees, Rush."

I didn't know what she meant beyond that I was missing a point, and then she nodded and was gone.

The hardest part was driving past the *Leaving Shades Run* sign. So many memories in Shades. Some good, some terrible . . . but all of them mine. My childhood. Billy and Noah. Havoc.

Ryker.

Every hour or so, I convinced myself that this move was a mistake, but I was too hard-headed to turn around. Also, I reminded myself that Ryker had let me walk—again—and although I couldn't blame him for doing exactly what I'd wanted him to do, I was still pissed.

I had to keep Ryker safe, which meant keeping Havoc safe. Which meant keeping the kids safe. Skipping town, leaving McKibbins and his wiretap request behind, should take the pressure off things.

All I knew for sure was that being angry sucked. Being selfless sucked just as much.

Both together? Fucking unbearable.

I'd opened the roof to catch the warm sunshine. I'd been on the road for ten hours, and I was almost to the new place when my phone rang. I glanced down at the ID and saw Gypsy's Bail Bonds. And my first thought, of course, was Linc.

"Hey Gypsy."

"Hey, Rush, wasn't sure I'd catch you. We've got a situation here."

"Let me guess—Linc?"

He gave a short laugh. "He's an Army buddy of yours?"

"I guess I'm supposed to acknowledge him. What did he do?" Because he'd been in Shades Run for, like, literally thirty-six hours at this point, and while not his best record, it was close.

"Ah, the police picked him up for getting a little rowdy at Bertha's," Gypsy said. "He called me for bail, mentioned your name. I'll bail him out if he's cool."

You know what? Shades needed a touch of Linc. "He dropped everything, and drove six hours in the middle of the night to get me what I needed. If you need me to come down to the station . . ."

"Nah, don't worry about it. He said he didn't want to wake you up."

I said a mental note of thanks to Linc for not revealing that I was already out of there. "Thanks, Gypsy. He's not staying in Shades long."

"That's what they all say, Rush."

HERE COMES SUNSHINE

I'd rented an apartment close to the beach, a one bedroom with a kitchenette. It wasn't a shithole by any means, and I could definitely afford better, but I wasn't ready to blow everything right now.

I furnished it with some cool secondhand stuff, plus a brand-new bed. And I painted the walls over the too-bright white. I bought pots and pans and pretended I'd cook. I got all the takeout menus I could. I took long runs on the beach, in the mornings before work and sometimes after work as well. I swam in the ocean. I went out at night and flirted shamelessly, but didn't kiss anyone.

Three weeks passed uneventfully, with me throwing all my excess energy into all things legal, trying to tire myself out too much to crave stealing, racing, or Ryker. The bonus was that the nightmares had ebbed.

Since my second day in Florida, I'd worked at a garage a mile from the apartment. I'd set up the job ahead of time through a Craig's List ad, and I was pleasantly surprised that the garage was as nice as it looked in the pictures. A family-owned operation, three generations, and none of them looked like car thieves. They were old Florida money, and the shop was run well. They were impressed by my work.

I was going to die of boredom, but hey, I guess you couldn't have everything.

Linc checked in by text. Told me he was still hanging around Shades, that my landlord said he could lease the apartment for another month if he wanted. I had questions I wanted to ask, but I didn't. I was ripping away from Shades completely, a clean break.

I never answered Linc's texts, but that didn't stop him from sending them. I'd been there a month and I hadn't been able to bring myself to get a new phone number—even though I didn't want to cut everyone off completely, I had to. I'd changed the address on my bills for a fresh start, and I didn't need Linc to get desperate and start breaking into cell phone records.

It was definitely on my list for tomorrow, I told myself as I pulled up to my apartment after a long day at work and found my car surrounded by Hangmen.

Because of course they had a Florida chapter.

"You Sean Rush?" a tall redhead asked me as I got out of the car.

"Who wants to know?"

The redhead stared at me. "Casey wants to talk to you."

"North Carolina Casey?"

"He's here," the redhead told me. "We're supposed to bring you to him. Now."

He pointed to a truck, a large four-by-four on too-big tires, with the windows open and music blaring.

"I don't want to talk to him," I said, but I climbed into the truck anyway, because they'd bring me to him no matter what. "Who's your president here?" I asked once we got on the road. The redhead turned to me and stared. "Ah, it's you."

Serious shit if the president of the chapter was sent to get me himself. I steeled myself for what would happen next. Pushed around like a pinball, bounced from club to club. And fuck, how the hell had Casey found me anyway?

Fucking *Linc.*

Casey was in the clubhouse, nursing a drink. "Thanks for coming, Rush."

"Like I had a choice," I practically hissed. "What the fuck are you trying to do to me?"

"Relax, Rush. No one's blowing your cover." He offered me a drink, and I took it down, and he poured me another. "Nervous?"

"Annoyed," I lied.

"I need your help, Rush."

"No one knows who I am here."

"I'll keep it that way."

"No one knows I'm here," I said through clenched teeth.

"Obviously, I did."

I threw up my arms. "Here we go again."

"Life's all about compromise, Rush. I've never said different." Casey looked determined.

"What's really going on?"

Casey leaned forward. "The Albanian guys who gave you trouble? They've got my Sergeant-at-Arms's old lady."

"And I'm the best person you've got for an extraction because they like me so fucking much?"

"You're the most unexpected."

I wouldn't deny that. "What aren't you telling me?"

"She's Greta's kid. Name's Donna."

My gut tightened. "Shit."

"Yeah."

I sat back down. "Give me the details."

"If you do this . . ."

I held up my hand. "I'm not doing this shit for favors or for threats. I'm doing this for Greta, and because I hate that there's an innocent woman dragged into this crap. Got it?"

"Got it."

"Then I don't want to hear anything but the details."

"You really push it, Rush, know that?"

"I've been told."

"I'd have fun with you over my knee."

"Casey . . ."

"Guy can dream, right?"

I scowled. "I don't think I want to be in your dreams."

He smiled wickedly. "Too late."

"Jesus. Details, Casey. Focus." I stared at him. "Why *are* you being nice to me?"

"Because I want to fuck you."

At least he was honest. "Ryker'd kill you."

"Ryker used to have no problem sharing."

And because I couldn't help myself, I asked, "When's the last time you guys shared?"

Casey didn't bother to hide his grin. "It was supposed to be you."

I tried to wrap my head around that and failed. "Change of subject. I thought we took care of Edmund."

"We did," he said. "But Edmund's associates had a little problem with letting go."

"All because of that shi . . . fantastic car of yours?"

"Yeah, Noah told me all about what's wrong with it." He rolled his eyes and stood. "And it's not about the car, Rush. It's about shit you should know better than to ask about."

I held up my hands. "Point taken."

"I can't ask Noah. They're familiar with him. And as much as I wouldn't mind handing him over, my daughter'll kill me."

I raised my brows but wisely kept my mouth shut on that subject. And I guessed that Jethro was still keeping track of Noah, so I wondered if he knew all about this new development. "So what do you need?"

He slapped down a list on the table in front of me. "These cars. By midnight tomorrow."

"Fine. But what's to stop them from doing this again?"

"Rush, you're going to steal me these cars. In exchange, no one's going to know who you are. Bring the cars to the address at the bottom. Memorize this shit. Clear?"

"Yeah, crystal."

CHAPTER 30

ARE YOU LONELY FOR ME

"You're not doing this alone."

I froze at the sound of Ryker's voice behind me. In my apartment. Where I'd come in ten minutes ago, saw no other cars or people out front, and I'd locked the goddamned doors and windows.

I turned and demanded, "How the fuck do you do that?" Because if I didn't, I'd either punch him or fuck him, and at this point, I actually wanted to do both. At the same time.

He looked so damned good. Black T-shirt. His vest with the cut. His eyes deep and dark and focused only on me. "Why'd you agree to do something for Casey?"

"Because I couldn't say no where Greta's concerned," I shot back and his expression softened with shock and then, "Ah, fuck, Sean."

"Don't. I can't do this if I'm all fucked up over you. Again."

It was his turn to demand, "What, you were over me?"

Jesus, talk about some serious arrogance. And I'd been doing a damned good job of pretending I was. Seeing him now, my body informed me that I was a fucking liar. So, of course, I ignored the question. "How long have you known where I was?"

When he didn't answer, I assumed both he and Casey'd been tracking me. The fact that they'd kept their distance . . . it pissed me off. What, would they have just watched me forever?

Fucking Linc. I should've told Gypsy to let him stay in jail, where he couldn't tell people shit, like where I was supposed to be secretly living.

"I'm doing the job," I said firmly. Crossed my arms and stared him down.

He mirrored my stance and my tone. "With me. Or else it doesn't happen."

We could be at this all night. "Alone. I work alone. You can talk to Casey."

"I don't have to fucking talk to anyone," he growled, and yeah, I was hard. His possessiveness turned me the fuck on. Sue me. "I will put you on my bike, drive you back to Havoc, and chain you to my bed before you do this alone."

"Right. Because I'm so wanted back at Havoc. Tell me, Ryker, in the very beginning, did you follow me because you wanted to make me part of Havoc? Was it a job interview?"

"Just the opposite," Ryker told me.

I frowned. "I was competition?"

"Complication."

I swallowed. Hard. "You were going to . . ."

"Get you out of the game."

"How?" I demanded. "Say it, Ryker. How did fucking me and killing me get mixed up?"

"Being real dramatic, Sean."

"Not kill then. Threaten. Push out."

"Yes."

"And if this thing between us doesn't work out?"

That got him more angry than my accusation that he was going to kill me. He was backing me into the nearest chair, pinning me there, his big body surrounding me.

"You," he said, his drawl like syrup, making me hard. Er. "Are. Mine. So where are you planning on going?"

"This mine stuff is . . ." Hot. So fucking hot it made me ache. But I couldn't admit it when I'd come so far—nearly a fucking month. But his hand was palming my cock, and it was really hard to figure out why I shouldn't admit it.

"This mine stuff is . . .?" His hand went down my pants now. His finger brushed my slit, pushed in, and I bit back a whimper.

"It's fucking hot and you know it," I managed, then, "Why, Ryker?"

"Why what, Sean?"

That echoing thing he did was mesmerizing. "Why do you want me as yours?" I managed. "Because I'm easy?"

He smiled then, a short laugh escaping. He cupped my balls. "You think you're easy?"

"I, uh . . ."

"You, Sean Rush, are the farthest fucking thing from easy. You're the most frustrating, intense man I've ever met."

My body—fucking goddamned traitor—completely ached for him. There was no chance I'd kick him out of my bed. "But if I'm yours, then . . ."

Then I am easy. Which meant, no challenge. No danger. No thrill.

He stared at me, like he was reading my fucking mind. Or hell, maybe I said it all out loud, because I could never tell what I was doing around him. "You'll never be easy, Sean. No matter how hard you try. And that's why I'm proud you're mine. Don't you get it, babe? This isn't a game to me. Way beyond that."

His face was inches from mine. We were both vibrating with anger and want and everything else in between. I don't know which of us leaned forward first, but it didn't matter. We were kissing, tongues dueling, bodies grinding, a dry humping slow dance that had me holding onto him like I'd never let go.

"Sean," he murmured as he brought me back to life. Because I'd been a goddamned zombie for the last month.

"What did you do to me?"

"Whatever I wanted to." He paused, then added. "For the record, it's the exact same thing you did to me."

At his words, my body was liquid—he could do anything he wanted to me, and I'd let him.

I *was* letting him. But I also couldn't help adding, "You weren't supposed to follow me here."

"Remember what we discussed, about how you don't get to tell me what to do?"

"You'll have to remind me."

Ryker's grin spread, the humor finally reaching his eyes. "Keep pushing. I'll put you over my knee and your ass will burn the entire time we're stealing those cars."

"We?"

Ryker nodded slowly, the intent clear in his eyes.

"You're not involved. I chose to help Casey. Nothing to do with the MC wars."

He continued to stare at me, pinning me to the spot with his gaze, shooting daggers at me from his eyes. But I wasn't backing down. He also knew that going over his knee was no hardship for me, no matter how hard I outwardly fought it.

And I would fight.

He pushed all my limits. Had from day one but this . . . this was new. Exciting. And scary as hell. And I was over his lap, my jeans pulled down, his hand on my bare ass. Just like he'd promised. There wasn't anger in those slaps. No, there was control. There was an apology. And a reassurance that he was always going to find me and bring me back.

When I thought about that, I came with a howl, stiffening in his lap. His hand caressed my sore cheeks for several long minutes, until I could breathe without hiccupping. I wiped my face with the back of my hand.

And then Ryker pulled me up and off his lap. I sank to the floor by his knees and he carded his hand through my hair. "Stop fighting, Sean. You don't have to. Not with me."

Bullshit. He didn't know that—or me—or anything about what I really wanted. And I told myself that while I let him lead me between his legs, press my head down to kiss his cock. I told myself that while I swallowed his cock, his grip now firm in my hair.

God, I loved that. I loved taking his control, the hard-earned victory of watching him, for just those few moments, lose it. Lose himself, because of me.

Triumphantly, I swallowed what he gave me as I watched him. His big body shuddered, muscles tense as his hips jerked erratically.

I was hard again. Rock hard. I rose as soon as his grip on my hair fell away. I led him to the bedroom, pushed him back on the bed, and climbed between his legs as I did so. My finger pressed his hole, and he stared at me and said, "Go ahead, Sean."

Go ahead, Sean, like he was going to be in control while I fucked him.

He was in control while I fucked him. If I wasn't the one inside of him, if I was watching a movie of this play out, I would've said that he was faking it . . . or that I was.

But from the second I entered him, I couldn't stop watching him, getting more and more turned on by his movements, the way he hissed. The way he enjoyed it.

And when I was buried in him, he flexed his ass, and I almost came. Yelled and holy fuck, he reached down between our bodies to put pressure on the base of my cock, stopping me from coming.

"Son of a . . ."

"Yeah, Sean. Fuck me. Take it all out on me, babe. All that anger and pain and frustration—pound me with it."

"You are not the boss of me," I growled back, began to pump into him—because apparently he was the boss of me, and I followed orders well, even though I told myself it was what I wanted too.

He closed his eyes while I set a rhythm, watching smugly, thinking, *Gotcha*.

As he thrust his hips up, riding me from the bottom, I pushed at his hips to stop him, but it was like his body had a motor attached.

I barely hanging on. His hands went to my hips, positioning them, showing me not only how he wanted to be fucked, but also how under his spell I was.

"Ryker!" I shouted, and he stopped me from coming again. A jumble of arms and legs later, I was on my knees, and he was on his in front of me, pushing back against my cock. I raked my nails down his back, and he practically howled.

"More, Sean. Come on."

I slammed into him as he took me, than I came in a blinding rush, murmuring, "I love you," in his ear.

"Pull out and clean me up," he ordered, and fuck it all, I did. He watched me lazily lick the cum spattered on his belly and chest. And he dragged me up and kissed me for a damned long time, holding me against him.

Finally, he broke the kiss, pulled back. "Sean, Jesus Christ, I fucking love you . . ."

I swallowed hard, realized I didn't ever want to go anywhere without him ever again.

WHEN PUSH COMES TO SHOVE

Ryker at least let me come up with the plan. Somehow, I had not only one Havoc MC guy, but four who were suddenly part of my car boosting team. Tug and Sweet, Chino and Lex. Gavin was there for backup, but he wasn't coming with us.

"He'll pinch hit, if necessary," Lex said and Chino nodded his agreement.

I supposed at least those two were involved in Havoc's car stealing ring, based on how easily they dealt with the list of cars, helping me find them and break them down.

Six cars. One night. The biggest obstacle was, of course, the rarest car that the Albanians had demanded, a 1962 Ferrari 250 LM. There were only thirty-two in the world, and they sold at auction for nearly seven million dollars. Nothing like stealing something that was being transported from two hours west of my new place to an auction house in New York for sale, since that's the one Casey was told they wanted.

We scoured the area to find one that wasn't being transported into the state, but no such luck.

"They said they did all the work finding it," Casey told me. "All you have to do is get it."

"Right, piece of cake," I muttered, echoing Edmund's early words. Which was not a good sign. I shoved that shit right out of my head and, when the others were busy with their boosts, Ryker and I worked together. Like he'd wanted.

In the end, I couldn't have done it without him.

It involved stealing the car off the back of the truck, which meant disabling the truck and driving it straight to the warehouse. After fucking with the GPS chip, which Ryker seemed to think wasn't an issue.

So we rode along the truck on the deserted stretch of highway. Ryker assured me it wouldn't be bodyguarded, because that would draw too much attention.

"It's the way we do it," was all he said, so obviously, he'd done this before.

So now I'd never be sure if I was seeing an actual delivery truck or a truck housing a stolen vehicle. "How can you be sure about this?"

"I called in a favor."

The favor was a big fucking deal, because the guy driving the truck basically got out and handed it over to us, no questions asked. He got an envelope from Ryker, which I assumed was full of cash and he took the junker car we'd been driving, and we got into the truck.

I drove. He let me. It was an hour to the warehouse, a tense, quiet hour as I kept thinking about how badly this could've gone without him. How this was almost boring.

And how, sometimes, boring was actually the better choice when it meant keeping Ryker safe. I guess he felt the same way about me.

Finally, we pulled into the back of an old warehouse, where Ryker directed me.

"We were a good team."

"Were?" Ryker rumbled.

"This doesn't change anything, Ryk."

"Nothing had to change, as far as I was concerned."

"I couldn't save Billy. I could barely keep Noah in line, and I put Havoc in danger without even trying. And the club's all about keeping each other safe. So yeah, shit has to change." I sighed. "I don't want to talk about this. Not now. Let's just get Donna back, okay?"

"Yeah, let's do that."

I was under no illusions that this would make up for everything, for Billy, or that this would bring me into Havoc. I couldn't live with that responsibility.

So of course, we weren't going to just hand everything over to the Albanians. They had five of the six cars, but we'd held ours back until we saw Donna. In the meantime, Casey had found out where Donna was being housed.

Before we turned the car over, we were taking Donna. From there, we'd give the kidnappers what they'd wanted, although Casey and Ryker planned to exact a little revenge of their own. Because they wouldn't go back on their word for the trade, but that didn't mean they were going to sit back and take what the Albanians had done to them.

Ryker and I got to the warehouse where Donna was being held. It wasn't the same place where we'd been directed to drop the cars. Ryker handed me a gun before he went in.

"We'll clear the place," he said as Casey, Chino, and Gavin looked on. "You go past when you can and grab Donna."

I nodded, and weapon in hand, I walked in behind them.

They definitely surprised the guys who were there, probably waiting for word from their bosses. I don't know if they'd have let Donna go—but a big part of me figured they wouldn't have.

The guards turned and then things happened fast. There were more men here than I thought there'd be. Didn't seem to bother Ryker or the others, though, and I stayed, half-outside.

But there was yelling, and I came in farther to make sure they were all right. At the same time, shots rang out. I froze for a second, the Florida heat baking the warehouse morphing into the heat of the desert. And I swear I saw Billy . . . he was trying to get to me, and he was pointing and bleeding. I turned and raised my gun at the man coming toward us, and as I stepped in front of Billy, I fired.

He dropped.

I heard yelling. More shots. I blinked again, and I was firmly back in the warehouse, and there was a man down in front of me. Another in the corner.

"Sean."

Ryker's voice. His hand was light on my shoulder, like he knew it might make me freak or bolt.

In truth, I had to fight that urge. But in the end, I did neither. For me, that was a big goddamned step. "Ryker, did I . . ."

And then I turned and noticed the blood dripping from Ryker's arm. "Ryker, did I do that?"

"You saved me." His voice was hushed with emotion and pain as he pointed to the man crumpled ten feet from us. "He shot me. And he wasn't finished."

When I thought I'd been saving Billy . . . it'd been Ryker.

Billy would've been pissed to think I'd put him between us. Ryker was my second chance. My redemption. My fucking everything. "Jesus."

"Come on, Sean." Ryker was easing the gun from my knotted grip. "Can you pull it together and grab Donna? Get her back to her charter?"

"Where are you going?"

"To end this shit. Trust me."

I did, and not because I didn't have a choice.

He did give me the gun back, and I found Donna in a backroom, tied to a chair.

She had a bruise on her cheek, looked like she was in shock, but otherwise she was fine. Physically.

I untied her while Ryker took care of the last of the guards in the main part of the warehouse, and when the coast was clear, Ryker grabbed one of the kidnappers, who he'd tied up. He put the guy in his own car and drove that away, but not before telling me, "Get her home, Sean, because then you're coming home with me."

Nothing had changed, except my perspective. It'd shifted, upright. I saw things as Ryker did. Because he'd always seen things my way.

I was delivering the girl now, and the car later. Ryker trusted me to do this first part alone, and I wasn't going to fuck it up.

Donna was so quiet on the ride to the assigned meeting place, where her husband would be waiting. Casey said he'd practically had to tie the guy down to keep him from coming with us, and that, I understood.

I turned the radio on, low, and I'd given her something to drink. I'd jacked up the heat because she was shivering a little. About half an hour into the hour-long drive, she asked, "How long have you been with Ryker?"

"That obvious?" I asked.

She laughed a little. That was a relief to me. "You're not Havoc."

"No."

"Probie?"

"No. I've just got a propensity to get into major trouble. And I like stealing cars," I added.

"So how did you meet Ryker?"

"At Bertha's. I was nervous. And I'm never nervous." I didn't know why the fuck I was telling her this. Probably because she'd just been rescued from being kidnapped, and she was scared we'd be caught before we made it back to the man she loved. "So I drank way too much tequila. And I uh . . . I told him that it was cool if he took me home at the end of the night. Jesus."

She put a hand on my arm. "Sounds like you knew he was right from minute one."

"I've been fighting it."

"Here." She tapped the side of my head. "Heart knows what it wants anyway. That night, you led with your heart."

I blew out the breath I'd been holding. Because she was right. I was too immersed in it to see clearly. "He said he wouldn't follow me."

"But he did."

"Yeah."

I glanced over and she was staring straight ahead, smiling the serene smile of someone who knew a giant secret.

I guess I knew it too.

"My mom wasn't happy that I didn't find a guy at Havoc. I told her to look at the bright side—this was the best way to ensure that Havoc and the Hangmen didn't go to war. I'd never let it happen."

"Is that the whole reason you married a Hangmen?"

"I married for love, Rush. Because it's the only thing worth doing anything for."

"Even after all of this?"

"Even after," she said softly. Because we'd pulled in, and her husband was headed her way. And that's when she let her guard down. Tears ran down her cheeks. She wasn't hysterical, but she did let go.

"I can't thank you enough," LT said. "Open invite. Any favor needed, anytime."

I didn't like favors, but this world—this MC world especially—lived by them. I shook his hand.

CHAPTER 32

YOU WIN AGAIN

Casey was going to pick the car up closer to the docks. After I dropped Donna off, I doubled back and waited three blocks away.

I was lying on the hood of the car, looking at the stars, when Ryker pulled up on his bike. He ambled over, stood over me and asked, "What're you thinking about?"

He wasn't going to let me get away with that *not telling you shit* stuff, but really, what could he do? I mean, I knew what he could do. He'd done what I was doing. He'd been there. And a part of me hated that he knew.

"Can't get away with anything," he murmured when I told him that. He smiled his slow, easy smile that told me he'd known that too.

Fucker. "You knew who I was long before last year, didn't you?" I asked him finally.

"Yeah. I didn't know that you were a car thief. I just knew you as the guy I saw in the clubs."

"I never saw you."

"I didn't want to be seen. But you did."

I couldn't deny that. "So when you started watching me for Havoc last year . . ."

"I finally got my chance."

"You were watching me as a job. So what, you were suddenly attracted to me?"

"I was *always* attracted to you."

"So why not approach me before that?"

"Because you weren't ready."

Now I did turn to stare at him. "Seriously?"

"Yeah, seriously."

At his words, I went to stand, but he pulled me down, half pinning me to the hood of the car.

"You weren't ready. You were too wild."

"I thought Havoc liked wild?"

"Not uncontrollable. You were."

I'd been, yes, but fuck him for saying it. "There's nothing wrong with that."

"No, of course not. Nothing." He was sincere. "But Sean, I couldn't risk that."

"Because of your family."

"Yes."

And we were right back where we started. "I don't want to be a part of Havoc."

"Do you want to be with me?"

I hadn't wanted him to ask me that. At this point, I'd realized that I couldn't live without him. That I'd be miserable. "Ryk . . ."

"Answer the question."

Jesus, he was going to fuck me right out in the open. Right on the car.

Just like my fantasy. Except . . . "You said these cars are too smooth."

"They are," he said seriously. "You're not. You'll give me the rumble." With that, he yanked me down toward him and unbuttoned my jeans. Stripped them off me, smiled at the fact that I wore nothing underneath.

"That's convenient," he said.

"Saves time."

He raised his brows. "You're only saving time for me, Sean. And I'd better hear you say that."

But he didn't give me time for anything like that, began putting my legs over his shoulders, unzipping his pants and gloving his cock. And there was lube, on his fingers, inside of me . . . and then it was his cock, sliding into me. Filling me.

"Missed this," I managed.

"Being fucked on a car?"

"Being fucked . . . by you. Only. You."

On the warm hood of the car we'd stolen together, he took me, hard and fast, and I watched him, imagined that people were watching us. Watching him take me.

I went to grab my cock, but he shook his head. I reached out to the side, but there was nothing to grab.

"Touch your nipples if you need to hold on to something," Ryker instructed. I did. Ryker's were pierced, and I loved tugging on them. Turns out mine were pretty sensitive too.

"You think I don't realize what you did?" Ryker told me now.

"I don't know what you're talking about."

"Bullshit, Sean. Bullshit." He held me down, thrust into me until all I could do was moan. "Tell me why."

"Ryk . . ."

"Tell. Me."

"For you, okay. So . . . fuck. I left so you didn't have to choose."

"I never had to choose, Sean. No one asked me to. I can have you both. And I will."

"It wasn't . . . always easy for you."

"It wasn't. It won't be. But nothing worth having ever is," he growled. "And you're worth having."

His words sent a shudder through me. My cock bobbed helplessly. Leaking. Red and angry, and he was hitting the right spot and he wouldn't stop until I came.

I did, with a strangled groan, splayed for him, the most painfully satisfying orgasm of my life.

He came a minute later, shouting my name. In that half-empty parking lot, where anyone could've seen us. We stayed in that position. I couldn't have said for how long. I was stunned. Submissive for him. And when he pulled out, he dressed me, got on his bike and waited for me to settle my weight behind him . . . just as Casey showed to claim the car.

I held on to Ryker, even though I didn't need to, and I buried my flushed face against his Havoc cut. By the time we got back to my place, my ass was sore, but I was hard for him again.

CHAPTER 33

COME BACK BABY

He fucked me in the shower, gentler this time. The soreness didn't matter, not when he kissed me the way he did.

He rubbed my hair dry with a towel. I had one wrapped around my hips as well. His fingers ran along my ribs, tracing a spot that was particularly sensitive on a good day. He was writing something there, then drawing. Then he placed his large hand over it, splayed out to span the expanse of skin like he was measuring.

And then he nodded, took his hand away, like he'd made a decision.

I knew what that decision had been when Gavin came in—the one who'd done Ryker's roses.

I lay partially on my side, with Ryker behind me, propping me up.

Gavin drew freehand over my ribcage using black marker with shades of gray, although he told me that the final version would have color. For twenty minutes, we were all quiet, and then he smiled at me, nodded at Ryker, and left.

I hadn't looked while Gavin was drawing. Now, Ryker urged me up and pointed to the mirror.

The drawing spanned exactly where his hand had been, although a few tribal swirls had escaped the confines of the space. The way it was drawn went perfectly over the planes of my body. It moved with me, looked like I was born with it there.

It was amazing, even though there wasn't color yet. A rose. A skull. My very own American Beauty. Not an exact replica. No, this was an original.

"Original, like you are," Ryker said, reading my mind. "Perfect spot. I knew it the first time I touched you."

That first night, his hand had strayed there. Stayed there, played on me, holding me.

I'd started to swear I could feel his heavy hand there, even after he left. When I'd still been enlisted, I'd sleep with my hand there for comfort.

It was why he'd looked so angry when he'd seen the bruises there. "Does this make me yours?"

"This makes you *you*." He paused. "Do you want it to mean that?"

"Yeah."

"You don't have to. That's for you—a gift."

"Suppose I wanted the ink to make me yours?"

"You're mine, Sean, ink or no ink. You know that, right?"

"I want the ink to remind me. I want that to be a part of me."

He grabbed me, tugged me to him, and kissed me. "My tough guy."

"Yeah." I rolled my eyes. "You know Billy did it for me. Stepped in front of me in the desert to save me from insurgent fire."

"His choice, Sean."

"That's what bothered me. He took it all into his own hands. I could've . . ."

"Died. You could've died, Sean. I know accepting what he did for you is hard, but you're too hard on yourself."

"I know that." I did. Really. Didn't mean it was going to change anytime soon.

Ryker took that opportunity to splay his hand over my side, stroking the drawing. My skin. "Going to be here to remind you not to be."

"I love you, Ryk. Probably from the first time you broke in. Definitely from the night you helped me."

"We're good together, Sean. Really good." He cupped the back of my neck. "You know I love you."

I did. He'd been saying it in a thousand different ways from the start, and I'd been running. In circles, it appeared. And he'd waited until I wore myself out.

Or until my brain cleared. "What do I do?"

He smiled, and I knew then that he wouldn't take away my freedom. "I've got an idea."

"Is it an idea . . . or something you've already done?"

"It's both. I've already discussed it with Noah. I figured you wouldn't mind."

"You and Noah, talking?" I raised my eyebrows. "And Noah's still . . . unbruised?"

"He's dating Casey's daughter, which isn't something I'd recommend to him, but I didn't add any additional bruises to him." Ryker paused. "Edmund's gone. But his shop's still there. The town needs it. So it'd be a shame to let it go to waste."

"So what, Noah and I should run it?"

"Run it. Own it."

"You're serious?" I stared into his dark eyes. "I'd have to steal a lot of cars to afford that."

"Shit, no. Please." Ryker's expression was genuinely pained. "I knew that's how you'd think, so I went ahead and loaned you the money."

"Ryker, I—"

"Loan. And you own it outright. You'll pay me back as you can."

"So what—the shop would be my front?"

Ryker rolled his eyes. "No, it's where you're supposed to be."

I'd fix up Harleys and cars. With Noah. And that way I didn't have to deal with Havoc or worry about how I'd take care of myself. "So I'd just own the place."

"The customers keep coming back for you."

That was true. In the year I'd been there, I'd become the most asked-for mechanic. Some of the guys were almost scared of their cars. They rode shotgun while I drove them. Rode their cars the way they needed to be ridden. Broke them in.

"You can't be bought, Sean. Never could."

CHAPTER 34

EASY TO LOVE YOU

The car ride home was kind of a blur. Ryker drove my truck while I slept on and off, the Havoc bikes guiding us home. To Havoc. The Harleys fell away once we got up the hill, and he parked in front of his house.

It felt like I'd been gone years. The crocuses were still there, blooming where they shouldn't be. Welcoming me back. "I'm worried, Ryk," I told him.

He shut the truck off and shifted to face me. "I know Greta told you how badly I fucked up when I was younger. How much trouble I brought down on the MC."

"Yeah. But that was once. You learned. I seem to have an issue with learning from anything I even moderately enjoy."

"Look, selflessness isn't what I'm after. I don't think you'd do anything to hurt the kids, no matter how strong your urge to steal is."

He was right.

"Did you want to leave?" he offered.

"No." I stared at him. "I'm fucking miserable without you. I'm miserable not being a criminal."

"I'd say you're more of a delinquent than a criminal. But I think there's a way we can work it to our advantage."

"Does it involve more of me getting fucked on the hood of a car?"

"It could." He paused. "I wasn't sure you liked it. I mean, yelling out that you're going to fucking kill me with your dick can be taken a lot of ways."

"I did not yell that out."

Ryker waited until I had soda in my mouth before adding, "Linc and Gypsy are fucking."

I spit the drink out. Ryker looked satisfied. I wiped my mouth with the back of my hand. "Fucker."

"Me or Linc?"

"Both of you."

I shoved him lightly, and he laughed and got out of the truck. I did too, but I waited at the steps of the porch. He'd walked a few steps up but stopped and turned to me. Waited.

"I'm in love with you, Ryker. You know that, right?"

His face broke wide open with the most beautiful goddamned smile I'd ever seen on him. "Doesn't mean I don't love hearing it."

I'd been bested at my own game. And I hadn't been playing a game. Or at least I hadn't meant to.

"You were protecting yourself," Ryker said after I'd explained that.

"From who?"

"Everyone. Everything. You can't get hurt if you can't get close enough."

"And neither can they," I muttered.

"Right. Forgot you've got that kind of power." He wasn't making fun of me. He never did that.

"Feels like it sometimes."

"I get that." He paused. "I can't promise that you'll know everything about Havoc. There's a lot we do. A lot one hand knows but the other doesn't. It's complicated."

"We don't have enough cars around here to steal."

"We have a lot of rogue members," he said. "We try to keep our nose clean on the compound."

"Suppose I fuck things up?"

"Don't," he said seriously.

"Ryker . . ."

"We stand by our own. You're with me, which means you're a part of Havoc."

Had I seen signs and closed my eyes against believing them? "Wait, *you* don't steal cars?"

Ryker shook his head. "I did, a long time ago. But Havoc does. Like you said, who are we hurting?"

I nodded, slowly. "You're in charge of the porn?"

"No. I'll bodyguard if need be, but I don't deal with it day-to-day."

"The kid stuff," I said finally.

"Yeah."

I stared at him. Because that was hands down the hardest, most dangerous job of all.

"Am I one of your lost boys?"

"You're not a boy, Sean. And you're not lost. Never were, really." He pressed a kiss to the side of my neck. "I love you, Sean Rush. Come on inside with me, and never fucking leave, okay?"

"So I'm home." It was more a statement than a question, but he reassured me anyway, like he always did.

"Yeah, babe. You're home."

Dear Reader,

Thank you for reading SE Jakes' *Running Wild*!

We know your time is precious and you have many, many entertainment options, so it means a lot that you've chosen to spend your time reading. We really hope you enjoyed it.

We'd be honored if you'd consider posting a review—good or bad—on sites like **Amazon, Barnes & Noble, Kobo, Goodreads, Twitter, Facebook, Tumblr,** and your blog or website. We'd also be honored if you told your friends and family about this book. Word of mouth is a book's lifeblood!

For more information on upcoming releases, author interviews, blog tours, contests, giveaways, and more, please sign up for our weekly, spam-free newsletter and visit us around the web:

Newsletter: tinyurl.com/RiptideSignup
Twitter: twitter.com/RiptideBooks
Facebook: facebook.com/RiptidePublishing
Goodreads: tinyurl.com/RiptideOnGoodreads
Tumblr: riptidepublishing.tumblr.com

Thank you so much for Reading the Rainbow!

RiptidePublishing.com

I'm thrilled to be able to bring you my MC series, and especially to be able to write it for, and with, Riptide. This one's been a long time coming (I started the first draft back in 2003, and the prologue especially, and several chapters remain very close to the original in spirit).

And for that, I must thank Sarah Frantz, who makes my stories shine. For Rachel Haimowitz for all the opportunities she's given me. For L.C. Chase and the gorgeous covers and layouts. For Keturah Jenkins, who is always on top of creating amazing book tours and other opportunities for my books. For Alex Whitehall, for her eagle-eye. For everyone at Riptide for making my publishing experience insanely wonderful.

As always, special thanks to those who keep my online spaces under control when I go into the writing cave: Andrea, LisaT, Susan, and Shawnie. Thanks for managing the havoc (!) so well. And thanks to all the readers I've met and the friends I've made in the ASK SEJ Goodreads Group and the Dirty Deeds Facebook Group and on Tumblr and Twitter—thanks for being so crazy right along with me. And thanks to all of you who have taken the leap into this new series. I think you'll all enjoy the ride.

Last, but never least, for my family. For everything, always.

Coming soon from the Havoc Motorcycle Club

Running Blind

Running on Empty

Hell or High Water (EE, Ltd.) Series

Catch a Ghost

Long Time Gone

Daylight Again

Not Fade Away

If I Ever (Coming soon)

Men of Honor Series

Bound by Honor

Bound by Law

Ties That Bind

Bound by Danger

Bound for Keeps (EE, Ltd.)

Bound to Break

Standalone

Free Falling (EE, Ltd.)

Dirty Deeds Series (EE, Ltd.) Series

Dirty Deeds

SE Jakes writes m/m romance. She believes in happy endings and fighting for what you want in both fiction and real life. She lives in New York with her family and most days, she can be found happily writing (in bed). No really . . .

SE Jakes is the pen name of *New York Times* best-selling author Stephanie Tyler (and half of Sydney Croft).

You can contact her the following ways:

Email: authorsejakes@gmail.com

Website: sejakes.com

Tumblr: sejakes.tumblr.com

Facebook: Facebook.com/SEJakes

Twitter: Twitter.com/authorsejakes

Instagram: instagram.com/authorsejakes

Goodreads Group: Ask SE Jakes

Truth be told, the best way to contact her is by email or in blog comments. She spends most of her time writing but she loves to hear from readers!

www.ingramcontent.com/pod-product-compliance
Lightning Source LLC
LaVergne TN
LVHW091129080826
845145LV00008B/2089

* 9 7 8 1 6 2 6 4 9 1 5 4 0 *